The Tenth Witness is the second novel in the Henri Poincaré series, the award-winning *All Cry Chaos* preceding.

Recognition for *All Cry Chaos*

- Translated into ten languages
- Winner, *ForeWord Magazine*'s Book of the Year, Fiction
- Winner, Macavity Award (Mystery Readers International) Best First Novel
- Edgar Award Best First Novel, Finalist
- Anthony Award Best First Novel, Finalist
- Chautauqua Literary Prize, Finalist

From Reviews of *All Cry Chaos*

"A startling novel. This is a thoughtful, beautifully written puzzle."
—*Booklist*

"It's a rare pleasure to find a protagonist who reads like a literary figure in a thriller." —*ForeWord Magazine*

"Beautifully well-written, with fully-developed characters, high-octane tension, elegant mathematical constructs, and human hearts that are both noble and black as the night. This is one of the best thrillers I have ever read." —*Daily Herald* (Provo, Utah)

"An ingenious debut novel." —*National Public Radio*

"Easily one of the best first novels of the past couple of years."
—*Mystery Scene*

"A richly descriptive thriller." —*Washington Post*

"Rosen has a fine detective in Poincaré."
—*New York Times Book Review*

"An intellectually provocative whodunit." —*Publishers Weekly*

"An international mystery that also confronts great moral and theological questions. Highly recommended." —*Library Journal*

THE TENTH WITNESS

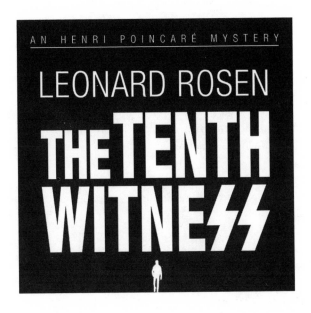

AN HENRI POINCARÉ MYSTERY

LEONARD ROSEN

THE TENTH
WITNESS

THE PERMANENT PRESS
Sag Harbor, NY 11963

This is a work of fiction. All of the characters and events portrayed in this book are products of the author's imagination or are used fictitiously.

For information, address:
  The Permanent Press
  4170 Noyac Road
  Sag Harbor, NY 11963
  www.thepermanentpress.com

Library of Congress Cataloging-in-Publication Data

  Rosen, Leonard J.
    The Tenth witness / Leonard Rosen.
        pages cm. — (Henri Poincari mystery; 2)
    ISBN 978-1-57962-319-7
        1. Engineers—Fiction. 2. Murder—Investigation—Fiction.
    I. Title.

PS3618.O83148T46 2013
813'.6—dc23   2013019229

Printed in the United States of America

For Linda

I still believe in man in spite of man.
—ELIE WIESEL, *Open Heart*

PART I

one

*E*very Christmas, for thirty years, my friend and former business partner sends me a basket of pears. With each delivery comes a note and the same unspoken question, posed in a teasing, left-leaning script: "Say the word, Henri. Your desk is waiting. Best, A. C."

I'm flattered to think Alec would have me back after all this time. For most of my career I could have used the money, and I could have done without the long stretches away from home and the violence and anxiety that attend police work. But I never was much of a businessman. During those first years, I turned down jobs that offended me. I took on clients who could barely make their rent, let alone pay us. Alec and I argued. In the end I'm convinced our venture would have collapsed due to what he rightly called my aggressive naïveté.

Once he suggested I quit business to join the priesthood. I might have, had I believed in God at the time. Now that I do, I'm too old—which is fortunate because these days I know how damaged we are and think it deluded, even dangerous, to hold to my former Sunday school view of the world. I would have made a bad priest, too.

Still, it worked out, my leaving Poincaré & Chin Consulting Engineers for Interpol. I got out in time to keep both a dear friend and the illusion that Alec and I could have prospered together. Better still, each December I sit with Claire at our farmer's table to enjoy good fruit out of season. It's a miracle of the modern age, eating an Anjou pear in December. I take one bite and there I go: off to an orchard in the shadow of the Andes, where these little jewels are grown.

It's Christmas Eve and my grandsons are asleep, finally. Claire dozes by the fire. Moments ago, she stirred and said, "Love, come to bed." We kissed and I laid a quilt across her lap. She drifted off again.

Outside, a thin crust of snow blankets the vineyards. With Alec's note before me, I'll consider once more his question in good faith. Which is to say, I'll review the events of that summer and ask: Did I choose well? Have I chosen well since? I must answer in all honesty. And if the answer is *no*, I will write my friend and ask him to dust off my chair.

He would do it, too.

I begin, therefore, as I have for thirty years: with the body of a man floating face down in the slack water of Terschelling Island. I can see him fighting the flood tide that runs off the North Sea. That tide is a relentless, galloping thing. The man knows it's coming and he can't outrun it. The water rises to his waist, his neck, his lips. Surely, he accepts his death. Why, then, the struggle? He swims until he can't, then sinks. His eyes bulge, the neck muscles strain, and here it comes: his first submerged breath. The brine freezes his larynx. His trachea collapses to protect his lungs. He's alive, yet. Starved for oxygen, his brain forces a second breath. More, but weaker, laryngospasms. Water leaks into his lungs. By the fifth cycle it's over.

And the world is well rid of him.

two

In June 1977, Lloyd's of London, the insurer, issued a request for proposals to design and operate a floating dive platform in the North Sea. Its aim: to recover lost treasure from HMS *Lutine*, the storied frigate that sank in a gale off the Dutch coast with a thousand bars of gold. Lloyd's took ownership of the wreck when it paid on the insurance claim in 1799. A hundred eighty years later, new technologies like side scan sonar gave the directors confidence that this salvage would fare better than earlier ones. Curiously, though the ship sank in only six meters of water, not more than a tenth of the gold, valued in 1977 at £10,750,000, had been recovered.

Longing to get out from behind our desks, Alec and I underbid the job and won the contract. We were young but respected, two newly minted engineers ecstatic to find work out of doors, on a treasure hunt no less.

We ended up retrofitting an old coal barge in Rotterdam and, in late May 1978, hauled it into position over the *Lutine* where it would float for the summer season. The workload had been crushing. On the day before the salvage began, our first real day off in months, I tried shaking Alec loose from his desk to go hiking with me onto the bed of the Wadden Sea.

The Wadden sits between the Dutch mainland and several barrier islands, one of which is Terschelling, nearest our platform. Twice a day at low tide, the Wadden empties into the North Sea and leaves behind a vast muddy flat, indeed the largest tidal flat in the world. Crossing the seabed from the mainland to any of the islands is something of a Dutch national sport. Thousands undertake the trek each summer, often families ranging from grandpa to grand-child, and I wanted to join them.

"At low tide there's no danger," I told Alec, "not if you go with one of the registered guides. They use walkie-talkies, ship-to-shore radios. They've even got a helicopter on call. It's absolutely safe."

He crossed his arms.

"It's a walk," I continued. "Mud, maybe some knee-high water here and there. And then, after five or six hours, we'll reach Ter-schelling." I handed him a brochure with photos of dunes and wide, white beaches. I described the starter hike I'd taken the day before, but still he showed no interest.

"It will be fun," I said. "Do you remember what fun is?"

We were standing in our temporary office, a fourth-floor attic in Harlingen on the Dutch mainland. The town felt more like a six-teenth-century fishing village than a modern shipping hub. There were masts in the harbor, steep tiled roofs, and working windmills.

"*Fun*," said Chin, "is a three-letter word for *lazy*."

Our lone window was crusty as a cataract, and I could just make out a group gathered along the wharf and our guide. She was tall, holding a pole longer than a walking stick, shorter than a fishing rod, the better to save "the weak and lame" as she'd put it the day before on my starter hike. That had gone well enough to invite her for lunch and a stroll through town; and that had gone well enough for me to sign up for a second, more strenuous hike.

Alec walked to the door and opened it. "We're expected on the platform at 5:45. That's A.M."

I grinned. "Here's my last, best offer: I'll buy you one of those inflatable tubes—the ones that go around your waist, with a duck on the front. You'll hit the flats looking like a Viking ship."

"Five forty-five, Henri. The launch leaves the dock a half-hour before."

"Learn to swim," I said.

three

$\mathcal{B}$y the time I climbed from the mud flats onto dry land, I looked and felt like a creature emerging from the primordial ooze. Exhausted, mud-spattered and, after a misstep in a tidal channel, half drowned, I sat heavily into a chair in a café by Terschelling harbor.

Liesel Kraus, my guide, approached from behind and clapped me on the shoulder. "I rescued you. On the Wadden Sea, that means you buy the beer." Without waiting for an invitation, she sat opposite me, called the waitress by name, and held up two fingers. "So," she said. "You're alive. Congratulations."

I made a show of checking my head to see if it was still attached. "I warned you. It's not an easy trek."

"You said it would be a *challenge*, not a death march."

I was wet and cold, trending toward miserable. My plan was to pay for the beer, drink quickly, and find a shower and a bed where I could be left alone to sleep or die, whichever came first.

Liesel had earned that beer by shepherding a dozen tourists through to Terschelling with the efficiency of a border collie. Out on the flats she was all business. If she talked with one hiker, she'd keep an eye on the others. Every few minutes, she'd scan the horizon or check her maps and compass. She maintained regular radio contact with a lighthouse keeper. She was focused, skilled, and smart. She was also long-limbed with auburn hair.

I found myself staring.

I paid with a sopping ten guilder note, making a little show of squeezing water from it. Liesel and the waitress laughed, and I offered a toast: "To my Moses of the mud flats. Cheers!" This time when she laughed, I saw a woman transformed. With no one to save any longer, a beer in hand, and a young man—me!—for company, she blossomed.

"If I'm Moses, then Terschelling is the Promised Land. I doubt it."

"Hold that thought," I said.

I rummaged through my pack for a camera, the one object I'd secured in a proper waterproof sack, and mumbled something about my children needing to know who saved me. I propped an elbow on the table and framed the shot. I was losing myself in the fine, bright weather and in my new companion.

"Children?"

"Future children."

We were all but strangers, Liesel Kraus and I, yet she settled her dark eyes on mine and searched the lens as if we'd long been intimate. Without the Minolta between us, I doubt we could have held the moment. A breeze lifted a strand of hair. It fluttered across her cheek. I waited, then clicked.

"Tell me," she said. "Yesterday, you mentioned you work on the *Lutine*. It's been lost forever, you know. The shoals out there form, disappear, form again. These are treacherous waters. How did you find it?"

Everyone loves a treasure hunt, but I had been working so long and hard on the *Lutine* platform that I'd steered our conversation in other directions. I didn't want to hear another word about the wreck. Yet I was eager enough to talk this time, for unless I was mistaken, she had taken an interest in me.

"We expect it's the *Lutine*," I said. I explained how the summer before, divers working for Lloyd's had found a ballast pile: rocks on the seabed laid out in a line at roughly the same latitude and longitude noted in the logs of previous salvage attempts. Liesel was right, these were difficult waters. Storms covered the wreck with sand in some years and uncovered it in others, which explained why the water's depth changed from one salvage to the next. Our divers were reasonably confident in naming the wreck, but not at all clear on how much sand we'd need to remove to get at her. We would know more when we started hauling up gold. Or not.

I had set the camera aside, but she continued watching me.

"Isn't the world strange? My brother Anselm and I grew up dreaming about the *Lutine*. It's one of the great stories of the island, you know. Papa brought us out here for summers when we were children, and we spent half our time digging up the beach, searching for treasure. There's a mass grave for the *Lutine*'s sailors on the island. And now you turn up, an honest-to-god treasure hunter. Anselm's going to love this."

As Liesel and I talked, the flood tide was creeping over the mud flats. In thirty minutes, the seabed would be covered. In two hours, the Wadden would be deep enough for ferries to haul passengers and provisions from the mainland. The café was a tiny place with a dozen tables and large terra cotta planters overflowing with geraniums and impatiens. By a spigot outside the kitchen, two Norwegians howled as they hosed caked mud off each other. At the table beside us, one of the trekkers, three beers gone, began to croak a folk tune.

"What do you do?" I asked. She avoided the topic the day before with as much determination as I had avoided the *Lutine*.

I waited. She offered nothing, and she must have realized I wouldn't be filling in any blanks to make it easy on her. Finally, she spoke. "I help my brother with a company our father started after the war. Our parents died when I was young. Anselm's fourteen years older. He raised me. When I completed school, I joined the family business."

It was her turn to wait and watch. I talked about work, how Alec was the more natural manager and how I traveled in search of new contracts—and in fact would be leaving for Hong Kong in a few days.

Out of the blue, she interrupted me. "Come to a party with me tonight."

I sat up.

"It's Anselm's birthday, and he's hosting . . . an event. Some people are coming. I bought him a sweater, like I usually do. But you're working on the *Lutine*! The two of you must meet, and I've been figuring a way. You'd make a much better present than a sweater."

The color rose in her cheeks when I asked if she wanted me to wear a bathing suit and jump from a cake.

"No, it's not like that," she said. "You'd be my date. I'm afraid Anselm invited one of his friends. I've met this one a few times in Vienna, and I don't much care for the man. But my brother's persistent. He's trying to marry me off to an über-industrialist. German, if possible. One after the next he brings them home. He says it's time. You'd be—"

"Your excuse!" I slapped the table, grinning. "Better still, your *French* excuse. I'll do my best to uphold the honor of my nation." I thought it would be great, good fun. "I accept!"

But that very instant my spirits sank as I recalled Alec's parting instructions: *five forty-five*. I couldn't not show for the first dive on the wreck. I told her, and never have I regretted two words—*I can't*—more. She looked disappointed, too, as if my company that evening might have meant something to her. "I can't," I added, "unless you can get me onto the dive platform at daybreak."

Liesel stood. "My brother or I will motor you over. You'll sleep at the house tonight. We're back in business, Henri! I'll introduce you as my French experiment." She smiled and held out a hand to close the deal.

It was a moment that has stood in sharp relief to the forgettable details of everyday life. I knew it even then. Her outstretched hand struck me like the blank signature line of a contract I hadn't thoroughly read. I was in the habit of being more careful than this. But there she was: smart, athletic, exotic (I'd never dated a German woman), taking a chance on me. And there I was, light-headed from beer and, I admit, feeling the onset of an adolescent crush. My goal in setting out that morning had been to reverse the normal curve of my life, if only for a few hours, by acting more and thinking less. So I agreed and shook her hand. "These are my only clothes," I said.

She reached for her pack. "It's a fancier party than that, in any event. You can borrow one of my brother's tuxedoes. He's a bit taller, but I can hem the pants. Shall we go?"

Tuxedoes.

Two cars waited in the parking lot: one a rusted Citroën, an island junker, and the other a Mercedes roadster, top down with gleaming grillwork. I watched her approach the cars, betting which was hers.

I was wrong.

four

The convertible flew down the backbone of Terschelling headed east, past fields as green as any I had seen in Ireland. The wind roared. I counted windmills and farmhouses, but not sheep. There were too many to count, thousands dotting the pastures like woolly, fair weather clouds.

"So . . . what's the family business?" I yelled.

Again, hesitation.

"Steel."

Ten minutes earlier, as I helped Liesel stow our packs, she'd removed her guide's jacket with its many zippered compartments to reveal arms as long and pale as those of the marble nudes I pretended to study at the Louvre as a twelve-year-old. I tried not to stare.

I cut angles through the wind with my hands. I considered how the barbed wire framed the pastures as if they were paintings. I watched everything but Liesel because what I wanted most was to study the sweep of her neck to her bare shoulder and the hollow at her collarbone.

"You're shivering," she said. "I'll draw you a bath when we get home."

Draw me a bath? I added up what little I knew until I felt certain of my hunch and said, "Kraus Steel."

She did not deny it. Her auburn hair was flying.

"Do you know," I yelled over the noise, "that I used Kraus steel on the dive platform? I looked everywhere for marine-ready steel. You're *that* Kraus!"

She shrugged, then smiled.

Now I could look. What an excellent coincidence it was. Liesel explained that she ran the family foundation, and I guessed—correctly—that she gave away more money each year than I would make in several lifetimes. She talked about her work, then stopped and pulled the car off onto a modest rise, little more than a mound that brought us to all of twelve or fifteen meters above sea level. On an island as flat as Terschelling, that offered a sweeping view to the east.

I wondered why we stopped until, gaping, I looked beyond her. "No way!" I said.

It made perfect sense.

"My family's summer home."

In the distance rose an estate built on dunes rolling down to the North Sea, as strange in that setting as the Emerald City rising over a field of poppies. The main house formed a massive gull's wing, with a pair of two-story corridors angled east and west that met at a central, turreted tower: an arrowhead, essentially, fronted by a stone turret. I had seen this tower, an old lighthouse sitting atop a promontory formed by the letters K R A U S. It was the logo burned into every piece of steel I received while building the dive platform.

I counted seven fireplaces and, connected by a series of board-walks to the main house, a dozen freestanding, single-story cottages cut into the dunes like satellites around a mother ship.

"Löwenherz," she said.

My German was passable: "Lionheart?"

She nodded. My eyes followed a long stone jetty to a dock, where I saw a boat that serviced three yachts moored offshore.

Liesel removed her sunglasses and turned toward me. "I want to tell you something and ask you something."

Before she began, she hit the hazard button with her fist and pointed. "This is what you're dealing with. I need to get it out in the open because I've been around too long not to know that my family's wealth screws things up. Half the men I meet see Löwenherz or my apartment in Munich and run because they'll never make as much money as I do. The other half think they've hit the lottery, and I kick them out because I can't stand them getting fat on bonbons and calling the staff at two in the morning for sandwiches. And this is good German stock I'm talking about. Which sort of man are you?"

It's not a question often asked on a first date, and I didn't walk around with a ready answer in my pocket. What kind of man was I? My father was a civil servant, an analyst for French naval intelligence; my mother, a university biologist. Our family read books, attended the symphony, and camped most August holidays in the mountains or at the beach. I owned a twelve-year-old Peugeot with torn upholstery. I owned no summer home and never knew anyone who *named* their home, summer or otherwise.

I told her this and said, "Does poverty disqualify me?"

She didn't miss a beat. "Not unless money disqualifies me."

I worked out a math problem on the palm of my hand with an imaginary pencil. "I may be wrong," I said, looking up. "But if half the men in your life run and the other half get bounced, you're talking one hundred percent. This would mean there's no man in your life. Currently."

My hopes soared.

"My brother's getting nervous I'll die an old maid, if that's your question. Which explains Anselm's friend from Vienna. He comes from the family that owns Bayer Pharmaceuticals. You know, the aspirin people. Their summer home is larger than Löwenherz, and they call it a cottage." She rolled her eyes. "There's something else," she said.

I waited.

"My father ran a steel mill during the war. In the late forties, factory owners all over Germany were being tried and sent to prison for using slave labor. Not Otto, because he saved people's lives like that man Schindler. Ten witnesses came forward to vouch for him. They signed an affidavit, and he was never charged with war crimes. But he was a member of the Nazi party. Some people, some of the men I've met, can't get past that. You should know now."

I knew her father's story, more or less, the instant I learned she was a Kraus. A few years earlier, there had been a boycott in Paris of products from German companies that profited through business with the Third Reich. The action was meant to force the companies to examine their wartime dealings, publish accounts, apologize and—if warranted—compensate slave laborers. The biggest names were easy to recall: Krupp, Siemens, and the I.G. Farben subsidiaries, including Bayer, which splintered after Germany's defeat. Kraus Steel was mentioned, which I had reason to recall when ordering beams for the dive platform.

"Do you understand?" she said. "My father wore a swastika lapel pin."

How could I understand? My father fought in the French Resistance. I was born in 1950 and had no direct memories of the war, though I may as well have lived through it for all of the stories I'd heard about the occupation. So, no, I couldn't understand Liesel or the German view of things much beyond this: that as a child, when I asked my father what he did during those years, I got answers that made me proud. When Liesel asked, she got news of affidavits and proofs of innocence. She had inherited a heavy burden along with that mansion in the distance.

"I enjoy your company," she said. "You liked me well enough yesterday, when I was just a guide. And today, in town and on the flats. You liked me, didn't you?"

This was true.

"Well, then." She hitched a thumb over her shoulder, pointing to Löwenherz. "Perhaps you could like me, even with that. But I want to make sure you understand. Hitler shook my father's hand. My father held my hand as we walked on the beach or in the city. At the café, I shook your hand." She fell against the seat as if she'd pushed a boulder up a hill, fully expecting it to roll back down and crush her. "That's it. That's all my monsters. I'm thirty years old. I was born in 1948, three years after the war, and sometimes I feel like I'm running from *my* Nazi past. It isn't fair."

It wasn't.

"I'm no German industrialist," I said.

"Thank God."

"Your brother won't be pleased."

"Sure he will. You work on the *Lutine*. That trumps everything."

Yachts rode their moorings as the tide ran. Farther out to sea, sails leaned into the wind while under the platform, a lost ship waited to yield her secrets. The broad Terschelling sky held it all: Liesel's burden and Liesel's beauty, honest work for my young firm, and the memory of a war that would not let go.

"I do have a question," I said.

She turned, her eyes red.

"I know we're playacting tonight. But will I have to kiss you?"

five

The estate buzzed with guests and staff preparing the banquet hall and ballroom. Anselm had run a bus service from the ferry landing that afternoon, and some thirty couples would be staying the night. I nodded my hellos to several as I made my way to the beach, where, after the promised bath and a change into borrowed clothes, I walked the tidal line.

Not five minutes later, I saw a boy, seven or eight years old, running with arms spread wide, making airplane sounds. He buzzed in and out of the dunes, onto the open beach, then back again making *eerrrrrm*, zooming noises. When he saw me, he banked right with a long sweep toward the sea, then back to his visitor. He was flushed and sweating when he arrived, his hair matted with sand.

This could only be Anselm's son. Liesel had run through the family I'd be meeting, and only one eight-year-old with wavy blond hair was on the roster: Friedrich Wilhelm Gustav Kraus. He'd blown through one knee of his pants and stained his otherwise white shirt purple with a juice of some sort.

"The beach plums are ripe," he said.

I looked for and found a hint of Liesel in his face. "Where can I find them?"

She had explained that the boy came into the world wearing the goggles and leather helmet of a combat ace. All he wanted to do was fly. He pointed to a dune fence half buried in sand and some low, scrubby bushes with flowers. "Magda and I are going to make plum jam tomorrow," he said. "You can have some. Come on, I'll show you. I'm a Stuka." He raised his arms and buzzed ahead, looking over his shoulder to see if I would follow. "Make machine-gun sounds," he called.

It was a fine afternoon in late May, the sun fat and yellow. We cast long shadows over the beach and dunes as we ran. I kept pace and gave him a lusty *Rat-atat-tat-tattt*, surprised I could move at all after my hike that morning. Friedrich was agile. He stalled to let me catch up, then banked hard right, dipping and pirouetting until he was on my tail. "I got you!" he cried.

When I banked into the dunes to lose him, I looked up the beach—and stopped dead on seeing a pair of large, heavily muscled dogs streaking toward me. My pulse rocketed. When Friedrich cried, *"You're dead!"* and caught up to me, I placed myself between the boy and the onrushing dogs, then reached into my pants pocket for a trusted, compact weapon.

From the age of eight, I've carried a metal T that my father gave me after a nasty episode. At a park in Paris, I was off running when a Rottweiler slipped its chain and chased me down. Before anyone could stop it, the dog had sunk its teeth into my calf and begun to shake me about. My father knocked it senseless with the lid of a trash barrel and would have killed the animal had its owner not tackled him. But the damage was done: my leg had been "tenderized," according to the emergency room doctor.

To this day, my calf aches at a change in weather and the approach of angry-looking dogs. It took months to learn how to walk and run again with a mangled calf. After a long convalescence, my father presented me with what he called a tool: a smoothly welded, stainless steel T of his own design that was, in fact, a small but very efficient weapon. He taught me to hold the cross of the T in my fist and to position the trunk between my ring and middle fingers.

He was more serious than usual the day he presented it, kneeling to my height and taking my shoulders in his hands. *Henri*, he said. *I won't always be around to save you. When you're attacked, always face the beast. Never run. If you must, let it bite you once, then aim for the eyes and throat.*

For twenty years I had carried that T in my front right pocket, prepared for an attack that never came. But I had formed a lifelong habit by that point. I'd left my wallet to dry back in my room at Löwenherz, perfectly willing to part with, and even lose, my money, IDs, and credit cards. Yet I took my father's T onto the dunes because I took it everywhere, just as I take my lungs and intestines with me on leaving a room.

As I tracked the dogs and set a firm stance, I was glad I had. The animals looked more like small lions than dogs.

"Hermann! Albert!" Friedrich yelled.

He ran from behind me and fell to his knees, his arms wide. When the dogs met him, they pranced and whined and licked his face. They were beautiful animals, I must admit: tawny-colored with thick, squarish heads and muscled like pit bulls though easily twice the size of that fighting breed. Friedrich tried climbing aboard the nearer one, which shook him off.

The dogs ambled over to me, sniffing, and I could guess why: they smelled Anselm's familiar scent on these clothes, mingled with mine. They turned circles around me, whining.

Friedrich leapt onto the one he called Hermann. "Giddy-up!"

A man approached. "Opa!" the boy yelled, slipping off the dog. He ran to his grandfather, already dressed in his tuxedo for the party and looking as out of place on the dunes as Löwenherz itself.

"Hermann, Albert. *Kommen!*"

The dogs trotted to their master, Anselm's father-in-law and Otto's partner in Kraus Steel. I bowed instead of releasing the T, keeping my hand in my pocket.

"A fine evening for a party. Viktor Schmidt, at your service." He was as kind and jovial as St. Nicholas. He was also short, with a thick bristle of white hair and a bull neck. He leaned forward as he spoke, as if into a stiff wind. "And you've come to Löwenherz . . . as a guest of—"

"Liesel Kraus. Don't worry. I'm not crashing your party."

"Ah! You're that French stray she pulled in from the flats. I know all about it."

"Opa, you promised to teach me to dance tonight!"

Liesel had never not known Viktor Schmidt—uncle by long association, not blood, just as the man who lived downstairs from my family's apartment in Paris was uncle to me. Every family seems to have one. Schmidt's daughter, Theresa, and Anselm had been crib mates after the war while their fathers built Kraus Steel. Their marriage twenty years later consolidated the partnership into a single bloodline.

"I don't know the breed," I said, nodding to the dogs. "Handsome animals."

"My boys! Indeed they are! South African Boerboels. Bred as lion hunters, in fact. Outstanding guard dogs. They're gentle with children and furiously protective of family. My boys. I trained them myself."

"Opa, what about dancing?"

"Yes, Friedrich. Fine. Enough already. The orchestra was setting up when I left the house. We'll have a grand evening. But I warn you, you'll have to dance with your sister."

The child made a face.

"Friedrich and I just met," I said. "He's a fine pilot." I reached to tousle Friedrich's hair, and the dogs growled.

"Don't mind them," said Schmidt, smiling. "Hey now, let's have some fun. Friedrich, do you see those rabbits over there?" He pointed, and I saw them just before they skittered for the cover of dune grass.

I could scarcely believe the discipline of these animals, which must have smelled the rabbits or detected movement well before Schmidt did. Yet they didn't flinch—not until he waited a five-count, then swept the flat of his hand toward the dunes and cried: "Hupt!" The dogs flew from his side.

Moments later, Friedrich called: "They've got one!"

I followed into the taller grass and found Albert and Hermann crouched on the sand, a rabbit paralyzed in fear between them. Friedrich sat on his haunches, staring.

"Ach hupt!"

The dogs closed in but didn't touch the rabbit.

"Friedrich. What shall we do?"

The boy looked at the Boerboels, then to his grandfather.

"You decide, Opa."

I glanced up and down the beach. We were alone.

"No, you'll be nine next month. You're a young man now and it's time you decide these things. Watch Albert and Hermann closely, their absolute obedience. There's nothing these fellows want more than a fresh kill. But see how they wait for my command? If you train your animals well, child, they'll serve you well. Now then, what shall we do?"

I slipped a hand into my pocket again, then removed it. What was my plan, to attack the dogs and end up in a hospital in order to save a rabbit? I prepared to turn away if Friedrich gave the command to kill.

"Hermann, unst!"

The dog nearer to me broke from his crouch and lunged for the rabbit, which bolted into the waiting jaws of the second dog.

"Brilliant!" cried Schmidt. "Excellent work, Friedrich!"

The child turned to his grandfather. "Opa, the rabbit's scared. Look at its eyes."

It was true. I, too, was scared. I had killed spiders and assorted bugs. I had fished and watched trout flop on riverbanks until they died. But I had never killed a sentient animal with eyes that suggested a soul. The child's color changed. The high, ruddy life in him drained.

Schmidt shifted his weight in the sand and said: "Yes, well, nothing leaves this world without fear. That's a fact. Shall we have rabbit stew for lunch tomorrow?" He folded his arms and waited.

"The command is Z-I-N-D with a hand movement?"

Schmidt nodded.

I was about to excuse myself when the child shouted: "Luft!"

The dog loosed its hold, and the rabbit escaped.

Schmidt laughed as he knelt and reached into a side pocket. "You're a gentle one, aren't you? *Kommen!*" he called to the dogs. They loped to his side, and he produced a plastic bag filled with neatly cubed pieces of raw meat. "Good, Albert. That's my Hermann. Good boys!" He stroked them behind the ears, cooing their names.

"Off with you, then," he said. "Take the boys to my apartment and get changed for the party." He swept a hand toward the mansion and the dogs took off, the child happy—a plane once more—zooming behind.

Friedrich disappeared into the dunes, and I turned to Schmidt. "Your grandson called himself a Stuka."

"A damned good choice! It was the best single-engine prop dive bomber ever built. . . . Isn't he a fine child! Isn't he splendid?"

He leaned toward me as he spoke, and I found myself leaning away. I could only agree. Friedrich *was* splendid.

"It's how we make them," said Schmidt. "Welcome to Löwenherz. You're *Herr* Poincaré in this house, not *Monsieur*. Make yourself at home."

six

"Shit and shit squared, Henri. We get perfect weather for the last two weeks—and now this for the first day of our dive? Low pressure from Greenland's going to hit us like a fist by sunrise. I may need that inner tube after all. You said it had a duck on the front?"

I'd left the beach for Löwenherz, determined to steer clear of Schmidt for the evening. Alec would want to know I hadn't drowned on the flats and that I'd be making my own way to the platform, so I called. On learning my host was Liesel Kraus, he accused me of gold digging.

"I should have gone on the trek with you after all," he said. "Really, between the two of us, would it even have been a contest? Women think I'm a fucking *prince*, Henri. They can't resist. And call your father. He's trying to find you."

"Any message?"

"No, he said to call, no matter how late. This Liesel of yours. She's really *that* Kraus?"

SHE WAS talking to Schmidt across the ballroom, touching his arm for punctuation as she told what must have been a very good story because Schmidt slapped his leg at one point, laughing hard enough for me to hear him over the music. Liesel's affection for her godfather startled me. Here I was drawn to her. She adored him. Must I, in that case, take this man on as a friend? I turned my attention elsewhere when they stepped onto the dance floor.

One could learn a great deal about Otto Kraus from the ballroom at Löwenherz. The coffered ceilings, the parade of gilt-framed mirrors suggesting Versailles, the crystal chandeliers, and the velvet-trimmed chairs all hinted at money that didn't know what to do with itself.

Two men to my right were puffing on Cuban cigars, observing the scene. One of them, short and rotund, looked like Kaiser Wilhelm with his waxed moustache. He was shaking his head. "Anselm flew in the string section from the Vienna Philharmonic, believe it or not. Landed them on the goddamned dunes in a helicopter."

The waltz ended, and Liesel broke away from Schmidt and crossed the room in my direction. She had made a definite change from her hiking clothes. Her shape-fitting black dress was cut low enough to fuel my imagination. She wore a long strand of pearls. Her hair beneath the chandeliers flashed reds and chestnut. It also tumbled to her bare, well-formed shoulders, and I found myself staring again.

"*You* clean up nicely," she said.

I kissed her right cheek, then her left.

"This is when you earn your rent money, Henri. That's Mr. Bayer talking to my brother. His real name is Hans Kellerman. Do you see, with Anselm—the tall one?"

As we edged around the dance floor, every few paces some new gray-haired eminence stopped to congratulate her. "Well done, dear! We're so proud of you!" Compliment followed compliment until we made our way to Anselm Kraus and Herr Kellerman.

"Why all the congratulations?" I asked.

"Never mind that. Here, meet my brother."

Anselm was the star around which the people of this room turned. I had seen it before, 'the great man effect': guests standing near to feel the warmth of the maestro or, better still, to let something clever slip and be noticed. Kellerman had one meaty hand at Anselm's shoulder, explaining something that required flourishes with the other hand. He stood a head taller than Kraus, who was tall—my height—and in place of a bow tie wore an onyx brooch as black as his hair. Kellerman possessed a quiescent, Cro-Magnon intensity that reminded me of Anthony Quinn, the actor:

handsome but, on a bad day, potentially volcanic. He caught sight of Liesel's hand in mine, and his color changed.

Liesel didn't hesitate to interrupt.

I extended a hand to Kraus, who hesitated as if we'd been introduced via phone across a transatlantic cable. I said *hello*. He paused before responding as if he risked tripping over my words. I didn't know what Liesel had said, but the man was clearly appraising me.

"My sister says you make things, Herr Poincaré."

It was not an unreasonable definition of engineering. "Yes, I do."

"My father believed you can trust people who make things. He didn't care if it was a chamber pot or an airplane. Industry is the proper measure of a man, he thought, preferably German industry." Anselm was looking at his sister, not me, as he said this. "We'll keep an open mind for the moment."

Was he marking territory? Laying out a grand view of the world? I said nothing.

"Liesel also says that you designed and built the dive platform out at the *Lutine*."

"We're hoping it's the *Lutine*. But yes, my partner and I built it."

"And that you used Kraus steel to anchor that platform over the wreck site."

His hesitation had meant nothing, after all. I had made a good impression before meeting Anselm Kraus because I was clever enough to have used *his* steel on my platform. I invited him for a visit and offered to show him around. Liesel stood beside me, her arm looped through mine.

Kellerman took a half step back.

"I'll take you up on that," said Kraus. "My sister has told you about my love affair with that ship. I can recite all kinds of facts and figures: where she was built, her tonnage, the number and types of cannons, her captains, her capture by the British at Toulon, all the salvage attempts since 1800. But I want you to tell me everything *you* know—tomorrow morning, when we motor out to the platform."

Liesel shrugged. "I forgot that I promised Friedrich a trip to Harlingen on the early ferry. I'm afraid you'll have to put up with my brother."

Kraus looked me up and down. "That's a damn fine-looking tuxedo!"

The three of us laughed. Kellerman, missing the joke, excused himself.

seven

At dinner, Liesel was obliged to sit beside her brother. Theresa was in charge of the seating and shoehorned me between two more of Liesel's uncles by long association, Eckehart Nagel and Franz Hofmann.

Nagel, a physician from Buenos Aires, sat to my right. He was a lean, aristocratic man, perfectly bald with a well-shaped head and fluent enough in French to give me a rest from my substandard German.

"Liesel told me all about you this afternoon," he said. His voice held an unmistakable note of approval, as if it were his right and privilege to pass judgment. He asked about the engineering business, and explained how he returned to Germany on occasion to consult with a few patients who insisted on seeing him.

"But after the war . . . *pfff.*" He waved a hand. "Germany was done. I wanted a new start. So we moved. The best thing I ever did!"

Schoolchildren know that Germans didn't resettle in Buenos Aires in 1946 for a change of climate. But I let it go and made the acquaintance of Franz Hofmann, a gray and gaunt man with food stains on his jacket and patches of white stubble he'd missed shaving. I'd seen him shuffle through a waltz with Anselm's wife. Off the dance floor, he used a cane, and I was shocked at the strength of his grip as we introduced ourselves. He could have pulled me into a grave.

Uncle Franz, I later learned, had suffered a stroke, and Anselm's family had provided a room at their home in Munich and here on Terschelling. He had no one else, apparently, and the Krauses were nothing if not loyal. Nagel whispered in my ear, "He's a shadow of his former self. He was a magnificent man."

This was a German-speaking crowd, men and women of distinct generations: snowy-haired contemporaries of Otto in their sixties and seventies, and gray-flecked friends of Anselm in their early to mid-forties. It wasn't a generous thought, but I wondered how the elders would have reacted had I lobbed a *Heil Hitler* into the room. They *had* voted for Hitler, after all; nearly everyone did who wanted to avoid a visit from their local Storm Troopers.

I don't remember the dinner, save for the fact that I was pleased not to be eating rabbit. Over coffee, Anselm stood at one end of a very long table and boasted about his sister and how she had founded the Kraus Family Charities.

"It's the Kraus one-two punch," he said. "Take Uganda, for example. When I learned of their iron ore deposits, I struck a deal with President Amin to dig two mines. Liesel met with the ministries of health and education to build schools and hospitals. We have all won in Uganda—the president, Kraus Steel, and the children! So tonight, just for a moment, and without letting it go to our heads, let's celebrate and feel good about ourselves. Cheers to you all!"

On cue, a waiter rolled out Anselm's birthday cake.

LATER, AFTER fending off more congratulations with polite thank you's, Liesel walked me onto the terrace. We were holding hands when I felt the first, painful cramping in my calf—the weather changing, just as Alec promised.

I glanced at my watch. The dive would begin in eight hours. It would be raining, not that the divers cared. The wind and wave action would be another matter if sand kicked up over the wreck and cut visibility.

"Let's walk," she said.

She was exhausted from the morning's hike and all the attention that evening. But given all the talk of Uganda, I had to learn if she'd met Idi Amin. In those days, you couldn't not know the man's reputation.

"Yes, we've met. Several times."

"And?"

"He's charming for a butcher. But what am I going to do? There's a hundred thousand million tons of high-grade iron ore in the east and southwest of Uganda—and a countryside filled with illiterate children and people dying of dengue fever. Anselm's in Uganda, like it or not; and I try to do some good wherever he does business. That's the model, and sometimes I have to hold my nose."

She felt me wincing.

"Oh, please. Would you let children die because Amin's a pig? It's better to accommodate the pig and save the farm."

We walked along a stone balustrade. The dune grasses were bending before a rising breeze. The moon danced on the water, and I considered every kind of romantic entanglement.

"I'm glad you almost drowned," she said. She stopped and straightened my bow tie. "No, that came out wrong. I'm glad that what happened, happened. I'm glad you're here."

"The experiment . . . it's going well so far?"

She smiled. "Yes, *Herr* Poincaré."

"And Mr. Bayer . . . he'll survive? He didn't look pleased."

"I saw him later with one of the servers, an island girl. I suppose he'll have a guest to his room tonight, after all."

There are no words to describe the pulse that shot through me as we kissed. That afternoon, when she led our group off the flats and turned to congratulate us, I thought, *Here is a woman who could make someone very happy.* Earlier that evening, as she crossed the ballroom heading in my direction, I realized that that someone could be me. When our lips touched, I found myself in full adolescent free fall. It was preposterous. I knew it and had no interest in stopping it.

I told her I was leaving for Hong Kong.

"When will I see you next? We're returning to Munich in a few days."

I had no pressing business in Munich, but Munich it would be.

eight

$\mathcal{M}$y father had called to tell me that Isaac Kahane, my own uncle by long association, had died. He was old and failing; we had all expected it, but just the same the news came as a shock.

On the balcony, I thought of him as clouds slowly blotted the moon. Here was Isaac in his bow tie on a favorite bench at the park, reading *Le Monde*; here, a five-year-old running, watching the man grow bright with a smile. He'd clear a spot and say, "Henri, come sit and tell me all about it." The "it" didn't matter. Life and our nearness mattered. He took interest in all that I said. I was precious to him and knew it in the way a child knows these things.

He had lost six sons in the war. And his wife. Freda had lost two children and her husband. They found each other in the summer of 1945 and decided the world was too dangerous and hateful a place to risk raising and loving children again. What a surprise, then, that the child who lived in the apartment upstairs on rue Jeanne d'Arc should melt their blighted hearts.

I was the beneficiary of their loss.

It took little time to discover that Isaac's great weakness was butterscotch. I'd save my allowance and go to the confectioner's as often as I could. Isaac, in turn, would accept my candy as long as I ate some with him; then he'd dip into his pockets for some treasure that always came with a story. Here was the pen the Tsar used to proclaim freedom for the serfs. Here, a cat's-eye marble so perfect it once started a war. I believed these stories, and once I was old enough to know they were stories, I believed *in* them, in their power to summon Isaac and Freda when I wanted them near.

—⁕—

LEGS SET wide, one hand steady at the helm and the other resting on twin throttles, Anselm Kraus gunned his sleek runabout, *Blast Furnace*, hard through the waves. Strong winds out of the north-west had collided with a flood tide running from the southeast, creating a vicious chop.

I shivered behind the windscreen, my stomach in knots.

"You should have told me about the seasickness!" he yelled over the engines. "I've got medicine back at Löwenherz."

At that early hour, all I could see of him was his chest and face, lit from below by the dim, orange lights of the instrument panel. Apart from that, the world was black. And, in my sea-sickened state, spinning.

"The *Lutine*," he called. "Why salvage her now?"

Even contemplating an answer turned my stomach. He directed me to a compartment beneath my seat, where I found a bottle of soda water. *Blast Furnace* slammed through some waves and skimmed the tops of others, bucking and heaving. I leaned over-board and retched, trying to make a joke of the fact that Alec's and my first substantial job should be at sea. I knew all about my weak stomach; still, I hadn't hesitated when writing the Lloyd's proposal.

"Cheer up, Henri! No one ever died of seasickness. I'll give us some throttle to take some motion out of the boat. Come on, take your mind off it. Talk. Why does Lloyd's think it can salvage the *Lutine* now, after all the other salvage attempts? And what the hell does my sister see in a Frenchman?"

I looked at him and threw up.

"Oh—I see," he said, listening to me retch. "It's your charm."

In between bouts of hanging my head over the side of the boat, I explained the technologies that had given Lloyd's the con-fidence to undertake the project: side scan sonar, vacuum hoses that pumped sand through a screen that would catch the smallest artifacts, improvements in the design of scuba gear and underwater lights.

"It's all about the technology," I managed. "If this salvage doesn't work, Lloyd's will wait another hundred years for better technology."

Behind Kraus, a dull line at the horizon cracked open like the eye of a drunk after a bad night. Soon I'd be able to attach a body to Anselm's face, which meant that soon I, too, would be visible.

He drove the boat hard and, after a few minutes, the sky brightened and he got a good look at me. "Good God, you've puked all over my new foul weather gear. Hose it off or buy me another set!"

I saluted him and drank my soda water, looking for Isaac's ghost in the darkness.

"My sister doesn't make friends easily," said Kraus. "But here you are, and I got all of two hours of sleep because she found some man who happens to be connected to the *Lutine*. It's my Achilles' heel, you know. Actually both are: my sister and that ship. I'm forty-two, and my mind's been stuck on the wreck since I was six. Once, my father had to send a boat to rescue me. I took an underpowered skiff out here because I wanted to be near her. I must have thought the *Lutine* would rise from the deep if I called her name. It means *tormentress*, you know. *Lutine*. Fitting as hell."

We hit a wave.

"Did you drown?"

"Damn near! By the time they found me, I was half swamped in a sea snottier than this one. Just so you know, I love my sister but you're not the reason I'm out in this slop at five in the morning. I need to be near that wreck. You're not offended, I hope. I give you a ride, you get me closer. It's how business gets done."

Despite the seasickness, I enjoyed his company. Anselm's passion for the *Lutine* explained a great deal about Friedrich's passion for his Stuka. What a fine thing it was, I thought, for a son to resemble his father this way.

We hit another wave that sent us sailing through the air. Anselm whooped when we landed with a satisfying *thwack*. "Really," he said. "This little boat could take on a hurricane. And you truly look like hell."

I retched again.

"You know, I tried checking you out, but I couldn't find a damn thing on P&C Engineering or Consulting or whatever you call yourselves. Do you people even exist?"

"I'm here," I said. "We're small. But yes, we exist."

"How small?"

"Two of us for the moment."

"My father started small. You have to begin somewhere. What's your next job?"

"The canal authority in Bruges. Repairs. After that, nothing just yet. I'm fishing, you might say, and in a few days I leave for Hong Kong to bid on a project. We've made the final cut. The job could launch us."

The prospect of steady work lingered in the salt air for a time, as Anselm worked the throttle and studied a confused sea. The wheel on *Blast Furnace* had a knob at six o'clock, which he grabbed and spun hard as a wave the size of a two-story building rose off our stern and threatened to swamp us. Anselm spun the wheel hard and surfed down its face, whooping again.

"How old are you?" he called.

"Twenty-eight. And I honestly don't see how I can make it another year. I feel awful."

"Right on schedule, Henri. I like it that you're going fishing in the East. I've got a ship-breaking yard in Hong Kong. Viktor Schmidt is going out there in a few days to check on some things. If your visits overlap, he should show you around. Manufacturing's moving east, you know. I can hire twelve men in Hong Kong for the price of one in Germany, and China's going to be even cheaper. Deng Xiaoping has positioned the country to take on textiles and manufacturing. I've met him, you know."

I stared.

"So Liesel's dating a younger man!"

"We've known each other for forty-eight hours, Anselm. Let's see if she takes my call when I return from Hong Kong."

"She'll take your call."

"And you know this because?"

"Because I saw the way she looks at you. You're French, but I'll make an exception for that because you build things."

The bow exploded through a wave that sprayed Kraus full on. He roared. "All of Asia is opening," he said, clearing the brine from his eyes. "Last week I signed an agreement with the new regime in Cambodia to build another ship-breaking yard. That's an even sharper deal for labor. Pol Pot is having currency problems just now. We'll set up, then Liesel will follow in a few months. Hospital clinics, schools. You know the drill."

"Pol Pot?"

He caught my meaning.

"You think I don't read the papers? He's a genocidal madman who's cash poor at the moment, which creates an opening."

"For the Kraus one-two punch."

He backed off the throttle and sat the boat hard into the sea. It rose, then dipped as it lost forward motion, and began to pitch violently. I threw up again. One wave nearly dumped me overboard.

"Don't lecture me, Henri."

I saluted him.

"Hell, forget that," he said. "Liesel thinks you're dating."

Seawater slapped my face, and I was liking him less and less. "Start the damn boat, Anselm."

"I don't care if you're poor," he said. "Everybody begins somewhere. I like your ambition, and I might even like you. I just need to know your intentions. Do you understand? My parents are gone, and I'm Liesel's older brother. So let's establish something."

I lifted my head.

"Tell me you're not leading her on."

I grabbed the windscreen and the gunwale and lifted myself to a sitting position. "She's thirty years old. Do you really think it's necessary for you to—"

"You're goddamned right it is! She's a wealthy woman, and men have broken her heart hunting for money."

German men, I nearly said. My own laughter sounded bizarre to me. The sky was the color of steel. The sea was slate, and the world spun. I hardly knew which way was up, and it struck me as odd that history should land me at so strange a moment, bobbing like a cork and about to lose my stomach lining because Anselm Kraus needed to interrogate me.

"Sorry to disappoint you," I said. "I fell for Liesel the old-fashioned way. Did your father-in-law question you like this? Start the boat. I'm suffering out here, Anselm."

He cocked his head. "Viktor and my father were friends. He knew me my whole life. I came pre-loved." He smiled.

A wave hit my face and Kraus stared, appraising me again. It wasn't the very best time to vomit, but I did.

"Look me in the eyes."

I tried my best. "What the hell? Get us moving."

"Tell me you understand."

"I do. I just don't want to vomit anymore."

"She's my sister," he said, as if that explained this abuse. "And that, I believe, is your dive platform. Unless you can think of anything else out here lit up like a department store." Kraus hit the throttle. "The *Lutine!*" he yelled. The engines roared, and *Blast Furnace* jumped like a sprinter at a starting gun.

nine

"*U*gly enough to be gorgeous" was how my partner described the dive platform when we first designed it. Alec had a talent for seeing projects in three dimensions while still in the drawing phase. I was made of denser stuff and needed to see the thing itself, under construction, before making judgments. But now that the platform was built and towed into position over the ballast pile, I agreed that it was both ugly and gorgeous—a magnificent blend of safety and function. I saw our achievement all over again in the face of Anselm Kraus as he climbed aboard.

We built the platform with a crew's quarters, a diving hut, a conservator's lab, a dining room and a lounge—all bolted, then welded, deep into the structure of the repurposed coal barge. Twelve people would live aboard during the weekdays throughout the salvage season, with a watchman posted on weekends. Lloyd's had hired six divers working in two shifts throughout the day, a sluice operator, a crane operator, a cook, a marine archeologist and her assistant, and us to serve as ongoing coordinators. But that was Alec's job. My plan was to stay as far from the North Sea as possible.

We had anchored the barge platform at four corners with beams of Kraus steel driven deep into the sand. Loops of heavy chain connected these beams to the barge, which rose and fell with the tides. I had consulted historical records, tide charts, and lunar cycles to calculate the maximum storm surge during a hundred year event. I spec'd the anchor beams five meters above that, figuring any storm strong enough to float the barge off its anchors would overwhelm northern Europe—in which case, a barge lost at sea would be the least of Lloyd's worries.

The risk, our employer agreed, was acceptable.

My head cleared as we climbed aboard the rig. With its mass, it moved like an enormous beast slow to anger. *Blast Furnace*, meanwhile, bucked against its line at the pontoon dock.

Before he said a word, Kraus surveyed the platform. Then he turned to me. "You designed *and* built this?" Beauty for a man who ran steel mills meant function. He approved.

"The *Lutine*," he said. "I feel it. She's down there."

Alec had just introduced himself. "Don't go all Ouija board on us, captain. We've got a one-in-fourteen chance it's the *Lutine*. I'm sure Henri explained all this: until there's proof, what you see on this platform is an expensive failure that we, thank God, are not paying for."

"What kind of proof?" asked Kraus.

Alec was quick to answer. "Gold would do. Or a cannon with a fleur-de-lis. Either would give Lloyd's a proper erection." He tucked a clipboard beneath his arm and smiled. "That," he said, pointing, "would not be proof. The divers belted it yesterday afternoon, but we're just now hauling it up."

The crane operator was lowering a long steel shaft onto the deck.

"Hardly from an eighteenth-century frigate."

"Storms must have pushed it onto the wreck site. The divers told me it poses a danger, and they wanted it clear."

We approached the crane, and Kraus inspected. "Steel," he said. "Pitted, fairly low grade with a heavy sulfur content. Do you see the way it's oxidized? It's a drive shaft, I'd say, submerged for decades. I would have heard about a commercial ship going down anytime in the last thirty years. This could date to the First or Second World War—and from the looks of the shaft, it was a large ship."

Several of the crew members were listening, and I heard some excited talk about another wreck in the vicinity. I gathered they'd be investigating in their spare time; divers earned major bragging rights on being the first to find and identify a wreck.

"In the last few hundred years, at least a thousand ships sank out here," said Kraus. "With our tides and storms, I'd expect you to find ship-to-shore radios pushed hard against eighteenth-century frigates. It's bound to be a junkyard down there." Kraus was clearly pleased to be aboard. "And to think I sit behind a desk all day. *This* is real work."

Alec pulled me aside to report that the Argentine government had contacted him about using our design to dive on a galleon lost in the River Plate, the *Preciado*. "They'll refit their own barge," he said. "They just want our specs and a welding scheme. Easy money. They're sending a few people out here soon. Evidently, they heard about us through Lloyd's."

"Everything you need, nothing you don't!" said Kraus, joining us. "Your platform is perfect." He looked again at the rig, then at me, as if piecing something together. "Are you related to Jules Henri Poincaré? The mathematician. A connection, perhaps?"

I walked him to the sluice box.

"He was my great-grandfather."

"Excellent! I see it in your design. Safety. Pragmatism. Elegance. It must be a comfort to know his blood runs in you. Listen to me. *Never* underestimate the importance of blood."

Isaac wasn't in the ground yet; but had he been, he would have turned at the thought of a German thirty years after the war extolling the virtue of bloodlines. I let it go. I pointed Kraus to the sluice box where, short of finding Alec's cannon, we were likeliest to prove the wreck was the *Lutine*. In addition to a thousand bars of gold, she had sailed with strongboxes filled with gold coins. It was the airlift, essentially a long vacuum hose, that would catch the coins. Finding a few bucketsful would be definitive.

Anselm didn't want to tempt the weather any longer. He shook my hand, and said, "Call my assistant in Munich. She'll give you Viktor's contact information in Hong Kong. I want you to tour our facility with him, Henri. Go see that, then let's talk. You've done a fine job here. Outstanding."

He was halfway down the ladder at the pontoon dock when I called his name. "She doesn't need anyone's permission," I said.

Kraus grinned. "Of course she doesn't. But she has it, for what it's worth. Happy fishing in Hong Kong. And tell your partner to call if your vacuum cleaner spits out a bar of gold. I'd like to hold it."

ten

"*I*saac Kahane lived and Hitler didn't. *L'chaim!*"

I raised a glass in celebration, two fingers deep, in what was threatening to be an even twelve rounds. A dozen of us sat in my father's book-lined study, where we retreated after the funeral to honor Isaac by serving pickled herring and potato vodka, his favorites. The fruit and vegetable seller, the fishmonger, the tobacconist, the baker, the launderette owner whose machines were always broken: these were the faces of my childhood.

For all my young life I ran errands for my parents and the Kahanes to and from their shops. I played football with their sons and kissed their daughters. We exchanged holiday presents and shared meals on summer evenings. After paying their respects to Freda, each in turn squeezed my hand; for after Freda, they knew, I was the one who would suffer most.

Of the assembled, the one couple I didn't know was the Zeligmans. Jacob had offered the last toast, and I figured him for family—from Poland, judging by the accent. Yet to the best of my knowledge, the Nazis had erased Isaac's relations. Some died in the Warsaw ghetto; some, in the remote villages to the east, standing over trenches they'd dug themselves; some, in the camps; some, in the cargo holds of repurposed furniture trucks, sucking down carbon monoxide.

Whoever this Zeligman was, he stood in my father's study like a centuries-old oak. Parts of him were broken. His fingers were bent. He used a cane to help with an arthritic hip. For all that, however, he was full of life. His white hair was thick, his face pocked with skin cancers. He wore a Star of David around his neck on a thick gold chain and, just as much a testament to his faith, a tattooed number on his left forearm.

Auschwitz.

He had wept at the grave. By the time we reconvened at the apartment, he was almost giddy in celebrating the life of a Jew who'd outlived the Reich. "The fucking *Deutsch*," he roared, pouring himself another shot.

"Yaakov, stop," said his wife. "Don't curse!"

"Why not? Isaac *lived*. And while we're at it, let's spit in the eye of Reinhard Vogt, that twisted bastard."

I raised my glass to the curse, though I had no idea who Vogt might be. Meanwhile, Tosha Zeligman swayed back and forth, whimpering, "*Gottenyu*, God, oh God," looking as if she'd never left her shtetl in Belarus. She wore black stockings rolled to the knee, a black dress and a black, lace kerchief. Wringing her hands, she looked across the room to Freda.

"Yaakov's right," she said. "Your Isaac died the normal way. The *Deutsch* didn't kill him."

My father was the next to stand. He was drunk, I could tell, though dignified. He steadied himself on the table where I worked out fractions as a child. "My parents and Allete's parents live in Lyon." He faced Freda, then turned to me. "We've visited when we could, a few times a year, but here in Paris, Freda and Isaac were Henri's grandparents and our friends. Isaac seldom spoke about the war, but I know this much: he saw enough to be bitter, yet he showed the world kindness."

At the open window, I smelled rain.

My father had told me we'd be gathering after the service. As I traveled to the cemetery from the airport, I considered what to say even though I had no words for death. I walked along rows of headstones carved in a Semitic script. I didn't understand the language, but then I didn't need a dictionary. Whatever its letters, a tombstone tells the same story: a newborn's wailing, a span of years, a hole in the ground, and dirt thudding onto a box. Isaac's life was so much more than this, but I could find no words to honor him.

I so wanted to honor him.

Surrounded by my father's books and photos of Poincarés past and present, I stood. I raised a glass: "Isaac gave me the world," I said. "I can't remember life before he and Freda moved downstairs. I have no practice living without the ones I love. I don't know how to do this."

My voice cracked. I looked at my parents.

Back at my apartment, I recalled my brief conversation with Zeligman. Isaac had shielded me from virtually all talk of the war. Yet here was a man who took the opposite view. Judging from what I'd seen, you couldn't shut him up. Zeligman knew Isaac from those days, and he promised to drink vodka with me and tell me everything I wanted to know. "By talking," he said, "I bury the *Deutsch* and keep them buried. You come to Bruges," he added, patting my hand. "We'll sit by my window and talk. I'll tell you plenty."

I told him to count on it.

That night I sat at my desk drinking coffee, trying to flush the alcohol from my system as I ran my hands across the beveled edges of a box on my desk. More than one visitor had examined its contents and wondered why I'd collect such junk. Item by item, I examined my treasures: the cat's-eye marble that started a war, the pen that freed the serfs, Charles de Gaulle's pipe. I learned later that De Gaulle never smoked a pipe, but that hardly mattered.

Isaac Kahane had presented me with sixty-two gifts but only sixty-one stories. I replayed each that night as I studied the gifts and recalled our time on the park bench. At last I came to his final gift, the one without a story: a medallion—a wafer-thin oval of steel that fit easily into my palm, stamped on one side with a pattern I sometimes thought looked like a boot.

For years I figured it to be a memento of Isaac's career as a shoemaker. I was eighteen at the time, headed off to University. He arrived at our bench first, as usual. He was reading the paper when I found him. He saw me and folded it, then patted the seat. I presented a large bag of butterscotch candies.

"Callard & Bowser," he said. "You went all the way to London for these?"

"How did you know?"

"You didn't, really."

"No, Uncle, I didn't. But they're the best."

We wouldn't be seeing each other for a long time, and already I felt the strain of it. As much as my parents, in some ways more, Isaac anchored me. Yet here I was leaving to make my way in a world that had murdered everything he loved.

He sat there in his bow tie on his day off, the Sabbath, smelling of his work from the week, of shoe leather and polish. Isaac didn't want to lose me, either, but he had the grace to say nothing. Maybe he still believed in the world. More likely, he understood that I was eighteen and ready to discover cruelty and benevolence on my own.

The worst excesses of history repeat themselves, I'm afraid, not because we love misery or don't wish to learn from the past, but because we're compelled to live and test ourselves in the present. Isaac's grief—and at that point I hardly knew its contours—could not be my grief; for I was young, full of vigor and eager to confront the beasts that had already burnt his life to a shell.

"Well, then," he said. "I have a little something for you." He dipped into a pocket and produced the medallion. I waited for the story, but nothing came. Only tears, which he tried to hide.

"Maybe another time," he managed. He kissed my forehead and my hand, then left.

He and I met often in the years between that visit in the park and his burial that morning. Yet no story followed, and it wasn't my place to ask. Since that day, when I'd held the medallion or recalled it, a mixture of dread and confusion settled over me. For I knew this last token concerned the war and that it was different, in kind, from the other gifts. He had come a long way, though only partway, in telling his story. The rest, I understood, was mine to discover.

So I pocketed the medallion and heard it jangle against that other piece of metal, long kept close: my father's T. On an impulse, not wanting to let Isaac go, I grabbed a few other trinkets for my briefcase. Armed thus with gifts from the men I loved best, I stood and stretched, then packed my bags for China.

PART II

eleven

*T*he trip to Paris had bumped me onto a later departure out of
Schiphol and, as it happened, onto Viktor Schmidt's flight to Hong
Kong. I had thought it might be Schmidt when from behind I saw
a stocky man with white bristle hair and a well-cut suit. He broke
into a broad grin when he saw me and, after I explained the cir-
cumstance, placed a paternal hand on my shoulder.

"A funeral? That's a bad business," he said. "I've never accepted
it, that one's reward for a long life is death, particularly the wasting-
away kind. I hope he didn't suffer."

But Isaac had.

"In any event, it's up to us to carry on. Isn't it, Henri?"

"It is, Viktor."

"Well, it's fine luck to meet you here. I promised Anselm I'd
treat you to a tour in Hong Kong. He told me all about your dive
platform. He's very impressed, you know—which isn't easy to do.
Exciting, eh?"

"It is."

"And what's this I hear about some sort of drive shaft at the
wreck site? These eighteenth-century frigates didn't have propel-
lers, did they?" He laughed from somewhere deep in his belly and
didn't seem to mind people staring.

"It's a junkyard down there," I said. "We'll be pulling up refrig-
erators before the dive is over. Count on it."

"Was it a commercial ship, military?"

I didn't know.

"Well, you keep me posted. I want a tour. Tit for tat, right?
Because I'm going to give you a tour. We arrive in the morning,

and the trick to getting on local time is to stay up and be active all day. If you don't have meetings when we land, my driver will take us to my hotel. We'll drop our bags, then tour the ship-breaking facility directly, so we won't be tempted to sleep. I tell you, that platform of yours must be something. I mean it, tit for tat. I give you my tour, you give me yours. What do you say?"

The frontal assault left me no choice. I had rescheduled my meetings for Isaac's funeral, and Schmidt's plan would work. In fact, I was as curious to see where my steel anchor beams had come from as Schmidt was to see the platform.

When we boarded, he turned left off the jetway into the land of linen and seats that reclined into beds. I turned right and found my own seat well to the rear, in cattle class, beside a woman who apologized for the two-year-old on her lap with a runny nose. "Ear infection," she said.

During takeoff, as the cabin pressure changed, the child wailed. *Just my luck*, I thought. The seven-hour time difference when I landed in Hong Kong would be difficult enough to manage if I were rested. The mother was no happier. "I can't get another dose of medicine into him for six hours," she said.

Every seat on the plane was taken.

At altitude, I ordered wine and asked for earplugs. I'd pulled a file on the parts manufacturer I'd be meeting and set it on the tray table before me. But the boy, tugging at his ears, was miserable. The mother bounced him and did her best to distract him. She apologized several times.

"Don't," I said. "I'll get my turn. I hope."

Which is when I smiled.

How many times had Freda or Isaac come upstairs to nurse me when my parents were off working? There's nearly a luxury in getting sick, though not seriously sick, as a child. The adults in my life doted on me. They smoothed my hair and dabbed cool compresses on my forehead and chest. Freda brought soup from downstairs. Isaac read to me, or we played chess.

I searched my briefcase for one of his treasures that I knew well, a hand-carved knight. I made sure the child saw it as I stood the horse on its legs. I could hear Isaac speaking as clearly as if he were perched on my shoulder. *Are you sure you want to move your Queen this far, Henri? Study the board. Think it through.*

He had carved every piece of that set. I asked him why when he could have bought chess pieces at a store. That's when he gave me a story.

I once had another set like this, he began. *In those days, we had to make our own pieces, and we drew our boards in the dirt so we could erase them quickly when someone came. It took months, but I found pieces of wood and used stones to smooth and shape them. I made a little sack for the pieces. It was a long time ago.*

Nine or ten at the time, I didn't understand that he'd gone back to the war for that story. I didn't understand, in fact, until the long flight to China. Where had he made it? At the camps? Had he played chess with his own sons before the Nazis shot them? I pranced the hand-carved horse across my files up to the very edge of the fold-down table, rearing as if the rider had come to a cliff. I could feel the child watching.

Then why didn't you use a knife, Uncle . . . to carve the pieces? It would have been easier.

I remember his smile and that he touched my cheek. *Because the Lord decided it would be better to shape the pieces with stones.* I could smell his aftershave; his fingers were stained with shoe polish. *Keep it*, he said, handing me the horse. *I'll carve another.*

I backed the horse up across my files and pranced through a series of high, looping arcs. By this point, the child had stopped crying. He watched me jump the horse through a last arc . . . and into his lap. He sat up and began to play. The mother's head went slack against the seat with relief.

She mouthed the words *Thank You*, and we all got some sleep.

—◊◊—

THE TRAVELERS in the customs hall at Hong Kong International Airport stood queued before eight of twenty active kiosks, each staffed with a control agent who sat on a high stool behind a raised counter. I had nothing to declare and nothing to hide, yet found myself nervous just the same. I scratched my chin, which didn't itch, and checked a watch I'd already reset to local time in an effort to look unconcerned. Behind me, Schmidt was pushing a flatbed hand truck loaded with his own suitcase and three large cardboard boxes, which I had helped him load from the baggage terminal.

The customs agent waved me through after a few routine questions, without opening my suitcase.

Schmidt was not so lucky.

"Your boxes," said the agent. "I will open them." The officer was a young man with jet black hair and a clipped British accent, his uniform starched and spotless. "What's inside, Sir?"

"Consumer electronics," said Schmidt. "I have a card here with the names of two officers on the customs staff. They're expecting me. Please find either of these men, and we can make quick work of your inspection—with all due respect, of course."

The agent read the card without touching it, then unzipped the suitcase as if Schmidt hadn't spoken. I watched the exchange from the far side of the kiosk, behind a bright yellow line which signified that I stood, officially, in Her Majesty's Colony of Hong Kong. The agent removed a shirt from Schmidt's suitcase and shook out its folds. He poked through undergarments and unzipped a toiletries kit.

Schmidt watched in disbelief.

The agent re-zipped the suitcase and looked up. "Tell me about these electronics. What kind?" He sliced open one of the boxes along a seam. "I see glass in here—it looks like a small television. There is also a keyboard built onto the unit. It looks like a typewriter. What is this?"

Schmidt leaned across the counter and presented his card a second time. "Contact one of these men."

"Do the other boxes contain the same items, Sir?"

Schmidt was losing control. I could see the veins in his neck.

"What is this?" said the agent.

"A computer."

The man looked at him. "I've worked with computers at the University of Hong Kong. Computers take up entire rooms and use card files for data. I see no mechanism for accepting card files. And the unit is too small. It cannot be a computer, Sir. I ask again, what is this?"

"It's called a *personal* computer," said Schmidt. "It's new, from America. I'm bringing it to show some people here."

The agent read something from inside the box. "What is this *Apple*?"

"A computer company. American."

"What are you intending to do with this Apple in Hong Kong?"

"*Business*," said Schmidt. "Call your supervisor!"

"We will open the other cartons now. And I must ask you to keep your voice down." He used his box cutter and read off two more names: "*Tandy. Commodore.* These are also computers?" The man placed a call and spoke to someone in Chinese, then re-inspected Schmidt's passport. "Mr. Schmidt," he said, flipping pages. "You travel extensively. Uganda, Cambodia, and Libya in the last six months. And with some regularity to Argentina. Why, may I ask?"

"Is this any of your business?"

"It is. This is our Customs Hall. I ask questions, you answer."

"Have I done something to offend you?"

"Answer the question, Sir."

"I *live* in Argentina. I work in Germany. I visit my wife. Satisfied?"

"I see a visa here to enter the People's Republic of China in three days. Why?"

"Business."

"Relating to computers?"

"Sir," said Schmidt, making a futile attempt at civility, "I'm a businessman traveling on business. Any more questions will have to come from your superior. I gave you two names." He crossed his arms and waited.

The impasse broke when a man in uniform, eyes puffy and hair dyed too black for his age, approached the kiosk. Without a word, he read Schmidt's card. He addressed his subordinate, then excused himself. The young man backed away.

Beyond the kiosks, passengers admitted to the British colony followed a walkway through a set of double doors that opened to a broad receiving area in the main terminal. An enormous banner read: W E L C O M E   T O   H O N G   K O N G. Down the corridor, I saw two uniformed agents and smelled a strong scent of Turkish tobacco that cast me back to the cafés of my student years. A tall man in a linen suit was leaning against the wall along the corridor, smoking what could only have been Gauloises.

How unlikely that a French cigarette would be my first scent of the Orient! But that earthy, acrid smell confirmed what Alec had told me: East collided with West in Hong Kong more violently than anywhere else in the world. "A total mash-up," he called it. "And frequently not pretty."

The lanky smoker must have been a Frenchman who'd lost his luggage in transit, for he hadn't yet stepped beyond the exit into the arrival hall, and he had no suitcase. *Waiting for news,* I figured. Schmidt was waiting, too, so I walked down the hall and introduced myself to a presumed countryman.

"*Comment ça va?*"

He looked up, cigarette dangling from his mouth.

"I couldn't help but notice your Gauloises."

He reached for a cellophaned package.

I held up my hands. "No—no, thank you. I tried once but couldn't stop coughing. At school all the intellectuals were smoking them. They were full of themselves." I gestured at holding a cigarette between my thumb and index finger, palm up. "Henri Poincaré," I said, extending a hand. "It feels good to speak French."

"There's a mathematician—"

"Yes, I know."

"Renard Malet. You're coming from—?"

"Holland, mostly . . . I've been working there. I live in Paris."

He ground out the cigarette on the tile floor and lit another after tapping it against his watch crystal. "I represent a men's clothier in Paris," said Malet. "We're searching for talent in Hong Kong to make custom suits and shirts for our clients. We fax our partners here precise measurements. That's the key, you see. Eighteen different measurements, not just neck size and sleeve length. Do you need a suit?"

I didn't.

"Well, if you do. Eighteen data points. We specify fabric. I take samples back home with each trip, and our tailors in Hong Kong send me finished suits and shirts at one-tenth the cost of custom tailoring in France. The workmanship here is as good or better than what you find anywhere in the world.

"Take this suit, for instance. My measurements are on file here. I made a call and five days later I received an airmailed bundle. *Voilà*—and a perfect fit! It's a new world, Monsieur Poincaré. Every type of business is going global. I'd hate to be a tailor living in Toulouse or Lyon just now. In one year or ten, he'll lose his job. It's just a matter of time."

In fact, I had noticed Malet's suit: a tightly woven linen, a blend of cotton and some other fabric that kept the material from wrinkling. With good lines, too, a handsome product.

Malet was a large, rangy man with bear-paw hands. In profile, he had the face one finds on old Roman coins, with a straight nose and strong chin. "Quite a racket over there with the old man," he said. "I saw you waiting for him. Are you two connected? Is he in trouble of some sort?"

"I know him slightly. I'm not exactly with him, Monsieur—"

"Renard, please."

"We met a few days ago. We were on the same flight. He invited me to share his ride into the city, which I'll do if I don't fall asleep standing up talking to you."

The senior customs agent returned to Schmidt's kiosk. "So sorry for the confusion," he said. He spoke a few hushed words to his subordinate.

The younger man nodded. Revealing nothing beyond dead-eyed obedience, he said: "Welcome to Hong Kong, Sir. Enjoy your stay. I apologize for my rudeness."

"That's my cue," I said. "He's through. I'll need to—"

"Take my card," said Malet. "This way if you need a suit, you can contact me. It's a local number for Paris. I promise you won't walk very far in this city without someone grabbing you to ask if you need custom-made clothes. I know the better tailors. And remember, eighteen measurements. It makes all the difference. Call if you have the need or if you have a sudden craving to speak French. I'm staying at the Peninsula. We'll catch a drink."

"Herr Schmidt is, too. The Peninsula. Perhaps you'd like a ride?"

Malet declined. "I came to meet someone," he said, "but it seems I missed him. I've got my own transportation." He left quickly through the double doors before it occurred to me to wonder why the guards permitted him to wait inside a restricted area.

Schmidt trundled his suitcase and boxes across the yellow line. "We're off," he said. "Damned Chinks."

twelve

Schmidt was pleased to announce that he had arranged an adventure for us. An old oil tanker slated for scrapping, the *Eagle Maiden*, swung at anchor a kilometer offshore. Through a translator, he had spoken with the captain via radio, and the *Maiden* would wait for us if we cared to ride her onto the beach at his breaking yard. "I've wanted to do this for years," he said. "It's an opportunity not to be missed. What do you think?"

Ride an oil tanker onto a beach? I could only agree.

His driver headed north, then east, in search of a water taxi.

Away from the high-rent district of the Peninsula Hotel, the streets narrowed and the sidewalks teemed with people who wore jeans and work shirts and uniforms, anything but suits. These were the workers who serviced Hong Kong's towers and glittery hotels, very likely the ones who would fill the manufacturing plant I hoped to build for a company in Stuttgart. After an hour or so of crawling through traffic, Schmidt determined we were close enough, and he leapt from the car to find a pier and a boat that would ferry us out to the *Maiden*.

Stepping from the limousine was like stepping into a fast-running current. The crowd pushed us past live chicken markets and butchers who hung geese and dog carcasses in window displays. Street vendors called to me, jangling cheap watches. Bead sellers were jammed next to fishmongers who shared stalls with jade merchants, tailors, and import-export companies where men in undershirts yelled into phones. Women sat on boxes shooing flies off carp, the buckets at their feet alive with eels. Everywhere, men and women smoked rank-smelling, filterless cigarettes. Drivers leaned on horns. At the windows in sagging buildings, old men on cheap folding seats picked food from their teeth, watching the show unfold. Scooters zipped around idling cars and trucks. The air was thick enough to make me spit, a soup of diesel and tobacco and pork sizzling on coal-fired braziers. It was an assault on all five senses.

Schmidt found his pier and negotiated a ride out to the tanker, using a map of the harbor with the *Maiden*'s position circled, a wad of cash, and hand gestures. And then I was on a boat again, a snug, freshly painted tender headed for open water.

Soon enough, so soon I didn't have a chance to get sick, we saw a reddish-brown object that rose in the distance much like the islands off the Kowloon Peninsula. But as we drew near, what had looked like a mountain resolved into a supertanker as long as the Eiffel Tower was high.

"Single-hulled," Schmidt shouted above the wind. "Twenty-eight years, a good run but not worth refitting. The owner sold it to us for two million US. We'll break her down and make four million after all is said and done. A tidy business."

Our boat approached the massive ship. Without its cargo of oil, she rode a full ten stories above the sea, with the bridge four stories above that. We were ants approaching an elephant.

It was no easy climb, up a narrow, rusted-out ladder—a steel hull hard to my right and thin air and a likely fatal fall to my left. Schmidt scrambled right up. Onboard, a gap-toothed Malaysian dressed in a faded blue uniform waved. I greeted him in French; Schmidt tried German. The man pointed to himself and said "Doud" in Malay, something else in Chinese, and finally "David" in halting English. He motioned for us to follow, and I was amazed to see him mount a bicycle—*a bicycle!*—wending his way through a grillwork of broad-gauge pipes, back to the bridge. The stench of crude oil stung my nostrils. We walked for ten minutes to reach the stern. It was like crossing the back of a city block, all the more strange because, as an engineer, I well understood the principle of water displacement. Still, I could scarcely believe how all this steel could float.

We reached the bridge. Doud led us up another stairwell to a rusting steel door with a thick glass window. He pulled hard, the door swung wide, and he addressed a short, sallow-faced man.

Captain Lee bowed to Schmidt, his employer, then spoke Chinese to Doud, who in turn spoke English to me. I translated to German. Mr. Lee, I learned, had just lately come aboard the *Maiden*. Others piloted supertankers across the oceans. Mr. Lee specialized in the controlled grounding of large ships, and he welcomed us for the *Maiden*'s final voyage.

Doud explained the maneuver. "When the wind is up and the seas are heavy, it is delicate work," he said, because a ship to be scrapped must land bow first, dead perpendicular to the beach. Tankers are not nimble things. The helmsman must execute the maneuver with care as well as with an eye on the tide clock.

"We must land at the highest tide to get as far up the beach as possible," said Doud. He pointed to his watch. "We are good. Very good. Tonight, 17:30."

The *Maiden* pulled anchor and we were off.

To be sure, the view was fine. The coast of the Kowloon Peninsula looked as if a creature had risen from the South China Sea and taken bites out of the continent, each bite a bay and each bay an unspoiled repetition of the one preceding, with thick green vegetation that ringed white, sandy arcs of beach. One bay would end, rising to a rocky promontory, then descend to another. The pattern repeated for a good hour until we passed a promontory atop which stood several steel towers.

The *Eagle Maiden* had reached her burial ground. This bay was larger than the others. Aligned like so many container trucks queued at an industrial park, eleven ships—some as large as the *Maiden*—sat high on the beach, bow first. We were too far offshore to see men with torches climbing over the hulls. But I knew they were working because I could see plumes of yellow-orange sparks raining down onto the beach.

The scale of this enterprise stunned me. I was prepared to congratulate Schmidt on his achievement, but as we drew closer, a second impression colored the first. A haze had settled over this beach, and what few trees I saw looked singed and dead. The off-shore breeze carried a bitter smell.

"What are those?" I asked Doud, pointing. I'd been studying the shoreline with binoculars. Some seventy meters off the sand, I spotted two bare poles rising from the water.

"Guideposts," he said. "At low tide this morning, we drove these tree trunks into the sand. If we can steer the *Maiden* between them, she will sit on the beach where we want."

The captain took his bearings and consulted the tide tables a final time. He took the wheel. He adjusted course and sounded the ship's horn. Aligned on the trees, he ordered the ship's engine full ahead.

I could feel the *Maiden*'s speed. The guideposts approached, followed by a sight sure to panic anyone who earned a living from the sea: the rapid onrush of land. No one needed to translate as the captain sounded the horn moments before impact.

We braced ourselves as the *Maiden* hit the beach at twenty knots in a last kamikaze run. At impact, the binoculars flew from the chart table and struck a metal pillar. Windows shattered. On any other bridge in any other body of water a captain would have been mad to push the engine as this man did, grinding his ship harder onto the beach. He backed off, then rammed forward, back and forward, rocking the *Maiden* to death.

And then it was over.

thirteen

The Kraus ship-breaking facility was a boneyard, a charnel house. To our right lay a ship, gone but for its huge aft section. To look inside, through the hull, was to see the crosscut of a mechanical drawing in actual fact: raw trusses and holding tanks, crew's quarters, half a bathroom, each sliced through, meant to be hidden and in their nakedness obscene. To the left lay the remains of another ship, rusted and half gone, its cables and pipes dangling like the guts of a freshly butchered animal.

Workers scrambled across the face of these behemoths like beetles over a carcass. Plumes of sparks rained onto the beach. The men below ignored the cascade. Many went bare-chested, their shoulders and backs scarred from burns and months of bearing heavy loads. They worked in open-toed flip-flops, one flimsy step from slicing their feet on sheared steel. No one wore hard hats or glasses, no one wore protective gloves. The air reeked of oil, acetylene fumes, diesel, and whatever fertilizers and solvents had been pumped onto the open cesspit of beach.

It was an ecosystem as complete and merciless as any in Nature. These men, sinew and bone wrapped in rags against the heat, cut and carried steel until the hulls disappeared and nothing remained but greasy sand and petroleum stink.

I could scarcely believe my eyes as a winch operator gunned an engine and *pulled* one ship higher onto the beach with steel cables threaded through holes cut into the bow. A tremendous belch of smoke rose from the engine. A marine winch turned, cables snapping tight, and the bow of a ship larger than the *Maiden* lifted and moved, millimeter by groaning millimeter, up the inclined beach.

Schmidt turned to me, rocking on the balls of his feet. "Every fourteen or eighteen months, seven hundred oceangoing ships are retired and new ones take their place. Anselm and I buy as many wrecks as we can. We've got a sister facility in Bangladesh and are building another in Cambodia."

He turned a circle, pleased with his creation. "It takes one month to cut a forty-five-meter ship to nothing. I'm amazed myself, frankly. We use every part of the ship. The oil and gas, the pipes and wires, bolts, even the furniture from the crew's quarters and the lifeboats. It's where the steel for your dive platform came from," he said. "We cut it to your specs from an old container ship."

Schmidt was pleased to explain that producing a million tons of steel from raw materials costs twenty times more than recycling steel from ships like the *Eagle Maiden*. For every ton of finished steel, Kraus and Schmidt had to feed their blast furnaces nearly five tons of iron ore, coal, and other materials, and 30,000 tons of furnace oil.

"Now do you see it?" he said, pressing me. "Do you understand why we break ships down? Anselm wants you to get a good look because he wants you to understand business done at scale. The world's a large place, Henri. The need for steel is great, and we've scaled our operations accordingly. Think of all the people on earth. They need shoes, don't they? If you want to compete, you must make shoes by the millions. It's the same with steel. Small-scale production is for small-scaled minds. It's fine, if you want to run a mom-and-pop store. But to be a global player requires a global mind. You must think large, Henri! You impressed Anselm with your dive platform. I believe he may have some work for you in Munich. But you must enlarge your thinking first. Watch closely."

I did, and what I saw unnerved me. The breaking yard lacked scaffolding, so the cutters hung from makeshift trapezes, eight, ten, even twelve stories off the sand. I watched a man twenty meters up banging a hammer against the hull until he got the attention of those below. The workers casually moved off. He relit his torch and made a final cut. A corner broke free and a steel plate half the weight of a car plummeted to the beach. Six men approached, their ribs visible, countable. They bent in unison; they jerked the plate onto their shoulders. One man's knees buckled. Another rushed to take his place.

An old man with a wispy beard and bone-thin arms squatted on the sand over a hole he'd dug, pants dropped to his ankles. He stared out to the bay, relieving himself, as dozens of other workers flowed around him as if he didn't exist. And in a way, he didn't, not to the men who ignored him. Further up the beach, a camp of rickety lean-to's housed crowds of off-duty workers in rags, squatting over their food. They slept on straw mats on the sand. On a hammock strung between two palms lay a teenager, inert, a bandage over one eye.

"What do you pay them, Viktor?"

"The going rate. They're not educated, you know. They're happy enough."

A week earlier, I'd heard Anselm Kraus tell his dinner guests that, like his father, he believed that business was war conducted by other means. If business was war and war was hell, then the Kraus ship-breaking facility of Hong Kong lay very near its center. I, too, had come to do business in Asia for a client in search of cheap labor. I wanted no part of it if this was how the company in Stuttgart intended to use its workers.

THE ROAD into the breaking yard passed beneath a large metal arch with lettering I couldn't make out from a distance. Trucks weighted down with metal plates passed beneath this arch; beyond it, I saw Schmidt's driver in his black livery uniform, standing beside the limousine. We walked on, and just on this side of the arch I saw a knot of men: Chinese, plump and dressed well enough to confirm them as managers. I saw a taller man, too, a European dressed in white linen.

It couldn't be, but it was: Renard Malet, laughing with these managers, speaking what sounded like serviceable Cantonese.

One of the men recognized Schmidt and waved, motioning us over. When Malet saw me, his expression froze for an instant, then relaxed. He wasn't there to sell suits at a ship-breaking yard. At once I understood he didn't want either of us to acknowledge our earlier meeting at the Customs Hall. He made the request without words, demanding that I choose sides.

The plump manager spoke enough German to offer a barely intelligible greeting. The others bowed and smiled. The first man pointed to Malet and said, in pidgin German, "Big customer, maybe. France."

Schmidt shook Malet's hand. After an equally inept greeting in French, he turned to me: "You've been drafted as translator. Introduce me, please, as a principal of Kraus Steel. Ask him his name and his business, and give him my card. S'il vous plaît!" He was all smiles.

I would have to betray one of them, a total stranger or Schmidt. I made my choice the way I might contemplate dashing across an intersection at a yellow light. I considered the data and figured the odds of a bloody collision.

My first lie was the largest. I took Malet's card, registered his new identity, and introduced him as Monsieur Roland Kempf, an independent steel broker from Paris. Schmidt clicked his heels and bowed.

"You're not selling suits?" I asked Malet in French, which only the two of us could understand.

He smiled at Schmidt and the others. "What I will say right now is that if you take sides with that one, you'll go straight to hell with him. I speak German and can understand every word you say. I'll speak through you for the moment."

"Why are you here?"

"Tell him—to buy steel."

"*And* sell suits? Maybe you make steel suits? Do you have many customers asking for those?"

He laughed and nodded. We put on a regular show for the others. Malet told me to say that he represented a design-build team that was bidding on several large projects in Paris. "Monsieur Kempf needs a large amount of steel," I said. "He's come out here looking for a bargain."

So I betrayed Viktor Schmidt, my host, for a total stranger. Behind his smiles, Malet suspected Schmidt of something, as did I. That was good enough.

At the end of the exchange we shook hands all around. We bowed, we shook again. Malet declined Schmidt's dinner invitation.

And then Schmidt and I left for Hong Kong, but not before I glanced over my shoulder to find my countryman staring at me. If Schmidt found out that I'd lied to him, I expected to need a suit made of steel after all.

We passed beneath the arch in the perimeter fence, and I could see two words welded onto the doubled bar, separated by the Kraus logo: S T E E L and S T R E N G T H. I'd seen this arch, or one very much like it. We stepped into the limousine, and I dozed on the ride back to the city. It wasn't until I closed my eyes that evening on the too-soft bed of a cheap hotel that I remembered another steel arch with other words: *Arbeit Macht Frei.*

Work sets you free.

fourteen

"Zeligman's *dead*? How is this possible?"

"How is it possible? He fell from a courtyard window at his home in Bruges. What can I say? He was an old man, and old men die."

"Papa, it can't be. You saw how fit he was. Days ago. *Days.*"

My father could only repeat the news and advise me to calm down. "Zeligman must have had some sort of fit and fell from an open window. It's sad, but there it is. Tell me, how did your trip go?"

I had called from Munich to share the good news that Alec and I had likely won our contract, pending final approval from the parent company. The Stuttgart plant would move its manufacturing to Hong Kong and save seventy percent on labor costs. P&C Consulting Engineers would play a crucial role. We were launched, but the news from Paris shocked me.

I called Freda and discovered that Zeligman had apparently staggered from his chair and fell three stories to his death. I didn't much care for my reaction to the news—not at all, because I didn't feel sad for Zeligman or his widow. I didn't know them. My main concern was that without Zeligman, I had no direct route to Isaac. The search for my uncle had become that much more difficult.

—◦—

MY OWN troubles preoccupied me when I called on Anselm Kraus at his estate. It was the first Sunday in June. Liesel hadn't arrived yet, which in retrospect must have been by design. Anselm gave me a tour of the home, then led me to a living room dominated by a large fireplace on either side of which hung, if I was not mistaken, an original Holbein and El Greco. He watched as I studied them.

"The Holbein my father bought. The El Greco was my doing. Look at the scarlet robe against that sky. And the priest's eyes. His backgrounds are always stormy, aren't they? Unsettled. And the priest knows it. I swear this could have been painted yesterday by someone on drugs. I love this painting."

He pointed to a desk on which sat two hard-shell plastic boxes, two keyboards, and a pair of portable television screens. Standing on the stamped and approved side of the customs line in Hong Kong, I hadn't seen what lay in Schmidt's cardboard boxes. But from that little drama, I gathered the contents looked very much like what sat before me.

"You're looking at the future," said Kraus.

The word *Apple* was stamped onto the side of one plastic shell. *Commodore* was stamped onto the other. On an adjacent table lay the electronic guts of a third machine, its plastic casing gone. "Personal computers, Henri. This is what they call the motherboard, this circuitry that makes the thing run. Look closely." Using the tip of a pencil over which he positioned a magnifying glass, he pointed to a series of slender wires attached to a small chip. "Damn if it doesn't look like an insect, like it couldn't just skitter across the room! Do you see it, the sheen on these connectors?" he said. "It's a thin layer of gold. These Apple people and the others use precious metals in their electronics because precious metals are the best conductors. And this here—" he pointed to another connector. "It's platinum. Yesterday, the gold markets in New York closed at $180 US dollars per troy ounce. Platinum at $220. Palladium at $65. Plus there's copper, glass, aluminum, and steel to strip from these machines. I've done my research. There's more gold in one metric ton of electronic scrap than there is in seventeen tons of raw gold ore. You saw the breaking yard in Hong Kong?"

He knew I had.

"I'm going to pursue the same model, but this time a salvage business for electronics. It's 1978, Henri. I'm willing to make a large bet that this market will grow, and as it does, people will want newer and faster computers. They'll be throwing away old ones. When they do that, Kraus Steel will be there to reclaim the gold and platinum from their used computers. I know the salvage business. I'm good at it. This will work."

I stared at him.

"In twenty years personal computers will be in every home and on every desktop of every business in the developed world. If I understood a damn thing about electronics, I'd get into the computer business myself. But I'm going to stick to what I know: how to make steel and how to strip value from other people's junk."

Anselm's Munich estate opened onto a woodland fronted by a vast lawn on which his son and daughter were kicking a ball. Hermann and Albert, Schmidt's Boerboels, ran and pranced with the children. Well to the left, in a formal garden, Theresa bent over rose bushes with pruning shears. She wore a broad-brimmed hat and gloves. When the ball flew and bounced into the rose patch, Hermann loped over and began to lick her face.

Hard to miss was a full-sized vintage airplane mounted on a steel post and buried in what must have been several tons of concrete. "A Stuka dive bomber?" I said.

"Very good. A beauty, isn't she?"

"On Terschelling, Friedrich pretended to be piloting a Stuka."

Kraus watched his son and daughter with obvious pride. "He learned to love the plane here. This was my father's estate, and after he and Mother died we moved in. Otto had the plane moved here in the fifties. His steel from the Salzgitter mills went into that very one. He had the engine lifted, but the controls are intact, all the cables and the rudders. Friedrich doesn't know it, but for his twelfth birthday I'm giving him flying lessons and for his sixteenth, a restored Stuka. I've got three in a hangar out by the airport, one in reasonable shape and the other two for parts. When he's twelve, he and I and a mechanic will begin restoring the plane. By the time he's ready to fly, he'll know every bolt, gasket, and control switch. What do you think?"

"He's certain to love it," I said.

A father couldn't have adored a son more. I liked this man. Rather, I wanted to like him despite everything I saw in Hong Kong. "What did you want to see me about?" I asked.

"Anselm!"

It was Schmidt, his voice booming from the entryway, around the corner.

"I want you to consult on a project," said Kraus.

"Ah, there you are. And Henri! How did your meetings go in Hong Kong? I told Anselm all about our ride on the *Eagle Maiden*. Some fun, yes? But I tell you, it's good to be back among the civilized peoples of the world. Did you get the contract?"

I nodded.

"*There's* a good man!" Schmidt looked at his son-in-law. "He's on his way."

I was explaining the work in Hong Kong, when Schmidt interrupted and asked if I had any progress to report on the dive platform. In fact, on my return I'd spoken with Alec, who'd informed me the weather had improved and they'd found a few coins with the proper dating. Kraus proved himself as knowledgeable as he'd boasted, asking if they were half guineas or spade guineas.

"They'd have to be dated somewhere between 1795 or so and 1600," he said.

In fact, they were: one showed George the Second in profile, and the other, George the Third.

Schmidt was more interested in the drive shaft. He asked if we'd found any new junk from more recent ships. "You let me know, all right? And get me out to that platform! Tit for tat, remember?"

Friedrich and Magda exploded into the room, the dogs right behind them. Magda took a running leap into her grandfather's arms. Friedrich, stopping before me, said, "You're the one I shot down on the beach. I'll give you another chance. Come outside."

Hermann and Albert turned circles around me, sniffing.

"Not now," said Kraus. "You two go along—upstairs. Get cleaned up for dinner."

Schmidt raised his arm and said, "Hupt." The children ran and the dogs followed.

We stood by the tables with the computers. Kraus picked up his magnifying glass once more and inspected the connectors on the circuit board. "Viktor, I was just explaining our plans for salvaging computers."

"Well, I suffered enough for those damned things in Hong Kong. What do you think, Henri? It's a good plan, don't you think? The success of this project turns as much on an understanding of human nature as on the salvaging process. People will throw away their old computers for new ones. If they do, we'll have an inexhaustible supply of valuable junk. Brilliant. Anselm is brilliant."

I hadn't known about the gold and platinum connectors. If it was true and the computers could be salvaged at scale, tons per month, the plan was indeed shrewd. I said so, and Anselm looked pleased.

"Good," he said, "because I want you to develop a process for reclaiming value off the circuit boards. I'll give you a workspace here in Munich and an open checkbook. Order whatever equipment you need. I'll pay you well for your time, and at the end of this enterprise I want a report telling me exactly what steps are needed to deliver gold, platinum, palladium, and the rest. Whatever will sell on the secondary markets."

Kraus opened a drawer and removed four glass vials. "This one's gold," he said, placing the first vial on the desk. "This one is platinum. Here's silver, and finally palladium." He gave me that same appraising look. "I bought these last week, two troy ounces apiece. In five years there will be hills of computer junk; in ten, small mountains; in fifteen, Himalayas. I need a process for extracting value at scale. You built a damned fine dive platform. I'm confident you can do this."

I wasn't. "I'm no chemist," I said.

He had invited me to a job interview I'd never sought. In fact, it felt more like an anointment than an interview because Anselm had made up his mind. Something, I realized, had been decided about my fate while I was away in Paris and Hong Kong.

"I don't really care about the particulars of what you studied, Henri. I bet on people. You've got a technical background, and your platform is all the proof I need that you can see a project through. I'm confident you can deliver."

"A process," I said. "You need a chemical process for isolating precious metals."

"I'll pay you well. The job will keep you in the neighborhood for the summer, at least. Then, who knows?"

I wanted to make sure he understood. "I took exactly one seminar in chemistry."

"We know," said Schmidt. "We checked your course roster at Écoles des Mines. If chemistry *isn't* your core competency, you can learn it. Look, you made it into that university, so you've got brains. We know you're ambitious. And your great-grandfather was Jules Henri Poincaré. You've got excellent bloodlines. We know all this and have made our decision. Do you realize who's making the offer and what is being offered—what this could become, young man?"

Kraus gave me no room to consider.

"This plan will work if you can make the process regular, knowable, and manageable. That's the thing. Discover a process that gives me measurable yields, that gives me thousands of these vials a year, and I will create a new subsidiary of Kraus Steel. Things lead to things, Henri. Small assignments become large ones. I'm in the business of placing bets on people, not on resumes." He found the magnifying glass and bent over a circuit board. "And I've placed my bets. What do you say?"

We heard a crash. On looking up I saw one of the men I met on Terschelling, Franz Hofmann, the old stringy one, standing beside a marble pedestal in pieces on the stone terrace. Schmidt and I followed Anselm outside.

"Uncle Franz," Anselm said. "Are you okay?"

"It moved!" said Hofmann. "It moved *before* I bumped it. Did you see it move? This wasn't my fault, Anselm. Look, it's shattered.

Oh . . . in so many pieces. Let me pick them up. Get me a can. Do you have cement? Any cement? Or glue? I could—"

"It's all right, Uncle. Please, sit. It's nothing."

In fact, it likely wasn't nothing. The chiseled pedestals and planters on the terrace looked to have been a matched set stripped from some Tuscan ruin. Schmidt took him by the hands. "Let's go, Franz. We'll find you a seat."

"Who's he?" Hofmann lifted a trembling finger in my direction.

Schmidt half walked him, half danced him to a chair. "March, Franz. One foot in front of the next. Step, step. There's a good soldier. Come now."

Hofmann pointed again.

"It's fine, Franz. Henri's a friend of the family. Don't be upset."

"I don't like him. I met him once, and I don't like him."

Kraus turned to me with an apology and walked me inside. "He was magnificent until last year. Franz worked on the line at our furnace in Duisburg until a stroke ruined him. He was one of the originals, you know. Maybe it was in 1948 or 1949 when my father took him on. Just like Viktor and Eckehart, he's never not been around. Speaking of which, Viktor told me about your own loss. I'm sorry for that. I swear, if you gave me a contract for eighty good years, then zip"—he made a cutting motion at his throat— "I'd sign in a second. No pain, no decrepitude, just gone."

"There's always arsenic," I said.

"That's the problem, Henri." He thought it over. "Most people won't kill themselves. When you're on this side of the grave, some life is better than no life. You can't see the indignity of your own decline even when you shit your pants every day. Tell me, who's going to kill you when you need it most? Who's going to kill that old man? Me? My affection gets in the way. But I assure you he wouldn't mind if someone shot him."

I cleared my throat.

Back at the computers, he pressed me to accept his offer, which was when Liesel entered the room wearing a sundress, her hair freshly washed. She kissed my cheek and looped an arm through mine.

"Anselm told me he'd be roping you into something. Watch out. Everything he touches turns to gold."

"Don't stare at her," said Schmidt, joining us. "You're not sixteen."

"We'll assume two months, Henri. I've got a mixed-use building in Dachau with some office space, a few apartments, and a rough warehouse. You'll set up there. My assistant will give you all the details." Kraus checked his watch. "Enjoy dinner, you two."

We turned to leave.

"Yes," I said, looking back.

They paused, not understanding.

"I accept your offer."

Kraus and Schmidt roared at what they thought was a good joke. Given what I'd seen of their model yard in Hong Kong, I was going to turn them down. But Liesel's arrival tipped the scales. Alec didn't need me on the platform. I was waiting to hear on fourteen proposals, and didn't dare submit any more on the chance that some, or most, would be accepted. That much new business could put us *out* of business. So I had the time, and Kraus had just given me a reason to stay in Munich for the summer.

Still, I dreaded what Kraus thought a computer salvaging operation might look like at scale. Would he locate it in Hong Kong? Schmidt had gone there with computers. But the customs agent had asked about a visa to enter the People's Republic. They were planning a new kind of breaking yard, I supposed, this one well out of view from prying eyes.

On the terrace, Liesel said, "Don't listen to Viktor. It's sweet, the way you look at me."

I very likely blushed.

"Anselm's very particular about the people he brings on. If you're working with him, you must be good." She opened a gate, and we crossed the garden into the shadow of Otto's Stuka.

"That or I've got an in with a member of the family."

"I had nothing to do with it," she said. "If you had no talent, Anselm wouldn't—"

"But the *Lutine* helps?"

"*That* helps. You did build the platform. He couldn't stop talking about it."

Liesel had grown up on the estate. To her, the Stuka sculpture was likely as invisible as a familiar couch or table. To me, it looked like what it was: a war machine that delivered death from above. Not even the engineer in me could find beauty in it.

"Let me show you the Isar River from the edge of our property," she said. "There's a hill. You'll like the view. . . . Then we'll walk through the English garden, past the pagoda. There's a fine little restaurant I know. It's such a beautiful time of year, Henri. I want you to like Munich. Over dinner, you can tell me everything about your trip to Hong Kong." She leaned into me. "Every detail. Did you see the shipyard? I've never been, but my brother's very proud of it."

I returned the pressure of her arm on mine. I had hoped to avoid, or at least postpone, an accounting of my trip. I gave her the short version. "I learned a lot—more than I expected," I said, and left it at that.

We reached the forest and found the trail that led through their woods to the public garden. It was where she learned to cross country ski and use a compass, she said. "I love these woods. Papa was always working or traveling, but I spent good years here. Anselm and Theresa wanted me to come back, after University. Can you imagine me at twenty-two, bringing a man back to my brother's house on Saturday night?"

My pulse ticked up. I didn't know if it was resentment at the thought of her with someone else or the discovery that she was no stranger to the bedroom arts. We followed the trail through a stand of oaks, the late spring sun streaming through the trees. The season had taken firmer hold here in the south. Large swaths of forest floor were covered with blue-flowered periwinkle. The family's groundskeepers had cleared the underbrush, so that one could look in every direction and find what in Europe passed for old-growth forest, oaks and beech trees with broad girths and splendid canopies.

The estate might have been an archduke's hunting preserve long ago. Otto had bought it after the war, when the old families were ruined and desperate for cash.

The trail led up a hill. Our breathing was heavier, and I caught myself thinking about straining with her in other ways.

Liesel had fantasies of her own, it turned out. When we reached the crest, she gave me a moment to consider the view. Below us, I saw the public garden and the gleam of the Isar. She tugged at my sleeve and walked me to a stand of pines.

"Here," she said. "This would be a nice spot."

"For what?"

"For what we've both had on our minds since hiking on the flats. . . . What's been on your mind, Henri? You've had a long week to think about it."

A bed of pine needles lay between us.

She stepped near.

"I could tell you exactly what I've been thinking."

She touched my hand. "Later, tell me anything you want. For now, show me."

I was done with words and imagining. We kissed. I dropped to my knees and lifted her pleated skirt, letting it fall around my shoulders. I held her in a dim light, a tent of my own making. I inhaled her bouquet and kissed the down of her thighs. She pressed herself into me, and I breathed like a man who'd held his breath for too long.

fifteen

*L*iesel slid a hand onto my abdomen. The sun streamed through the windows as we sat on a couch, covered by a sheet. Dust motes floated in the light. The vendor on Mandistrasse, which bordered one edge of the Englischer Garden, was already sizzling bratwurst. In the distance, I could just see the peak of the famous pagoda. It was early, but the beer drinkers would be lining up soon.

With its steel and blonde wood and Nepalese rugs, the apartment looked like a spread in *Architectural Digest*. Liesel had divided the double-height warehouse loft into two floors, with the sitting and dining areas open to the full height of the loft. Glass and steel beams dominated, with large white walls reserved for oversized art. It was Euro-chic, the reclaimed upper stories of a bombed-out turbine factory.

I had been speaking with Alec every day or two to exchange progress reports. I knew he rose early, so with the phone on my lap and Liesel curled at my side I placed the call. It still amazed me that I could pick up a landline and, via a switching station in the Netherlands, reach him on a barge at sea. I waited through the clicks and whistles, eager for updates but just as eager to tell him about my work for Anselm. When he answered, I spilled the news in a torrent. He was pleased.

Alec's news was also good.

"The dive team found three cannons," he said. "We've hoisted them onto the deck. At the moment they're encrusted with limestone at the fat end. That's where the ship's name would be, or a fleur-de-lis. Hillary's put—"

"The conservator?"

"Yes. She put one of the cannons in a chemical bath, but lime-stone sets like concrete, and it may take months to dissolve. I'm for chipping it off now, but she won't hear of it. We're prospecting, Henri! The news gets better.

"The Argentines visited this week, and we're set. They want a duplicate of our barge. We're selling them the specs and they will oversee construction. All *you* need to do is visit a few times over the next year, look wise, and collect money. How's your Spanish?"

"Serviceable. That government is a retread of the Third Reich. Really, why would we do business with them?"

"I grant you the junta's a bunch of thugs. I knew you'd be sensitive, so I asked and they said the dive on the *Preciado* is strictly a cultural affair. They assured me that whatever they haul up is going into a museum. Just hold your nose and go, would you? Their money is good, and our cash flow is not exactly the best just now."

This was true.

"Alec," I said. "There must be better ways."

"This is not a discussion, Henri. I asked about it, they answered. It's a fucking *cultural* expedition. You're going. Charm them, accept the check, and come home."

"I'll think about it."

"No, you'll do it. And now for some truly alarming news."

I sat up.

"You left some notes here . . . on one of the procedure check-lists. Three lines that you crossed out a half-dozen times. It's a god-damned poem, Henri, and it's awful. It *is* your handwriting. Don't deny it."

"That was supposed to be private."

"Why?"

Liesel straddled me. "What's supposed to be private?" She had leaned her head against mine and heard him.

"Are you there, Henri?"

"With a friend, yes."

"*That* friend?"

~ 82 ~

The best way to take a friendly beating is in public, all at once. I held the receiver up so we both could listen. "Full disclosure," I told her, "is the foundation of any relationship. Liesel Kraus, meet Alec Chin. Alec, Liesel. Speak up, Alec. We're all just dying to hear."

He cleared his throat. "No title. Here goes:

The festive ballroom.

Sunlight and shimmering birch.

I see her. Liesel!

"A haiku? Ms. Kraus, you'd better take care. He's known you two weeks, and already he's writing bad poetry. It's a very bad sign."

You didn't. She mouthed the words.

"Alec, it's not that bad. It sounds better in Japanese."

"You don't speak Japanese."

"It's Sunday. Don't you have something better to do?"

I hung up.

"Shimmering birch?" she said, kissing me. "I *like* it. No one's ever written me poetry." She pulled the sheet over us, then slid onto the floor.

"Your knees," I said. I passed her a pillow.

"No, not that one. My mother embroidered it when I was born."

I looked, but the string of letters didn't add up to her name. A B L v K.

"The *A* is for Antonia," she said. "I like Liesel better."

"And the *B*?"

"My mother's maiden name. Shh. Sit back and close your eyes. I'm busy."

IT WAS the best Sunday of my life. We lounged and made love and napped throughout the day. When we were hungry, I shuttled between the street vendor and the apartment, carrying bratwurst and sodas.

I endured one odd moment, though. Before breakfast, I left Liesel sleeping to investigate noises I heard coming from the living room, where I found a young woman in a maid's uniform dusting furniture. I'd forgotten that Liesel told me to expect Dora. As I pulled the bedroom door closed behind me and introduced myself, I was the more bashful one. I'd thrown on a robe Liesel had left and, bare legged, nothing beneath but the suit I was born in, felt all but naked before this stranger. I was embarrassed for another reason, too. No one ever cleaned my apartment but me. My parents cleaned their own apartment. With Dora standing there in her black dress and white apron, I felt suddenly, strangely, like apologizing.

"Good morning, Sir. May I get you some coffee?"

I started to plump pillows on the couch and straighten papers.

"No, no. This is my job. Sit, please. Coffee? Will Miss Kraus be up soon?"

Her frankness was disconcerting. She knew what I was doing there. I knew she had a job to do. No doubt, she needed the money. But it was no easy thing for me to sit and let her tend to me. Finally she disappeared—to wash the kitchen floor and wipe down the counters.

I settled down to read the biography of Liesel's father, which lay conspicuously on a coffee table. *Steel and Service: The Life of Otto von Kraus* was a hefty book with plenty of photos, some of Liesel and Anselm as children. I'd been at it for thirty minutes when the bedroom door opened and a yawning Liesel found me. She wore a silk robe cinched loosely at the waist with the Kraus logo at its breast.

She nodded at the book. "What do you think?" Without even looking to the kitchen, she called, "Dora, coffee, please. And grapefruit juice. Not the bottled kind. Fresh squeezed, if you would."

In fact, I had formed an early opinion of the biography, having read fifty pages. It was a puff job written to make Otto von Kraus look heroic. Insider histories generally make founders into saints or geniuses. Still, the Kraus story intrigued me. Even allowing for exaggeration and the smoothing of rough spots, Kraus Steel had played a role in saving Europe from Soviet domination after the war. Without his tens of thousands of girders and beams and trusses at good prices, Europe could not have been rebuilt. Without durable buildings and bridges, no postwar economy could have put people to work. And without work and at least a dream of recovery, no idea would have been potent enough to resist the communist vision of the greatest good for the greatest number. Stalin would have won.

So despite the writer's too generous use of *visionary* and *bold*, the Kraus biography had something to say about the mood of those years and the reconstruction of a devastated continent. Yet as I skimmed the book, nowhere did I find an honest accounting of Otto's direct involvement in the war, nothing to suggest he'd gotten his hands dirty making steel for the Führer. Even so, I would read it through and find something good to say.

Dora arrived with the coffee and juice on a tray, with toasted muffins and jam set on fine china. "How are your studies going?" Liesel said.

"Very well, Ma'am. Thank you."

"Henri, I'm paying Dora's college tuition. Her parents worked for my family for years. Way back when, sometimes we played together, didn't we?"

Dora was, perhaps, twenty. She smoothed her apron as Liesel spoke.

"Dear, please clean the toilet in my bedroom before you leave."

I watched the young woman step into the bedroom and through the open door saw her picking up my boxer shorts and pants. I cringed as she folded them over a chair. At last she left, and Liesel and I fell into each other's arms again, ransacking the freshly made bed. I drifted in and out of sleep, wondering if, and how much, Liesel knew about the breaking yard in Hong Kong. I said nothing because I wouldn't dare risk ruining our day.

As it turned out, a phone call did that for us.

It was late afternoon by that point, the shadows creeping across the Englischer Garden. As Liesel listened, I watched her expression slide into something hard and focused. She reached for a pencil and paper. She said *yes* several times, *I understand. Of course.* She hung up.

"One of our iron mines in Uganda. An explosion and cave-in, with thirty men trapped. Anselm wants me to go out there to meet with government ministers."

"You were just there. Did you have any idea?"

"That's my brother's end of the business. He does mines and blast furnaces. I do schools and clinics."

"And you . . . you'll be the pretty face."

She paused. "He uses me like that sometimes."

I could see, in fact, that she felt used; but she wouldn't take me into her confidence just yet because I hadn't earned that. Her eyes flashed as she packed her bags. Night fell, the streetlamps blinked on. Neither of us was happy when the driver arrived.

"Stay," she said, heading out the door. "You'll get the apartment in Dachau set up tomorrow. But stay tonight. It would make me happy."

She gave me a key and left.

sixteen

*T*he next day I met with the senior management of Steinholz Precision Auto Parts in Stuttgart, an hour's train ride west and north of Munich. The Hong Kong contract needed some fleshing out, so after moving to the apartment in Dachau and inspecting the warehouse space that would become my lab, I took a ten o'clock train.

The trip to Stuttgart proved doubly useful because I'd be visiting the chemical supply house Anselm had recommended, not a ten minute walk from the Steinholz headquarters. It had been a while since I stood over a lab bench. Notwithstanding my concerns about how Anselm would ultimately put my work to use, I was actually excited to begin. New projects always get my attention. Anselm had already delivered eight personal computers, all new, to the warehouse. These were to be the patients on which I would perform a caustic surgery.

Even without conducting research into the chemical extraction of precious metals, I knew the process involved dissolving the metals into a solution with acids and then crashing them out of the solution with salts. I'd be working with a pantry full of nasty materials, and I made sure to put protective gloves and goggles on my shopping list.

As the Munich–Stuttgart train rumbled along, I continued to read the biography of Otto von Kraus, written by A. Bieler, an historian at Hanover. The *von* in Otto's name was an old-world salute to nobility that Liesel and Anselm had dropped. There were *von* Habsburgs and *von* Rothschilds; apparently Otto was one of them, which I didn't quite understand, given his humble origins. But I supposed great men have a habit of surprising.

My opinion of the biography didn't change for reading more of it. Still, I enjoyed a middle section of glossy photos, especially the image of Liesel flanked by her brother and Otto at the lighthouse on Terschelling. The caption read 1960. They each held shovels for the groundbreaking of Löwenherz. Liesel, twelve or thirteen, all arms and legs with short wavy hair, wore fisherman's boots that reached to her knobby knees.

From the photographs I could see that Otto Kraus was a pugnacious man. With his beefy hands and thick forearms, he had the look of a dockworker one would do well to avoid in a bar. Yet by the time this photo was taken, Kraus had moved well beyond fighting with his hands. By that point, he could pay lawyers.

Good for him, I supposed. He had waltzed into the lucrative business of steel fabrication after the war, anointed by the German, Flemish, and Dutch governments to be their provider of choice. How he had managed that was anyone's guess. But the more contracts he won, the more furnaces he built, the cheaper his steel became, the more demand he created. All he had to do was deliver a reliable product, which by all accounts he did.

I saw in these photos the supreme self-confidence of a man who understood his advantage and would yield it to no one. Anselm had more refined edges, a university education that gave him a high-caste vocabulary and manners. But whatever toughness Anselm possessed, and I guessed it was plenty, he had learned from Papa. And Papa had learned on the farms and in the foundries of Lower Saxony. I read this:

> *Otto von Kraus was born in 1902 in the village of Beddingen, which after the municipal consolidation of 1942 became the town of Salzgitter. His parents farmed, but with iron ore deposits in the district, he worked autumns and winters at the local mills. These were the crucial years in which von Kraus developed his passion for steel.*

Kraus's rise had been meteoric. Prior to the four-year run-up to the war, the Reich depended heavily on iron ore shipped from suppliers beyond Germany's borders, which Herman Göring regarded as a strategic weakness. A solution lay close at hand. Known since the 1300s for its low quality but plentiful iron ore, the mines of Salzgitter could provide for all of the Fatherland's needs if a new method could be found to work that ore into usable steel. Kraus devised such a method, and Göring chose him to lead the new Reichswerke. Berlin invested millions, and Otto Kraus, the local man who knew the district and the mines, prospered.

Not without a cost, however. Kraus took what his biographer called "the necessary but unpleasant step" of joining the Nazi Party. He contracted with the SS for labor: Jews from the east and Slavs from the north—all from conquered territories—and express-shipped in cattle cars to the newly constructed Drütte concentration camp. In a triumph of efficiency, the SS built the camp inside the gates of the sprawling steel mill. Bieler noted that Otto was sickened at the necessity of working men like animals.

I had had enough. Between Bieler's wretched mythmaking and the rhythmic shaking of the train, I was nodding off as I thumbed through the final section of the biography, devoted to the postwar triumphs of Kraus Steel. It was titled "Ten Witnesses and a Clean Slate."

Many who directed the factories that supplied the Reich with war materiel faced prosecution for their use of slave labor. Of those, dozens escaped justice by passing as refugees and escaping the country. But Otto von Kraus, a principled man confident of his innocence, did not run. As would be expected, the Americans arrested him on a charge of war crimes. Yet one month into his captivity, and prior to his scheduled trial, military prosecutors received an extraordinary affidavit stating that von Kraus had acted honorably during the war. Within the areas of the Reichswerke Hermann Göring that he controlled, von Kraus treated workers with humane consideration. Indeed, he opened an infirmary on the factory grounds where the sick and the most seriously injured could recover.

Von Kraus could not change the deplorable conditions at the Drütte concentration camp; but even there he demanded that the SS increase food rations in order to give his laborers the strength needed to make steel for the Reich. The sad fact remains that many perished at Drütte, a loss that von Kraus mourned deeply the rest of his life.

When news spread that Allied forces had arrested Kraus, ten survivors of the camp approached a military judge and swore to the following:

1. Otto von Kraus resisted Nazi barbarism.
2. He treated workers the best he could in terrible circumstances.
3. He saved lives.
4. We know him to be a good and honorable man caught up in evil times.

As sworn to and attested by the undersigned in the presence of Col. Richard Starr, military judge.

I scanned the names and sat bolt upright as I read the last one: *Jacob Zeligman.*

"Stuttgart," called the conductor. "Stuttgart is next."

I didn't walk far along the station platform before finding a pay phone and calling Freda Kahane. The phone rang. *Pick it up,* I muttered. I reached into my pocket and held Isaac's medallion.

"Henri! Are you upstairs? Come, visit."

I asked the unlikely and heard the improbable. She was crossing the kitchen; in the background a tea kettle whistled. "We buried Isaac two weeks ago, and here I am leaving to sit shiva with Jacob's wife? God isn't kind."

She had plenty of evidence for that.

"It's true, Jacob survived Drütte. He and Tosha talked about it all the time. But Isaac? You know he wasn't a talker. When I asked

Jacob to tell me how he knew him, he said 'Ask Isaac.' Some kind of agreement they had, that he wouldn't say. It was that way for thirty years, Henri. I would go to Isaac and say, 'Tell me about the war, what you saw.' And he would say, 'Why, so we can compare whose horror was more horrible?' He wouldn't do it. I could never get him to talk, aside from the fact that I was his second wife and that he had children once. Sons."

She waited. "Visit, Henri."

"You know I will."

"Give me a few weeks. Tosha wasn't a well woman even when Jacob was alive. I may need to stay."

PIGEONS ROOSTED in the rafters of the station and pecked at trash in the train beds. Businessmen folded papers beneath their arms, waiting for the first-class coaches to open, and suddenly I felt both alone and scared. The years collapsed and I saw these same men and women in winter, yellow stars sewn onto their coats. I heard orders and harsh, guttural shouts. Truncheons fell. Old men dropped. Soldiers pushed and clubbed hundreds into trains meant for cattle.

Someone tapped my shoulder. "Are you done? The phone?"

The possibility that Isaac had worked alongside Jacob Zeligman at Drütte, making steel for Otto von Kraus, struck me dumb. Had they occupied the same square of German soil at the same moment? I found myself wishing that Kraus was the hero his biographer made him out to be. Never mind that his steel was turned into Hitler's tanks and bombers. Von Kraus was part of the Nazi apparatus, but he could also have been one of the righteous who saved Jews at great peril to themselves. These people existed, and I desperately wanted Liesel's father to be one of them.

Zeligman could no longer help establish that; nor could he tell me Isaac's story. But others from Drütte, the witnesses who signed the affidavit, could. I decided to find them.

seventeen

$\mathcal{T}$he noble metals do not degrade in the presence of air and water. A chemist would explain by saying they don't oxidize easily. That's why jewelers prefer gold, silver, and platinum over steel, which rusts, and copper, which turns green. Find a gold necklace in a 3,000-year-old crypt or salvage a saltwater-soaked guinea from the *Lutine*, and the gold will shine sun-yellow. Or spray a thin layer of gold or platinum to connect circuits on a computer's motherboard and the circuits will transmit electrons faithfully for years until some other part of the board fails.

I understood the risks Anselm's assignment posed the moment I accepted it. My strategy would be to use great care in pursuing two extraction techniques: a chemical approach using acids and salts and, more promising for production at larger scales, electrolysis— running a current through a chemical bath to release metal ions.

The chemical supply house delivered my order the day after my visit to Stuttgart, and I spent the remainder of that week assembling shelves and directing the small army of plumbers, electricians, and carpenters that Anselm had made available to me.

I had claimed one corner of an otherwise enormous, vacant warehouse located in the suburb of Dachau, by a train yard. Kraus Steel owned ten of these warehouses and had converted one to furnished apartments for employees cycling through the Munich headquarters from the far-flung corners of the empire. My situation was ideal, with a comfortable apartment and a four-minute walk to the lab. I took a long-term rental on a car and settled in for work.

With Liesel in Uganda for at least two weeks, I had no obligations other than building the lab. At the end of the first week, given all the assistance I received, the only missing piece was a proper ventilation hood. This would arrive the following Thursday and, in its place, I bought two box fans that I set in the windows to draw fumes from the workspace.

I was proud of my effort and took photos with my trusty Minolta as proof I had built a serviceable lab. In neatly labeled trays were my pipettes, graduated cylinders, stir plates, and beakers. I had purchased carboys for hazardous waste. I set up a desk with a lamp and a phone. I read everything I could about the extraction of gold from mixed materials, a process that turned out to be relatively straightforward, though by all accounts dangerous.

When I had nothing left to read and no shelves to build, I prepared for my trip to Buenos Aires. I copied our designs for the dive platform and made notes for likely alterations. The Argentine wreck, the *Preciado*, sat at the bottom of a river, unlike ours at the bottom of the sea. They would need a barge with a shallower draft, which affected both the size and capacity of the crane they would use, as well as the number of sheds that could be built. I re-spec'd the barge and prepared a presentation.

By the following Monday, I had nothing to do but wait for the vent hood. All that was required was that I be patient. I could have devoted my days to walks in a park or reading a novel or technical journals. But I've never been one for sitting idly. So I set to creating a supply of aqua regia, one part nitric acid to three parts hydrochloric acid. The "king's water" is a solution strong enough to dissolve most noble metals.

I knew full well what a mistake in mixing these acids would mean, and I believed in safety protocols. If I checked my lists another dozen times I couldn't have been more prepared. I slipped on my goggles, my flame-retardant lab coat, my rubberized apron, and my nitrile gloves. I turned on the box fans for exhaust.

I did everything according to plan, except wear a gas mask. The man at the supply house had forgotten to mention I might need one, in addition to the ventilation hood, or I had forgotten to ask. Either way, my sworn enemy couldn't have planned a more potent attack if he'd shot a canister of chlorine gas into my lab from an opposing trench. In my haste to begin work, I inadvertently produced a weapon of mass destruction.

All by myself.

I mixed the acids too quickly or overlooked a drop of water in one of the beakers. Whatever the cause, when I poured the nitric into the hydrochloric, the mixture fumed. The first whiff knocked me backwards, the chlorine blistering my throat and lungs. I collapsed in a fit of coughing, but not before dropping the beakers into the steel tub, which had enough residual water to create a billowing, yellowish-green cloud.

I clawed my way across the warehouse floor. I reached the wall and flung open a window. Breathing seared my lungs. I hacked into the sleeve of my lab coat and saw phlegm and blood. My eyes burned. Had I not worn goggles, the gas would have blinded me.

Stupid, stupid, stupid. I sucked down ragged breaths and stared across the tracks to a stand of trees, grateful that I could see them. *Stupid.*

WITHIN THE hour, still spitting blood into a handkerchief, I fashioned a makeshift mask, wrapping wet towels around my mouth and cinching them in place with my belt. Protected, barely, I vented the chlorine and neutralized the acids. Within an hour, I could feel my lungs clearing and decided against a trip to the hospital. I staggered, instead, to my apartment and took a hot shower.

As I gulped down the cleansing steam, I could imagine no likely scenario in which Anselm's salvage of circuit boards would leave his laborers unharmed. I'd had protection, and look what happened. They would have none, and they would be maimed or killed. Unless, that is, I reported faithfully on the dangers and convinced Anselm to take precautions. I made a conscious choice to continue my work and deliver the report he'd asked for, but with a detailed appendix titled "Safety."

Still, I imagined the worst. The men who'd work at an electronics salvage yard in the People's Republic of China would be desperate to feed their families. They would sign whatever document Kraus Steel waved in front of them for the privilege of navigating a landscape of chemical filth. Anselm was going to create a dead zone more toxic than his ship-breaking facility in Hong Kong.

I showered until the water ran cold. I damn near cried from exhaustion and from anger at my stupidity, both for having injured myself and for having accepted the job. The physical symptoms would clear in a few days. Weighing more heavily was the question of what to do with what I'd learned.

Alec would have told me to shrug my shoulders and get over it, that business requires the occasional bending of one's finer instincts. My father would have lectured me on the dangers of doing business with Germans, even thirty years after the war. I couldn't confide in Liesel because I had spent no more than a handful of hours, albeit intimate hours, with her. What would I have said, in any event? That I suspected her brother of a crime he had not yet committed?

I fell asleep spitting blood and phlegm into a handkerchief.

eighteen

I had no business returning to the lab before I could mix aqua regia with a steady hand. Each time I coughed and tried to clear my lungs, I'd risk splashing hydrochloric and nitric acids. I'd had enough of that. With Liesel gone for another week and no compelling reason to stay in Munich, I left for Stuttgart, where I would sign the revised contract with Steinholz Precision Auto Parts.

My pallid color and cough alarmed my friends at Steinholz, who accepted my explanation that a bad allergic reaction had sickened me but that I was on the mend. We clinked glasses and agreed to break ground on the new Hong Kong facility the following April, after Alec and I worked with their architects on a design that would maximize workflow. We parted company with earnest hopes all around: for Steinholz to save on labor costs and for me to ensure that its laborers didn't lose in the deal, as they did with Kraus. The Steinholz manager seemed a decent enough fellow. Then again, so did Anselm.

I made a day of it in Stuttgart. Just north of the city lies the town of Ludwigsburg, home of the Zentrale Stelle, the Central Office of the State Justice Administration for the Investigation of National Socialist Crimes. I went in search of contact information for the nine remaining witnesses who, after Zeligman, might have known Isaac Kahane—possibly at Drütte. I assumed that if the Allied military authorities had contemplated a case against Otto von Kraus for the use of slave labor, the Nazi archive at the Zentrale Stelle would have a file. The original affidavit might have recorded the last known address of each signatory. Without these, I would never find the remaining witnesses; without the witnesses, I had little hope of reconstructing Isaac's life during the war. The Zentrale

Stelle would have answers, or not. It was a slender connection, but a connection. I boarded the local train to Ludwigsburg.

The Archive was located on the site of a former women's prison. Set behind tall stone walls, the main building was a three-story behemoth retrofitted with bulletproof glass and security cameras. In former times, the keepers wanted to prevent prisoners from breaking out. These days, they defended against former Nazis and neo-Nazis intent on destroying evidence of war crimes. For the Archive stored millions of records and photos neatly filed on metal shelves, waiting for prosecutors to dig, discover, and bring charges. Extremists would have counted it a banner day to see the building burn.

I had called the day before requesting research privileges. As I stood before a steel gate, I announced myself by speaking into a call box, then looked squarely into the lens of a security camera. A guard buzzed and pointed me down a long hallway to the office of Gustav Plannik, the director. Off this hallway I found numerous small rooms, former prison cells.

Plannik sat in a double-sized cell, bent over a desk stacked with black and white photos. He waved me over as he held a magnifying glass to one and positioned it so that I could see a German soldier posing beside a gallows occupied by six corpses. Plannik taped that photo to a sheet on which was typed a place, a date, and a name.

He rose from his chair. "I'm glad to meet you, Herr Poincaré. Names to faces," he said. "It's what we do, attach one to the other. This particular crime occurred outside Lyon. In the Klaus Barbie years, the hanging of partisans, and worse, was commonplace. If by markings on the uniforms or, sometimes, a staff car, we can identify the unit, we can sometimes identify a perpetrator. We Germans have kept very good records, even when killing people. It makes my job easier."

Tacked to the walls of his office were maps of occupied Europe, a pyramid detailing the chain of command in the Gestapo and the same for the SS. The fourth wall had a double-windowed view of a courtyard and an apple tree. The window was open, and I could hear birdsong and the chattering of squirrels.

"Drütte," said the director. "After you called, we pulled together files on the camp for you. It was one of the eight sub-camps of Neuengamme. *Vernichtung durch Arbeit*. Do you know the term?"

I apologized for my German.

"It's peculiar to the war. It means 'extermination through labor.' The workers lasted on average four months. There are some stories of survival, of course, but these are the exception. We've set up an office for you with several hundred photos and fifty or so files. We've also included a sheet to help you with our reference system— a series of colored index cards. Files lead to other files lead to others. Pay attention to the color markings. Making copies is no problem."

As the Archive's founding director when it opened in 1958, Plannik wore three hats. He was a conservator who preserved documents, a librarian who indexed documents so historians could find them, and a jurist who supervised prosecutors as they conducted preliminary investigations into war crimes.

Plannik was a balding, fleshy man with a heavy face and black-rimmed glasses that magnified agile but tired eyes. He eased himself into his chair. "Here at the Zentrale Stelle, we maintain one of the largest catalogs of misery ever assembled. It's a peculiar but necessary sort of treasure, Herr Poincaré, and you're very welcome to dig. My office door is open."

I was shown to a former prison cell, bright and white-walled with a view of the exercise yard. I opened the window and leaned outside, where I found three surveillance cameras. On the plain metal desk were folders, including photos captioned just as I had seen in Plannik's office. I had no plan other than to plow through it all. A quick survey of the images revealed what I was in for: preening soldiers posed beside bodies piled like cordwood or hanging from ropes or meat hooks. The document files contained hundreds of yellowed pages with official Nazi letterhead. I had brought a French-German dictionary; the woman who showed me into the room left me with a magnifying glass.

I didn't expect to find a photo of Isaac, which would have confirmed his imprisonment at Drütte. But I found something nearly as definitive, a stamp on a worker's pass that identified the bearer as a member of the factory air defense system at HGW, the Hermann Göring Werke. Drütte was part of the mill complex, and on the pass, stamped in faded red, was the HGW logo: a thick ring connected to a square, seated atop a bar.

All these years, I'd assumed the stamped pattern on Isaac's medallion was complete in itself. I had seen a boot in it, and why not? He had been a cobbler; it made sense. I set the medallion on the table before me:

It was not a boot. I turned the metal ninety degrees and saw it at once:

Isaac had picked up a sliver of stamped metal off the floor of the mill. What had happened there that he couldn't tell? I went to the window and stared at the perimeter walls. It must have been a daunting obstacle when the Zentrale Stelle was a prison. Branches of a large oak arched into the yard. The roof lines of neat and trim houses rose beyond, and I imagined children in earlier times spying on the inmates from attic windows. On the pale walls I saw Isaac shuffling in the striped uniform of a prisoner, head shaved, lice infested, wearing ill-fitted wooden clogs as a defense against winter. They had tried killing him through work. How close had they come?

I let him go and returned to the image of an SS guard with a truncheon in the act of beating a prisoner he'd hung by the wrists, followed by an image of that same guard posing in the countryside on what must have been a rare day off. He toasted the photographer with a stein full of beer.

I rose from the desk and closed the door to my cell, then tore through the remaining folders in search of Otto Kraus and Reinhard Vogt, the man Zeligman had cursed. I read several documents signed by Kraus, pro forma letters detailing steel output versus monthly quotas set in Berlin. It was true, Otto was a producer: twelve tons ordered for March 1941, fifteen tons delivered. Eighteen tons ordered for July 1941, twenty delivered. And here were photos of Kraus at his desk, in a business suit. Here he was on a catwalk overlooking a furnace and there, standing before a mountain of finished product destined, said the caption, for the Opel plant, owned by General Motors.

Otto's hand was in it all. Using the magnifying glass, I could locate the Herman Göring stamp on many pieces of steel. I read a letter of commendation signed by Hitler himself, praising Kraus for taking the poor quality ore of Salzgitter and finding a process for creating high quality steel for the Fatherland. I held a letter signed by, touched by, Adolf Hitler.

I found no evidence that Kraus secretly saved hundreds, nor did I find evidence that he participated directly in the abuse of prisoners. Despite my urgency, the documents did not establish the facts one way or the other. I saw dozens of SS guards, repeating faces from one photo to the next, though none with the name Vogt—until I stopped at a sheet on which was printed, as a caption, the following:

Salzgitter HGW, October 1943. Otto von Kraus,
Reinhard Vogt, Menard Gottlieb

Gottlieb I had never heard of, but here were Kraus and Vogt mentioned together. The photo was gone, and the page was coded with a green tab. The reference sheet told me that green pointed to an additional file, one started for a preliminary investigation into war crimes. I walked down the prison corridor to the administrative office and asked to see it.

The administrative assistant soon arrived at my cell with fresh folders. She leafed through them, scanning the summary memo clipped to each. "The evidence of war crimes was sufficient to refer the cases out for prosecution for both Vogt and Gottlieb, but they were returned as non-actionable because the men could not be located. It's common enough," she said, looking over her glasses at me. "Vogt and Gottlieb may have died during the war. If they survived and were on the run, they likely changed their names. Whether they left the country or stayed, it's very difficult to track these people down. We couldn't find them, and it appears there are no other photos. It happens, these dead ends."

She set the files on the desk. "Remember to sign and date the files you review. There's a log inside the file jacket." I opened the top one, Gottlieb's, and read the summary memo: wanted for murder, torture, and rape. The second file, on Vogt, was another catalog of horrors. In both files, I found photo sheets with captions but no photos. I signed the log, noting that von Kraus's biographer, A. Bieler, had visited and read these same files in 1973. No surprise there. I made a note to contact Bieler and learn what had become of the photos of Gottlieb and Vogt.

The administrative assistant knocked on the door. "You had asked for this as well, Herr Poincaré, but we had to go to another office to find it. Otto Kraus's file." She stood in the doorway reading the summary note. "Prosecutors from this office didn't initiate this file. It's an earlier one that came to us from the days the Americans administered part of Germany after the war. The American military courts ran their own judicial process to prosecute war criminals. This file was begun on Kraus for using slave labor, and it looks as though he was going to be prosecuted. But the evidentiary materials are gone and the investigation was abruptly ended. What we do have here is a statement, a document signed by ten men dated February 11, 1946."

I was looking at the original affidavit.

I signed my name, again after Bieler's, and found a second sheet listing each witness's address in April 1946. Of course, they would have moved, but now I had a place to begin my search.

I heaved a huge sigh of relief.

Outside, shadows were cutting long angles across the prison courtyard. I had to catch a train back to Stuttgart, then to Munich. I selected documents from the combined files and asked the administrative assistant to copy them.

The woman nodded. "I'll just be able to finish before I leave for the day, Herr Poincaré. While you're waiting, why don't you take a walk in the courtyard? You look like you could use the air."

She couldn't name what she saw in my expression. But I could: sudden despair at the difficulty of locating witnesses thirty years after the fact. Who would be living at the same address? What had I been thinking? I needed advice and asked to see Gustav Plannik.

But he had been called away on family business and was leaving early the next morning, on holiday, for three weeks.

"To Australia," said his assistant. "The bottom of the world. Imagine that!"

nineteen

$\mathcal{T}$he documents I had copied were singeing my fingertips. In them was evidence of crimes so horrible that I felt, on leaving the Archive, that I was carrying some dread virus into an unsuspecting world. I didn't want the burden of their sitting unprotected at my apartment as I worked in the lab. I needed to park them somewhere; so on my way from Ludwigsburg I stopped at a bank in Stuttgart and rented a safe deposit box, figuring I'd take the late train to Munich.

A security officer directed me to an elevator, and I descended three levels below street grade, where a woman buzzed me through a steel gate. I filled out some forms, and fifteen minutes later was seated in a tiny room behind a closed door, transferring the files from the Zentrale Stelle into a steel box that would be locked in a vault. They'd be out of harm's way until I could figure out what, if anything, to do with them.

I reviewed Vogt's file before leaving. He was known for pulling prisoners from morning assembly and beating them with a rubber truncheon. Other prisoners learned to stare dead ahead and make no sound, for if they revealed the slightest unease or showed any sign of compassion Vogt would pull them from the line for their turn. In this way, he trained prisoners into a kind of studied numbness. At Drütte and, I suspected, the other camps, one learned to live for oneself.

I copied the names and addresses of the signatories to the von Kraus affidavit. This information I needed with me and could safely hold, for only someone who knew about the case would have reasons to raise questions.

I was packing up the steel box when, incredibly, the door to my private viewing room opened. No knock. No request to enter. These are privileged rooms, and I was about to stand and complain loudly when Renard Malet, or was it Roland Kempf, closed the door behind him, a finger raised to his lips.

"What—what is this!"

"Shh. You'll wake the neighbors."

I placed my hand over the safe deposit box.

"Get out! Right now!"

Again, the finger to his lips.

"How did they let you—? Only the police . . ."

Malet nodded. "What's in the box, Monsieur Poincaré?"

I didn't answer.

"I could get a court order, you know."

"Who are you this time?"

He was wearing another of his linen suits.

"My name is Serge Laurent, and I work for Interpol. Your friend Anselm Kraus has a problem and, if I'm not mistaken, so do you."

"What!"

"May I sit?"

"Laurent? What, a third name? Why should I believe—"

He produced a badge. "I had to speak with the bank manager to get in. He called my headquarters in Lyon. The manager was satisfied, and so should you be. I'm international police, Monsieur Poincaré. How else does a man talk himself into a private viewing room in a bank vault?"

"How did you find me?"

He shrugged. "You're close to the Kraus family. I've been observing the comings and goings at the estate. I saw you meet with him and decided to follow you and have a chat. You see, I'd like to know someone on the inside, someone with information."

"Jesus," I groaned.

"No, Jesus won't help you. But I may be able to."

I could not have been more amazed.

"You said I have a problem. What problem?"

"I've been following you the last day and a half, and I discovered someone else following you, too."

"No! Why?"

The steel box that I was intending to lock into the vault might have been one reason. But I had only discovered the files that afternoon. I did not understand why I'd be followed in advance of my visit to the Nazi archives.

"You were in China with Schmidt," said Laurent. "You've become friendly with Anselm's sister. And I believe you're doing some work for Anselm. I'm assuming you have information that could be useful to me. To demonstrate good faith, I helped you out just now. The other tail—I ran his plates—he's a private detective out of Munich. I had the Stuttgart police detain him for resembling a man wanted by Interpol. It's not true, but it got him to go away for a bit. Aside from me no one knows you're here, although the detective and those he reports to know you visited the Archive." He pointed. "What's in the box?"

I said nothing.

"Let me put the matter more clearly. You visited the Zentrale Stelle, which does only one sort of business. The question is not what is in the box. They are files, obviously. *Whose* files? You're investigating someone."

"I'm *not* an investigator."

"Of course you aren't. You're an engineer. But that's the name for people who go looking for information in obscure places and find it. Someone besides me is interested in you. Why?"

The examination room was tiny. Malet or Kempf or Laurent, whoever he was, sucked the air out of it. He was a bulky man, all legs and arms. One of him hardly fit in the room. With me, it was impossible. "Who are you really?" I demanded. "First, we meet at customs, in Hong Kong. You're selling suits. Next, I see you at a ship-breaking yard, buying recycled steel. Now this. Do you import suits, broker steel, or both?"

He crossed and uncrossed his legs, his knees bumping the wooden viewing shelf. "Interpol," he said again. "Kraus has installations around the world. I assume you heard about the disaster at their mine in Uganda? They've got another breaking yard in Bangladesh that's as bad, or worse, than the one in Hong Kong. Kraus has been moving operations into the Third World to take advantage of cheap labor. He's a pioneer in shipping Euro-manufacturing offshore, and you can believe that manufacturers in every sector are paying close attention. That's why I'm hoping to make an example of him. It will serve as a warning."

I volunteered nothing about Steinholz Precision Auto Parts.

"For the moment, I'm still collecting information. But I hope there will be an indictment. Did you see the condition of his workers?"

I nodded.

"What did you think?"

"A bit rough."

"A bit? Kraus Steel charges them rent to sleep in those miserable huts, charges them for food, and if they injure themselves, charges them for medical care in a facility that would outrage anyone in the developed world. The company prepays their rent and food allowances, then garnishees their wages. It's meant as a loan the workers pay off through labor.

"But the workers never pay it off, you see. It's called debt slavery, and I'm in the process of building a dossier that will kick his ass. If I make a case, I'll pass it to a prosecutor in The Hague." He lit a Gauloise and left the pack and a silver lighter on the shelf.

"You can't smoke in here." I pointed to a sign.

He shrugged and leaned back in his chair.

"You don't sell suits," I said.

"In fact, I do."

"You don't."

"One has to have a cover story. If you and I end up doing business, I'll introduce you to a tailor I know. Your first suit's on me, as a gesture of good faith. Call it an installment."

"On what?"

He blew a plume of smoke at me. I may as well have been sucking the exhaust of a city bus. "I want to know about your relationship with the Kraus family."

"No. I'm not talking to you."

"How well do you know the family?"

"I don't see—"

"Have you gotten close to Anselm? I would like a source on the inside."

If Laurent was who he said he was, I had a great deal to tell him about the dangers of salvaging gold from electronic junk. But I said nothing. I had heard too much, too fast. "Anselm's a good man."

"Charming, I understand. By all accounts, devoted to his family."

"We've met a total of three times. I'd hardly call it a friendship."

"Have you formed an impression?"

I was forming one, yes. I said nothing.

"The customs officials in Hong Kong told me that Schmidt was bringing computers into the colony and had a visa for the People's Republic. Would you know why?" Laurent jabbed at the wooden viewing shelf as he spoke. He was a hydraulic jackhammer dressed in linen, and I wouldn't have been surprised if the shelf exploded under the force of him.

"No," I lied. "I don't know why he'd bring computers to China."

"Do you suppose they're planning some sort of business, Henri? May I call you Henri?"

"No, you may not."

"Perhaps you know Anselm and Schmidt well enough to appreciate their business model. If not, it goes something like this. They travel the wide world, looking for a good deal. They shit wherever they build a facility, then they bring the profits home to Munich. Remember that the next time you're drinking their champagne."

He handed me a business card, then stood, bumping his head on the door frame. "I believe you could use a friend, Monsieur Poincaré. Really, it's not my style to give advice. But don't let your affections get the better of you. This is a criminal investigation, and if you help that man I won't hesitate to take you down. Stay in touch."

twenty

I couldn't stay away from the lab, despite my resolve to leave the circuit boards alone until I stopped coughing. When the ventilation hood arrived a day early and Anselm dispatched an electrician and carpenters to install it, curiosity got the better of me. By Thursday evening the lab was operational, and I began work mostly because I couldn't *not* begin it. The problem of extracting pure gold from junk, as a problem, fascinated me. To the naked eye, the circuit boards contained nothing of value. But I knew better.

I would be the alchemist squeezing gold from slugs of lead. I would take a worthless board, crush it, bathe it in obscure solutions, and produce a glittering fortune. Never mind Kraus and the hellhole he would need to scale this process and make it profitable. The *problem itself* seduced me.

Liesel was due to arrive from Kampala late Saturday evening, and I had seventy-two hours to advance the cause before greeting her at the airport. The following day, we would visit Anselm for another family barbecue, and there he would press me for news. I would give him news, though at the same time would commit a rather large sin of omission: I'd say nothing of Interpol's investigation, not to him or Liesel. Which meant that from this point forward, I would be lying every time I was in their presence.

My accident had given me a newfound respect for the tradecraft of chemistry. This time I wore a gas mask *and* worked beneath the ventilation hood as I ground and crushed two circuit boards, soaked them in aqua regia, and boiled a mixture that quickly turned to sludge. I had already used nitric acid, alone, to dissolve the silver and copper into solution as ions. Filtering the sludge a first time, I used sodium chloride to crash the silver from the decanting. This I collected and purified. I had salvaged my first noble metal—and heard Isaac at my shoulder, applauding.

Years before, at our park bench, he'd presented a piece of mica. I could hear him clearly. *When I was your age, my father let me walk with him behind the plow and hold the reins. One day, the blade turned the earth and I saw something shining. I picked it up and said, 'Papa, look! It's silver, like Mama's candlesticks! We're rich!' My father laughed and laughed. 'It's mica,' he said. 'A mineral. Look, pull it apart.' So I held the mica and discovered that I could peel thin sheets off it. 'It's fool's silver,' my father told me. 'Don't go thinking you're rich. You'll need to work harder than that!'*

Isaac handed me a large mica flake that day, as long and wide as my hand. He must have seen his amazed younger self in my face. He laughed as I peeled thin, silvery sheets and held them to the light. I could see through them, each sheet glass-like but flexible. Twelve years later, at University, I chose in my geology course to use a powerful microscope to study the crystal structure of mica. I wrote Isaac long letters all about it and mailed him my final report. As a student, I could still scarcely believe this mineral came fully formed from the earth without humans having shaped it. My learning only deepened my wonder.

Nor could I believe, six years later, that I'd caused pure silver to drop out of a clear, watery solution. But there it was, silver, sitting in a flask before me, nothing foolish about it. Anselm Kraus and his money-making venture aside, I found the *chemistry* of my chemistry, the bonding and unbonding of materials at scales invisible to the naked eye, miraculous.

And to think I was getting paid for it.

I pushed on and found copper to be trickier. After considerable trial and error, having consulted several textbooks, I added sodium hydroxide to what remained of the decanting after harvesting silver. The copper crashed out of solution as copper hydroxide. I heated this, dissolved it in acid, and treated the solution with zinc metal to crash pure, solid copper—not a precious metal, but valuable nonetheless.

I was two for two.

Next came gold, and here I found myself as absorbed in the process as any prospector working the streams of California. Throughout my career I have found that work can impart a welcome form of amnesia. Standing at the lab bench, I forgot about Laurent and his threats to bury me should I side with Liesel and her brother. I forgot the dead eyes of laborers in the ship-breaking yard. I forgot my disgust at Schmidt's saddling a child with the decision to kill and calling that a lesson in manhood. For a time, I even forgot the photographs at the Nazi archives. Work brought amnesia, if only a temporary reprieve, and I welcomed the break.

In search of gold, I added aqua regia to the ground-up boards already stripped of silver and copper. The next morning I filtered that solution, which contained gold ions—invisible, but present the way sugar is present after it dissolves into a cup of hot tea. I added sodium metabisulfite, and damn if pure gold didn't crash out of the solution, sun-yellow gold falling like flecks in a snow globe. I let out a yelp. I collected it, melted it, and let it solidify into shiny pellets.

An excellent start. I had proofs of concept but nothing useful to report regarding a process that could liberate these metals at scale, when Anselm would be collecting tens of thousands and, one day, millions of circuit boards for salvage.

My more difficult challenge concerned palladium and platinum. To recover these precious metals, I had to dissolve circuitry from the boards once again in aqua regia—but this time boiling it! I used tongs to swirl the flask over a Bunsen burner. The solution threw off fumes, as before, though a manageable amount. In an abundance of caution, I had used compressed air to dry the flasks before mixing the acids. I switched the ventilation hood to its "high" position. My gas mask functioned properly—the lenses didn't fog. So I had conquered the fumes.

Even so, if the flask cracked and splashed aqua regia onto an open flame, I risked a flash, if not an explosion. I arranged for a serviceman to install a second phone at the lab bench in the event I needed to make an emergency call.

All day Friday I worked at isolating palladium and platinum. I tried to crash the platinum out of solution first, using ammonium chloride. It wouldn't go. I tried using different ratios of hydrochloric and nitric acids. I varied boil times and the intensity of the heat. I refreshed my chemical supplies, thinking my original batches might have been tainted. Nothing worked; so at the end of a long shift, I killed the flame and set the solution beneath the exhaust fan to cool.

It was seven o'clock. I pulled off the mask and was closing windows and shutting off lights when I heard a knock at the door and turned to find a visitor who'd taken the liberty of letting himself in.

"Permission to come aboard, Captain?"

"Viktor," I said. "You're always welcome."

"Anselm told me I might find you here. A young man like you, alone in a lively city. Surely you have things to do tonight." He looked at his watch. "Music. Bars."

"I'll share a secret. I'm boring. Please don't tell Liesel."

"Hah! I'd call it industrious. Seven o'clock on a Friday evening, still at your bench?" He rose on the balls of his feet and leaned my way. "Anselm mentioned your Argentina connections. Liesel must have told him. She's very proud of you, too, you know. She was boasting. A second treasure ship—in Buenos Aires. Imagine that. It's becoming something of a specialty of yours, hunting treasure."

"Not by design. But we'll take the work." I removed my lab coat.

"Well, if you go to Argentina, you should meet my wife, Greta. If it's possible, you should meet our friends, too. We gather every Friday afternoon at our home. We call ourselves the Edelweiss Society. We all moved after the war. Europe was such a depressing place. But I go so far back with Kraus Steel that I couldn't give up my position here. I spend at least one week of every six in Buenos Aires. I'll retire soon enough and move there permanently. It feels like home, this collection of friends. I miss them."

I hadn't a clue why he was visiting. "I may not go," I said. This was the truth. It was a long trip, and I figured I could get everything accomplished using courier services. Plus, I could spare our client, the Argentine government, an expensive airfare.

"But another treasure hunt? How can you resist?" He joined me at the bench and held an empty beaker to a lamp, turning it in his hands. "It's good to know people, Henri. Anselm and I do, here in Germany. My friends in Buenos Aires are well connected, and you should know them—if you go, that is."

"Viktor, you're very kind, but it's been a long day."

"All right, then. To the point."

The warehouse was large enough to hold several modest-sized apartments. I had claimed a tiny corner by a bank of windows and a water supply—hard by one of the two doors, near a freight elevator. The second door was some forty meters distant. If I had a rock in my hand, I couldn't have thrown it that far. But I could see that door plainly, and when it opened I saw a tall man with short hair like Schmidt's, only blond. He wore a dark suit and closed the door behind him. He stood at attention, his hands clasped before him, and said nothing.

"Henri, you've visited the Zentrale Stelle and pulled a file on Otto von Kraus."

I stared at him.

"How would you know, Viktor?"

"Any business that concerns a Kraus or this company, I know."

I doubted that. I doubted he knew that an Interpol agent had been watching his little drama with the customs agent in Hong Kong.

The bastard.

"Yes," I said. "I went to the Archive."

"Why?"

"I don't really think that's your business." I fought a bizarre impulse to run. I had located my lab at the butt end of a building that, in flagrant violation of code, had only a single exit along the corridor, which led directly past the second door and Schmidt's assistant. "What's your problem, Viktor?"

Schmidt stepped past me and turned the valve of the Bunsen burner. The gas hissed, and he reached into his pocket for a lighter. The butane ignited with a *whoosh*. "The problem arises when you or anyone researches this family. I find that rude. If you have questions, ask. Anselm or Liesel or I will be happy to answer them."

I didn't understand why he had brought an assistant, this silent goon. Schmidt was frightening enough on his own. He was twice my age, but with his bull neck and thick chest communicated a threat that made matters perfectly clear: our present exchange was civilized, but he would not hesitate to break me and eat me if he had cause. I couldn't resist him physically, let alone his assistant.

I gave him the slimmest version of the truth. "I went searching for information about my uncle, my adopted uncle, the one who died. Remember, you offered your condolences."

"That's right. But why go to an archive of Nazi-era crimes?"

"I don't understand that it's your place to ask."

"Humor me. Why the Zentrale Stelle and the file on Otto von Kraus?"

I explained Isaac's vague connection to Zeligman, and Zeligman's name on the list of ten who had vouched for Kraus. "I thought that if Isaac knew Zeligman and Zeligman signed that document, the others who signed might have known Isaac. So I have the list and thought I would call on them. It's a bit of unfinished business, Viktor. I want to know more about my uncle."

"That's admirable. But you pulled other files as well."

It had to have been the administrative assistant, the woman who'd seemed so helpful. She must have retrieved the files and called Schmidt. I could scarcely believe this interrogation.

"I'm filling in holes," I said. "This is about my uncle. I owe him this, a little research. Now please explain your problem."

"Leave it alone, Henri. Those witnesses are long dead."

"It's been thirty years. If they were twenty or thirty at the time, it wouldn't be unreasonable—"

"Suit yourself. If they're alive, I very much doubt you'll find them. Scattered to the winds. America, South America, Europe. Good luck."

"All right, then. Are we done?"

Schmidt killed the flame on the Bunsen burner. "You seem wise enough to take advice. Ours is a tight-knit family, Henri. My daughter married Anselm. I was Otto's right hand in building this company. I'm Liesel's godfather. She's quite fond of you, and I can see why. You're a clever man with great promise." He surveyed the lab and nodded. "Here." He handed me a business card. "My address in Buenos Aires. I give it only to friends and family, and despite your indiscretion at the Archive I would like to think we're friends. I take you at your word, Henri. Should you go and find yourself there on a Friday afternoon, stop in. You've already met Dr. Nagel. He would be there. You know, a home-cooked meal in a faraway land never hurts."

Schmidt stepped past me into the corridor.

"What about him?" I nodded to the second door.

"He keeps me company . . . how shall I say it? The Zentrale Stelle is about the past. The future is what matters. Let's not get ahead of the facts, but Liesel is fond of you. Anselm thinks the world of you. You should visit our family in Buenos Aires. Get to *know* us, Henri. . . . You're good at math?"

"There's some talent in my family. Yes."

"Well, then. Add two plus two. By the way, I really do want to get out to that platform of yours. I'm waiting for an invitation."

"I'm busy here, Viktor. But I'll let my partner know to expect you. Go anytime. Really."

"Well, thank you for this little talk. I feel better." He looked at his watch. "I'll see you at the picnic, yes? Sunday?"

At the far end of the warehouse, Schmidt's assistant opened and closed the second door. Two sets of footsteps receded down the corridor, then died. I turned back to the lab trying to understand what had just happened. That evening I found that a can of shaving cream, which I usually kept on a shelf above the sink, had moved to a ledge by the tub.

I wondered if it was time to call Serge Laurent.

twenty-one

I woke Saturday morning to find Schmidt's muscled assistant waiting outside my apartment. The heavy-handed reminder should have infuriated me, yet I realized I must have gotten close enough to something at the Archive to raise alarms. The administrative assistant had said that prosecuting wartime criminals was difficult because perpetrators moved and changed names. Perhaps Schmidt was worried I'd find his name.

Why wasn't I surprised?

The man stood across the street, leaning on a car and pretending to read a newspaper, pitifully obvious. I had no doubt he'd follow me at least for that day and report back to his master. This surveillance wouldn't do, and I could make the point in one of two ways. I could drive to Schmidt's home, knock on his door, and tell him to stop the nonsense; or I could demonstrate how futile his attempts at surveillance would be.

I opted for a demonstration.

Early Friday morning, I had spent a few hours checking two local names from the Otto Kraus affidavit. One, Felix Schumpter, had given an address in a suburb of Munich. A phone book and a call to the tax assessor's office quickly established that no one by that name currently lived at the address, though the records did show a Schumpter in residence before 1939. The assessor's office gave me a phone number for the address, and the woman who answered had never heard of him. Her father had bought the apartment before the war, and that's all she could say. Perhaps she didn't care to know more—for instance, that prime German real estate often sold for a song after the original Jewish owners fled or were shipped off to the camps.

I tried the next closest city listed on the affidavit, Vienna. I found a phone number and called. To my delight a woman answered the phone and said that yes, Aaron Montefiore, her grandfather, was alive and well but was napping at the moment and couldn't talk. I thanked her and said nothing more because I wouldn't risk an easy rejection by phone. My plan was to visit Vienna, unannounced—a possibly flawed tactic, I knew. He might be away. He might resent the liberty I'd taken, ambushing him. But if I found Herr Montefiore and he refused to answer questions about Drütte and Isaac Kahane, he would have to deny me to my face. He needed to *see* my love for Isaac. If he knew Isaac and still said no, I could do nothing but move to others on the list.

Given my frustrations in the lab with platinum and palladium, I decided to spend the day walking, as I sometimes will when encountering a problem. My habit is to keep a notebook close at hand and divert my attention elsewhere. As often as not, answers will suggest themselves when I'm admiring the patterns of a leaf or lost in contemplation of an article I've read.

Schmidt's man settled the matter. I would go walking . . . but in Vienna. I thought it through, packed an old suitcase, and stepped out of the apartment.

I behaved as if unaware anyone was following me and boarded a bus bound for the Munich rail station. I wore tan pants, a darker tan sports jacket, and no hat. At the station, I bought a ticket to Stuttgart, sure to say *Stuttgart* loudly enough so that anyone standing within six meters would hear. I was first in line at the platform and first onto the train when it was ready for boarding. I assumed that Schmidt's man would not be bold or stupid enough to sit in the same car. As a precaution, I took a seat in the last row of a car with forward facing seats, so whoever had an interest in my affairs would need to turn to see me.

When the train departed, I gathered my suitcase and stepped into the lavatory. Inside my suitcase was a smaller day bag in which

I had packed a change of clothes, a gray suit and a black felt hat. I stuffed the clothes I had worn from my apartment into the day pack and zipped the larger suitcase shut. I grabbed the hat and my day bag and waited. By this point, I had made the trip to Stuttgart several times and had chosen a local train, not the express, knowing that within twenty minutes it would take on passengers at Augsburg.

When the train stopped, I exited the lavatory in my fresh set of clothes and new bag, returned my original suitcase to its position on the luggage rack, and stepped off the train. I immediately turned my back to the train and opened a newspaper, which I'd bought at the Munich station as a prop. Schmidt's man didn't move. The train to Stuttgart left the station with him aboard, which gave me just enough time to follow the passageway beneath the tracks and emerge onto an adjacent platform, where I stepped onto an eastbound commuter back to Munich. From there, I boarded an express to Vienna.

Again, I chose the last row of a forward-facing car. I recognized no one from the Stuttgart-bound train. I checked the car behind me and found three people, none familiar. A conductor waved and blew a whistle. I settled into my seat and pulled the list of witnesses from my suit jacket.

I STEPPED outside the Vienna station looking for a taxi—but not before an odd event. As I exited the train, on an adjacent platform another train was idled, about to depart for the airport. I saw a familiar-looking man: tall, impeccably dressed, and completely bald—his head shaved. He looks like Dr. Nagel, I thought, the physician from Buenos Aires. I looked a second time to be sure, then called across the platform.

"Herr Nagel!"

The woman beside him heard clearly enough. A raised voice bordering on a shout can be alarming in public, and she looked in my direction. The man I thought was Eckehart Nagel didn't move, however.

"Herr Nagel!"

Others stared, but he didn't. He boarded the Airport Express, and I went about my business, forgetting him. I left the station, and a fifteen-minute taxi ride brought me to the edge of a neighborhood of townhouses outside the center of the city.

"You'll have to walk," said the driver on encountering the flashing lights of a police car. I paid him and made my way up the street, checking an address on a scrap of paper against the numbers on the houses, rehearsing what I would say all the while. I was nervous, about to throw myself at the mercy of whoever answered that door. As a habit, I avoid placing my fate in the hands of others. I prefer to rise or sink by my own efforts. But in this business, I was the supplicant. *I* needed information. There I was, a stranger about to make a very strange request.

Complicating matters was the voice of my father ringing in my ears, an old argument he used whenever my mother wanted to visit Vienna: the Austrians, he grumbled, were more enthusiastic Nazis than the Germans. Why would anyone willingly visit Vienna? My mother would protest and point to the architecture, the music, and the food. My father switched off the radio whenever Mozart played.

I was not visiting a Nazi, I reminded myself, but a man who survived Nazis. Would he be more like Zeligman, a large personality who freely discussed those years, or Isaac, who didn't? I walked up the street, ignoring a gathering commotion ahead of me—a knot of cars and more flashing lights—and rehearsed my appeal to Aaron Montefiore. To build confidence, I recalled Isaac at our bench and dinners downstairs on Friday nights as he chanted over the wine. I reached into my pocket and grasped his medallion. I could do this. I would knock and state my case simply.

I didn't get the chance.

The flashing lights belonged to an ambulance and a second police car. An officer had set a perimeter barricade with yellow tape. A crowd watched someone being carried on a stretcher down marble steps. I checked the number on the scrap in my hand against the number of the building. They matched. There were three apartments, I assumed, each floor-throughs.

"Who?" I asked a woman.

"Ah, Herr Montefiore. His granddaughter ran screaming from the house that he'd collapsed. I live over there." She pointed. "I called the ambulance. Such a good man."

Not possible, I thought. I was so upset I nearly blundered into one of the horse-drawn carriages that serve the tourist trade near St. Stephen's Cathedral. The mare clip-clopped on the cobblestones, making a cruel sound. She stopped, I stopped. The driver asked if I needed help.

I sat on a curb to collect myself.

Within the hour, I was leaning my head against the window of the return train to Munich, confused. The odds were against it, my wanting to talk with two men and their dying before I got the chance. I recalled Montefiore's handsome street with its white limestone townhouses and black wrought-iron lamps and shutters. Flower boxes sat at each window. The buildings were narrow and tall, elegant. Montefiore had prospered. I convinced myself he would have spoken to me.

The train lurched, and I crossed another name off my list.

twenty-two

*L*iesel ran into my arms after clearing customs. I had hoped for some small sign that our affection would hold after our delirious weekend in bed. I needn't have worried. She ran to me as if we were lovers long separated by a war and reunited, miraculously, on the far side. What she had seen in Uganda had unsettled her.

She needed to talk.

"The mine," she said, clutching me. "It's awful, Henri, and our name is all over it. Thirty men died. Trapped, suffocated. The *Times* of London had a reporter in the country. He'd already called in the story by the time I landed. I met with the widows and children after he interviewed them."

Her shoulders began to shake. She fought the emotion and stepped away, wiping her eyes. "Government ministers were screaming. The widows and children threw dust on their heads. It was a nightmare. More reporters came. They were swarming like insects. We would never stand for something like that in Europe, Henri. How did Anselm let it happen? He should have *fixed* this!"

Did she really not know? Could Anselm have separated her that sharply from the business arm of Kraus Steel?

That night, after a bath and with a Scotch in hand, more composed, Liesel reported more or less the Ugandan version of what I'd found in Hong Kong, and what Laurent had found in Kraus facilities worldwide. Anselm's workers lived in shanties with roofs of thatch or, if they could afford extra payments to the company store, corrugated tin. "We don't give them the hardhats or headlamps," she said, pouring another drink. "They pay the store for that. I give my staff office equipment. I don't make them *pay*. Christ."

She sipped her Scotch.

"The collapsed mine is a tomb. We shut it down, but Anselm has his geologists drawing up plans for a new shaft several kilometers to the east where he can work the same deposits. This time he had better do it right. What a fiasco."

The hour was late and the lights low, though still bright enough to make a mirror of the window overlooking the Englischer Garden. We sat on the couch in her living room, watching each other's reflection in the glass.

I wondered aloud if Anselm was in the habit of visiting his facilities.

"He visited the mine when it opened, yes. But they hadn't dug the shafts deep enough to create any hazards. The store and the huts were all new and fresh-looking then. That was twelve years ago, and he never went back. Now he says he's as shocked as anyone and that he didn't know. How is this possible? He *runs* the business. I can tell you one thing. Our facilities in Europe are all safe and well run. Anselm assigns the management of our offshore holdings to his vice presidents. That's why he didn't know."

"And they report to—?"

"Uncle Viktor."

That night Liesel nearly consumed me in bed. Our first efforts were a sweet, if hurried, welcome home. When I turned on my side to rest, she turned me back and, nearly pleading, asked me to hold her. I did, but that wasn't enough. I woke while it was still dark to find her straddling me. She turned on a night-light. We thrashed. I urged her to get some sleep, but she woke me again at first light and called my name: "Hold me," she said.

Later, when I rose and crossed the apartment to sit by the balcony, I felt her watching until, finally, I returned and sat beside her, smoothing her hair. I kissed her forehead and she closed her eyes. "I'm not going anywhere," I said.

She looked at me and wept.

—◦◦◦—

WHEN WE parked at Anselm's estate, I stepped from the car to hear Friedrich from his perch in the Stuka in furious aerial combat. *Eeeerrrrrr rat-at-tat. Eeeerrrrr.* He was too consumed to wave, and I could imagine one day having children, hoping they'd have a passion, any passion, as pure and beautiful as his.

The day was hot and sunny. Anselm worked a barbecue grill, and Theresa, arms held wide, came to greet us. She was a sturdy woman in the way opera singers can be sturdy. Heavy, not fat. Strong and big bosomed. Also tender. Magda, sucking her thumb, had attached herself to her mother's skirts. Theresa kissed Liesel on both cheeks and did the same for me, with equal warmth. I hesitated to think so, but her greeting felt as cheerful and easy as if I were already a member of the family.

"Opa!"

I wasted no time when I saw Schmidt.

I walked directly to him, shook his hand, and whispered, "This is idiotic. Stop the surveillance." I didn't do him the discourtesy of making a scene, and I wouldn't be telling Liesel that her godfather didn't trust me enough to leave me on my own. My disagreement with Viktor would remain between us, if he listened to reason.

He returned my whisper. "Just a reminder to take care, Henri."

"It's heavy-handed and insulting."

"True. But I wanted to be sure you *heard* me yesterday. You don't think it's just as insulting that you'd check on this family in a war crimes archive? Exactly what and who do you think we are?"

He said this over his shoulder, having turned toward the house as Franz Hofmann shuffled by with his cane. It was not the stroke and the resulting deficits that made Hofmann so unpleasant. I didn't mind that he'd taken an immediate dislike to me. But after fifteen minutes in his company, I'd concluded he was a bitter man who looked at the world through a lens that colored everything and everyone deficient. He saw me but didn't acknowledge me. *Tap tap shuffle. Tap tap shuffle.* One could wake screaming in the night at the sound.

I offered my hand in greeting, ready for his grip.

"I remember you," he said. "I didn't like you."

"I bet you still don't."

His lower lip flapped. The stroke had affected his voice, which sounded as rough as if he'd spent the previous week shrieking. He stepped closer: "You're French, aren't you? That's the problem."

"*Mais oui.*"

"Go to hell."

He shuffled on, and his aide joined him for a walk in the rose garden.

Flanked by his Boerboels, Schmidt reappeared with a tray of drinks. "Schnapps for the adults," he called. "Lemonade for the children." The dogs raced from his side to Liesel, prancing about her. They sniffed around my shoes and pants, smelling my uneasiness. My calf seized up, but I resisted reaching for the T in my pocket. With Schmidt present, I figured I was safe. Even I believed he controlled these animals. On cue, they broke away from me when their master called, "Hupt!"

"I shot down four planes, Opa! Two American Thunderbolts and two British Spitfires. Shot them right out of the sky. Four on one, and I got them all!"

"That's my boy!"

"Papa!" Theresa scolded her father. "The Americans and British are our friends now. Have him shoot somebody else down."

"Leave it be. Friedrich, run this drink over to Uncle Franz. Don't spill any. And for God's sake, don't *drink* any."

"Really, Papa. He should be shooting down space aliens or Russian MiGs."

"Ach! It's a game."

Anselm called to Friedrich: "Watch out—two Spitfires on your tail, five o'clock. Dive hard!" Anselm waved to us, and Liesel and I joined him after relieving Schmidt of three glasses of schnapps.

"We've got to talk," Liesel told her brother.

"I know," he said. There were circles under his eyes. He was taking the news from Uganda seriously. That gave me hope.

He kissed her cheek. "I heard you met President Amin. You sent my regards—and condolences? And you, my friend," he said, turning to me. "Viktor tells me you've set up the lab. Have you begun work? Any insights yet?"

Anselm saw me watching as Liesel walked off. "You know, I still look at my wife that way. It will be twenty years next month. . . . Tell me about the lab, Henri."

I was in the man's house drinking his liquor, knowing more than I cared to know about his business and unable to say a word. Besides Uganda, he had a disaster-in-waiting in Hong Kong. He had Interpol perched on his shoulder and didn't know it, along with the sure prospect of a chemical wasteland if he decided to salvage circuit boards the way he salvaged ships. In spite of it all, I wanted to like Anselm Kraus, not the least reason being his affection for Friedrich and Magda. Somehow the man disarmed my criticisms. If at that moment he swore he didn't know about the conditions at the mine, I would have believed him.

I didn't ask.

I dug into my pocket and produced three small vials. Gold in one, silver in the next, copper in the third. "Proof of concept," I said.

Anselm grinned. "Viktor, come look!"

"Don't rush to conclusions," I told him. "Wait until I finish my report."

He clapped my shoulder. "Well done, Henri! I was going to give you this in any event today, but now I'd say you've earned it." He produced a check. "Funds to get you started."

I looked at it and looked at him. "Anselm, this is ridiculous."

"I'll be the judge of what I pay a valued consultant." The grill flared, and he excused himself, laughing. "Really, extracting gold from junk. I love it!"

Schmidt walked over to inspect, the dogs at his side. "I'll grant you this," he said, flicking the vial of gold in the sunlight. "You're competent. Competence matters, but it's not enough. You must set up systems, then perfect them. Everything depends on well-run systems. Clear methods. That's the thing."

Theresa called us to lunch, and we found our way to bed sheets spread across the well-tended lawn. The children led Uncle Franz from the rose garden, and he sat beside me.

SERVANTS CLEANED up after us. I played soccer with the children and engaged in a bit of aerial combat with Friedrich. He and I ran across the lawn, into the woods and back, with the same result as on Terschelling. The child was happy, and Liesel embraced me openly as I returned to the terrace.

"You're a good sport, Henri."

"No," I answered. "I'm not. I wanted to beat him but couldn't. He's faster and more agile, and that makes me angrier than hell!" We were laughing as Friedrich walked by, sweating and gulping lemonade. "You're the best combat ace I know," I said, tousling his hair.

The dogs perked up.

Magda, sitting beside her grandfather on a chaise lounge, pointed to the thick picture book propped on his knee: *Kinder- und Hausmärchen* der Brüder Grimm. Grimms' *Fairy Tales*. Schmidt reached an arm around the child, who leaned against him. "Opa," she said, "let's read the silly one about the man in the thorns."

"*Again?*"

"Please, Opa!"

I helped myself to a lemonade as we all settled in for a story on a pleasant afternoon. Schmidt was clearly pleased to be taking directions from his granddaughter. He consulted the table of contents. "Let's see now. 'The Jew Among Thorns.' That's the one."

I looked at Schmidt, then to the others. Only Liesel's eyes flashed as Magda clapped her hands. "Read the part where the old man with the billy-goat beard gets caught in the thorn bush. The good servant makes him dance by playing his magic fiddle and he gets all scraped. *That one*, Opa!"

Anselm and Theresa were watching and smiling. I wondered what could possibly be happening as Schmidt read and came to the part Magda had requested. " 'When the Jew was fast among the thorns, the good servant's humor so tempted him that he took up his fiddle and began to play.'"

"His *magic* fiddle," cried Magda. "The one that makes everyone dance!"

"Yes," said Schmidt, continuing: "'In a moment the Jew's legs began to move, and to jump into the air, and the more the servant fiddled the better went the dance. But the thorns tore his shabby coat for him, combed his beard, and pricked and plucked him all over the body. *Oh dear,* cried the Jew, *what do I want with your fiddling? Leave the fiddle alone, master; I do not want to dance.*'"

Liesel set her drink down. "Uncle Viktor, please. It's enough."

Schmidt stopped his reading. "What? What's wrong?"

"The story offends me. Please. The old *Jew*? Enough already. It's a thick book. Find another story. As I remember it, the Jew gets hanged in the end mostly for being a Jew. Just stop."

Schmidt looked to his daughter then to Anselm for help. "Liesel, these are children's stories. It's the brothers Grimm, for goodness sake. This book—" he lifted it—"is a national treasure. It's part of our heritage."

Liesel turned to her brother. "She's your daughter. Tell him to stop. You know exactly what I'm talking about."

"Magda, come. The rose bushes you and I planted last autumn are flowering." Theresa stood, extending a hand. "Papa, put the book away for now. You can read later."

Schmidt looked at his goddaughter. "Well, that wasn't very pleasant."

"Uncle Viktor, it's stories like these that—not around me. Just stop it."

Anselm shrugged. "I don't see the problem. It's a fairy tale. And Viktor's right. It *is* our history."

"Anselm, we live in *Munich*, for God's sake! Do I need to spell it out? Magda's five years old. Wait until she's fifteen, when she can think for herself. Really, how could you, Viktor?"

Uncle Franz, with greasy hands and chicken bits on his chin, was gnawing at a drumstick.

"Liesel, our father read these same stories to us. That's my copy of Grimm."

"I *hated* that story. You're poisoning her."

They must have accepted me as Liesel's boyfriend after all, arguing in the open as they were. Not that anyone asked my opinion. I walked behind Liesel and whispered a soft *Bravo* in her ear.

Schmidt announced that he was suddenly tired and went into the house. Anselm looked at his watch. Liesel had ruined a perfectly good picnic, and I couldn't wait to congratulate her in a more private setting. I was waiting for her signal that we should leave when Friedrich bolted off the terrace and cried: "One more dogfight. You're the Spitfire. I'm the Stuka."

This time I was ready for him. Before he even finished his challenge, I cleared the porch and caught up. I grabbed his shoulder and he tumbled and spun, laughing, this time making sounds of a plane with a sputtering engine. This child knew how to lose with grace, which endeared him to me all the more. I was enjoying this last installment of our game a great deal when I hoisted him into the air and caught him.

Friedrich laughed. "Again, do it again!"

I threw him higher, and by the time I saw the dogs streaking towards me it was too late. Schmidt was inside the house when Albert and Hermann broke from the terrace and raced across the lawn. The child was mid-toss, airborne, and I had to choose: catch Friedrich and let the dogs attack, or face the dogs and let Friedrich fall.

I caught the boy and shielded him with my body.

Theresa saw it from the garden and began screaming. Anselm was up and running. Liesel shrieked. And Friedrich, who was so casual with these animals, knocking them about and riding them like ponies, cried as the Boerboels loosed their fury on me.

I heard Schmidt shouting: "Hupt! Hupt!" But he was either too far off or the dogs, in their bloodlust, ignored him. I covered my head with one hand and reached into my pocket with the other, coming up with the T. The animals didn't bark or growl. I felt their hot breath and their teeth, and I heard Liesel's and Theresa's screams and Anselm's shouts. With one eye open, I saw a shoe, then a pant leg.

"Albert! Hermann!! Hupt, goddamnit! Hupt!!"

My hand and ankle burned.

And then it stopped with one pained yelp followed by another. Schmidt had taken a fireplace poker from the house and beat each dog across the flank, once. "Hupt, hupt!"

The dogs cowered, but I didn't release my hold of Friedrich. I waited for Schmidt to leash his animals and yank on their choke collars, hauling them off. Beneath me, the boy wept.

When I raised my head, I saw Theresa, Anselm, and Liesel. I rolled off Friedrich, who was shaken but otherwise unharmed. Theresa lifted her son and ran him into the house. Anselm knelt. "Are you okay? They must have thought you were attacking him. I'm so sorry, Henri. Viktor trained them to protect the family."

Liesel pushed her brother aside. "Tell me you're okay!"

I was, more or less. My first thought on realizing Albert and Hermann weren't going to kill me was that I'd carried my father's weapon for these twenty years and hadn't used it. But I couldn't have used the T and protected Friedrich at the same time. My hand and ankle hurt, but I could still move them. The Boerboels hadn't crushed any bones, but I would be plenty sore.

I examined my wounds and agreed that Liesel should call a doctor because a dog's mouth is a cesspool for bacteria. The wounds would need cleaning, and I'd need antibiotics. Stitches, too, from the look of things. I slid the T into my pocket, but sensed something missing.

Theresa appeared with clean dishtowels and a pitcher of water. Schmidt approached from the car park. "I locked them away. I'm sorry about this. They thought you were attacking Friedrich."

"*Vater!*" screamed Theresa. "I *hate* those animals."

I stared at Schmidt. It had all happened quickly, but from my crouch above the child I had seen Schmidt's shoes and pants a full three, maybe four, seconds before I heard him beat the dogs and call them off.

It has happened to me since, this strange warping of time in tense moments, when seconds stretch and minutes shrink. Who could tell how long Schmidt had stood there watching before acting? But of this I was sure: he had delayed.

I reached into my pocket and couldn't find Isaac's medallion, which in my rapidly clouding frame of mind had become an urgent problem. My hand and ankle hurt like hell. Anselm, Theresa, and Schmidt were standing over me. Liesel, on her knees, was bathing my hand.

"I lost something in all the commotion," I said. I described the medallion and asked them to look. Everyone dropped to their hands and knees for the search, even Uncle Franz, who had shuffled over to investigate.

"They wouldn't have attacked unless they thought one of us was threatened," said Schmidt. "I was very clear about this in their training. It's the only explanation. Did he threaten the child?"

"*Vater*, this is insulting! Search like the rest of us."

While the others looked for the medallion, Anselm knelt beside me. "Thank you. I saw you playing and knew he wanted to be tossed higher. I see how easy it is for Friedrich to be with you. We're all fond of you, Henri. You let yourself be bitten to protect him." He placed a hand on my shoulder. "I'll speak with my father-in-law about the dogs."

"I found something!" said Hofmann, spittle hanging off his lip.

They gathered around me as I held out my good hand. But Franz didn't place the medallion into my palm just yet. He examined it, first one side then the other. He handed it to Schmidt and croaked: "Where did he get this?"

In their eyes I saw a flash of recognition.

twenty-three

*T*he good news: X-rays showed no broken bones. The bad: I took twenty-eight stitches in my hand and ankle and an IV bag of broad-spectrum antibiotics.

"Boerboels?" the emergency room doctor said. "Never heard of them."

Liesel couldn't watch me being sewn together and left for the waiting room.

"I don't know the breed, but judging from their bite dimensions and depth I'd say they're bigger and likely stronger than Rottweilers. Good for you they missed the arteries. You'll be sore, but that's all."

I left the clinic with ointments, bandages, and a prescription for both antibiotics and a pain-killer. "Finish the erythromycin," the doctor advised. She was a wafer-thin Asian woman who, even with heels, barely reached my chest. "You don't want to know what can grow in you after a dog bite. And don't be heroic. When the lidocaine wears off, this is going to hurt. Stay ahead of it, take the codeine, and take some time off."

Liesel looked worse than I did. Six hours after the attack, sitting in her apartment, she was brooding, drawn and worried, with dark half-moons under her eyes. I didn't know she smoked; but she did then, one cigarette after the next, tapping her foot and rattling keys long after I made a point of putting Albert and Hermann behind me.

"Look," I said, "I don't have good dog karma. Let it go."

"It's not *your* fault, Henri. I could never understand why Viktor keeps those animals. They scare Theresa and me to death, but he insists on teaching Friedrich the art of canine obedience. I mean, really, what's this about?" She ground her cigarette into a glass ashtray and lit another. "Friedrich is *not* Viktor's son. I'll speak to Anselm. Those Boerboels could kill the children."

Codeine is a marvelous drug. Nothing much hurt at that point and, realizing that my happily clouded mind wouldn't function well for a few days, I suggested a trip to Terschelling. Liesel needed the break more than I did. The Uganda trip had rattled her, and she didn't sound too confident about how she'd left matters with her brother. In the heat of the crisis, Anselm had pledged to take direct charge of improving working conditions at Kraus facilities worldwide.

"He's a profit-driven man," she'd said. "But he's a good man. He couldn't possibly have seen what I saw and done nothing." Still, speaking the words suggested she may have had doubts.

Add that doubt to the shock of the dogs' attack, and Liesel was needing a few days off. She drove as I drifted in and out of a medicated dreamland, listening to her stories about family hikes out on the Wadden flats at the end of each summer.

"You'll join us this year, Henri. It's settled. In five weeks, your ankle and hand will be healed. Anselm will be the guide this year. We alternate, you know. It's so much fun. We march out with the children, that's the main thing—that they enjoy the trek, and march back. Everyone gets muddy and laughs. And," she said, reaching for my knee, "I promise not to let you drown. Will you come? It's the last Saturday of August."

Under the influence of codeine, I would have agreed to anything. I felt good enough, in fact, to extend an invitation of my own. I fumbled with my wallet and found a scrap of paper. "We need a map," I said.

"A map? I've driven from Munich to Harlingen a hundred times."

"But have you driven to Bruges?"

She'd been home just a few days from Uganda, and I hadn't said anything about my visit to the Zentral Stelle. So I told her. I said nothing, however, about Schmidt's very strange visit to the lab.

Liesel knew all about Isaac Kahane and what he meant to me. She said she'd never seen the name Zeligman, yet she took a keen interest when I suggested she had—on the affidavit for her father. "It was in the biography. He was the last one who signed, so he was at Drütte. If he knew Isaac from the war, they may have met there. But the man died before I could ask. That's why I'm going to Bruges, to talk with his widow. Maybe she knows something." I could see my visit to the Archive troubled her. I explained and explained again my motives. "I needed addresses for the other witnesses. That was all, Liesel."

Her hand dropped away from my knee.

"You found files on my father?"

"There was nothing about your father other than the affidavit. I had to request his file to find that. I found the addresses."

"It's an archive of Nazi *crimes*, Henri."

She looked the way she had on Terschelling, when she pulled off the road to confess her "monsters" to me. Perhaps, that first day, she thought she could defeat them by naming them. But they hadn't gone *puff*, in the air, and vanished.

"You're saying that Isaac was at Drütte, the camp at my father's steel mill?"

I nodded.

"Of all the concentration camps? And you went searching for him, not Otto?"

I nodded again.

We drove on in silence.

LIESEL'S TAKING her family to task for "The Jew Among the Thorns" had changed something for me. At the same time, I was amazed, and disappointed, that Anselm had defended it. Schmidt, I knew, was a lost cause. So pernicious was the tale that had Liesel found it as harmless, even endearing, as Schmidt had, I would have left her within a week. But she protested, strongly, and that protest was a beautiful thing. I found myself taking a step toward her, beyond infatuation. I was going to Bruges. With its canals and medieval center, it was a fine city, a romantic city. Why not take her?

"Maybe Zeligman talked with his wife about my father," she said. She seemed to have figured something out for herself and was suddenly enthusiastic about visiting the widow—at precisely the moment my last dose of codeine was wearing off and I was concluding the visit was a bad idea.

We were on a ring road, somewhere west of Frankfurt.

True, Zeligman might have spoken of Otto. But I warned her against expecting too much. "Survivors continue fighting the war," I said. "I'm not sure it ever leaves them. The widow will still be bitter. And it's complicated by the fact that Jacob was a slave laborer at your father's mill. Even if Zeligman did stand up for Otto, the larger story of those years was a bad one." I held her hand. "Come to Bruges, but why don't you wait in a coffee shop while I visit the widow. I'll only be an hour."

"After thirty years, you think she'd still be bitter?"

I stared at her.

"Okay, that was stupid. But I would still like to meet her." She was determined. "I'll shake her hand, at least. All the old ones are dying off. I won't get to meet her husband, but I'll be one step away. That's closer than I've been. It would mean a great deal to meet these people and learn more about my father."

We agreed to rest up first at Löwenherz and visit Alec on the barge. He was reporting that the divers were hauling up more rusted steel and were taking bets on what it might be. We reached Harlingen late that night and rented a room, waiting for the morning tide and a trip to Terschelling by ferry.

LÖWENHERZ, EMPTY, wasn't the mausoleum I'd imagined. Liesel had called ahead and asked the staff to stock the refrigerator in her apartment and then leave for the week. We arrived at the east end of the island to a contrast of the powerful and delicate. The North Sea pounded the beach, and I felt its thunder in my bones. Winds gusted with a force that could have toppled children. Yet at the tide line, shore birds on matchstick legs skittered just beyond the sea foam, pecking for crabs. The dune grasses trembled, and the broad sky made me feel small and expanded all at once.

We burrowed into Liesel's apartment as we might have into a cave. On the second morning, we negotiated the stone jetty and sunbathed on the dock, nude. That evening, Liesel set up a make-shift dinner table in the ballroom and entertained me by skating on the parquet in her socks, as she had as a child. She threw open the doors, turned up the lights, and played Strauss on the stereo as she waltzed with an invisible partner who looked, she said, just like me—only one who danced better. By Friday I quit my cane and gave up the codeine for cabernet.

I was on the mend.

I had brought my copy of the biography to read, and Liesel hounded me for a reaction. She'd linger in the room as I read, pretending to read herself when in fact she was watching my facial expressions. If I set the book aside to stretch or nap, she'd sidle over and ask in a dozen ways what I thought. *What do you think of the writing? It's not too scholarly is it, with all the references? Does it tell a good story, Henri? It's the story that matters most. Do you see Otto in it, the real Otto?*

How could I possibly know? When she pressed me, I pointed to the photos of her as a gangly kid and we laughed. She would point to photos of her father. "He never liked wearing suits. He'd come home from the mills and rip off his tie and jacket. Look at his hands, Henri. Big and rough. He grew up working with them, but he ended up wearing a suit in an office, signing papers. I think part of him regretted success because it took him off the shop floor. Do you think this comes across in the biography?"

What I could say in good conscience was that I never appreciated before how men like Otto von Kraus played a role in rebuilding Europe. This was a real and significant contribution; and the biographer, A. Bieler, had documented Kraus's heroic, postwar phase with care. But I couldn't yet comment on the question that mattered most because the author had left gaping holes about Otto's wartime service. Liesel pressed me for opinions until I realized that all her questions pointed to a single question, more the plea of a child than the sober assessment of an adult: Do you think my father was a good man?

Ten witnesses had sworn he was; but I didn't know, and I didn't think that Bieler knew or had even pursued the issue. The main thing was that Liesel didn't know, not really, though she spoke of her father with the reverence one reserves for saints and lesser gods.

"Damn!" I heard her shout from the bedroom.

I found her shaking an upended suitcase, searching for something that clearly wasn't there. "Oh, please! I left my birth control pills on the counter in Munich so I wouldn't forget them. I forgot them! And now that you're healing, I had such plans for us."

"*That's* a loss," I said. I must have been feeling better.

"No, it doesn't have to be. But there's no pharmacy on the island. Did you bring any . . . protection?"

I hadn't. When some very small, disciplined part of my animal brain managed to pause that first time beneath the pines and ask what we were doing for birth control, she managed a few syllables that both urged me on and told me not to worry. I dropped those concerns then and forever.

But Liesel wasn't one to let a package of birth control pills back in Munich defeat our holiday. She removed her blouse and unsnapped her bra. She shimmied out of her jeans. "We'll be creative," she said, "but I'm keeping my panties on just in case."

"Give me a little credit."

She grinned. "You're clueless. It's *me* I don't trust. I'm not taking a chance on children."

It wasn't the moment to ask. But I ignored the second, nearly dominant brain between my legs and said, "Why not?" Her hair tumbled across her shoulders. Her eyes, bright and playful, held secrets, though she'd not keep them for long. One curve flowed to the next: supple neck to shoulder, shoulder to flank to hip, the coastline of a continent I would never tire of exploring. I felt the sea's thunder in my chest and my own rushing blood. I began pulling off my clothes. "I've watched you with Friedrich and Magda," I said. "You're brilliant with children. They love you."

"Other people's children, Henri. Not mine. I'm contemplating an operation, you know, because these pills are a damned nuisance. In any event, if I had children they'd give you competition for these." She took my hands and placed them on her breasts. "Stop talking."

— ᴍ —

THAT SUMMER, I personally brought out the worst in the North Sea. The evening before we planned to motor out to the platform on *Blast Furnace,* my aching calf predicted violent weather. Sure enough, a low pressure system out of the south forced us to delay the trip, which hardly broke my heart. Alec and I spoke by phone; he urged me, again, to visit Buenos Aires even though I explained my plan to mail a revised set of specs and save the Argentine government money.

"You don't get it," he said. "They *want* to trot us out before a general or two." He laid out all the reasons it had to be me, and while I made no promises, I told him I'd reconsider.

The good news was that the conservator, Hillary Gospodarek, had confirmed the frigate beneath the barge was the *Lutine.* Apparently, Alec had lost his patience and took a hammer and chisel to the limestone accretion on one of the cannons. Before Gospodarek could stop him, the limestone fell away to reveal a perfectly cast fleur-de-lis.

The team was over the right ship, but the *Lutine* wasn't yielding much in the way of treasure: a few handfuls of coins and a gold bar or two. Besides that, the divers had found beads and crockery, nothing much to set anyone's heart thumping.

Alec had a keen sense of marketing, and he tried out an idea on me that I thought was brilliant. From a commercial standpoint, the *Lutine* expedition was shaping up to be a failure. It had cost Lloyd's at least a million and was yielding trinkets. Alec read the situation and suggested they turn the dive into a BBC documentary that would interweave a bona fide treasure hunt with the nearly 300-year history of the venerable insurer.

"Lloyd's should send a film crew," he said. "Win or lose on the gold, they could tell a first-rate story. They could call it *The Last Grand Salvage*. People will eat it up." And he was right. He made the call, and a week later Lloyd's got back to him with news that they'd hired a production team. More than a century earlier, salvagers had found the *Lutine*'s bell, which Lloyd's rang in its underwriting room on learning news of the ships it insured—once for bad news, twice for good. The documentary would open with a shot of the bell, they said, then plunge into the sea after one of the divers for a shot of the ballast pile. As conservator, the well-spoken Gospodarek would take a star turn. Alec would get a cameo.

The real mystery of the dive was turning out to be the rusted metal the team had been hauling up from the seabed. More and more, the curved bulkheads and fragments of a steering mechanism suggested a military vessel, possibly a submarine. They hadn't found the main wreck, though it had to be near.

"I don't get it," said Alec. "The water's too shallow for a sub to be anywhere close. Anyway, it's good entertainment. A solid month of finding shards of glass hasn't exactly lit the place up. Go to Argentina," he advised, signing off. "And to tell you the truth, stay away. Every time you get within a hundred kilometers of this platform, the weather goes to shit."

twenty-four

I knew Bruges from visits as a child. Each August, for fifteen years, my parents would pack the car for a holiday by the sea, and we'd stop overnight in the old Flemish capital. These annual visits had a comfortable rhythm. We'd stroll along the canals of the old city, making the usual stops at the chocolatier's and lacemaker's. At the one, I would gorge myself as my parents debated which was the superior chocolate, Belgian or Swiss; at the other, my mother would watch the women at their lace tables, their hands a blur of motion as they worked the wooden bobbins and pins. Each August she would purchase a doily that she'd tuck into a drawer and never use.

Because I was so fond of Bruges, I made a point when starting out in business to pursue Requests for Proposals issued by the city or companies in the area. Happily, in 1977, the city's public works department issued an RFP for consulting engineers to manage the ongoing maintenance of stone walls lining the canals. The mortar was in constant disrepair, and the town budget, already distressed, had money enough to hire a consulting engineer but not new, full-time staff. I made the trip from Paris to plead our case and was rewarded with a modest contract. When the dive on the *Lutine* ended in September, I planned to live in Bruges and direct three construction crews. I would have full authority to reinforce canal walls and bridges with steel, as long as all modern touches were faced with stone and continued to *look* old. Alec, meanwhile, would travel to Hong Kong and oversee the project for our client in Stuttgart.

On our return from Terschelling back to Munich, we turned west at Cologne. I found a hotel with a car park on the rim of the old city center and walked arm-in-arm with Liesel to our first stop, Dumont Chocolatier on the canal by Saint Anne's Church. With its striped brown and white awning, Dumont's looked no different than it had twenty years earlier. When we stepped inside and the smell of cocoa and butter hit me, time collapsed. I had pressed my nose against these very same display cases, studying which treats I'd claim as reward for enduring a long car ride. The shop was little more than a narrow, brightly lit corridor that opened in the rear to a larger working kitchen from which escaped the rich, simmering smells of chocolate ganache.

Anton Dumont, fourth-generation chocolatier, charmed Liesel and astonished me by saying, "I know you." It was a friendly, preposterous greeting reserved for his out-of-town customers. But then he added, "All you Frenchmen come rumbling through here in August. You were on crutches one year. Is it true? I have a good memory, you know. And you remember me, perhaps?" He patted his ample belly, his apron smeared with that day's confections. He *had* remembered. That was the summer I recuperated from the Rottweiler attack.

We bought far too much chocolate, and I introduced Liesel to the same café where my parents and I would sample each other's selections. Pancake flat, old Bruges was timeless with its churches and canals and crumbling bricks. A carillonneur sat at his console in the playing cabin at the tower in Market Square, ringing his bells, first practice scales and then "Ode to Joy." Our café table wobbled on the cobblestones, and I folded a matchbook cover, as my father had, to steady it. A bargeman waved to the chocolatier, who stood at the door of his shop surveying a scene that hadn't much changed in centuries. People lived in Bruges as if on a stage set. I had come and left and returned, and the illusion was complete: I had aged, but the city hadn't. My life was unspooling, and I realized I no longer wished to live it alone.

Liesel drank her coffee, and I avoided saying what was plainly in my heart. It was too soon for such words, so I said nothing even though our visit to the chocolatier's marked an anniversary of sorts. We were one month strong. I could imagine years, but I said nothing.

"Are you certain you want to meet her?" I said. "I could ask about Otto for you, and about her husband and the affidavit. It should take an hour, then we'll spend the day here."

"I'll be fine," she said. "I *want* to meet her."

"Liesel." I chose my words with care. "I've talked with many people about the war. I've spent years trying to fill in the blanks about Isaac and Freda. Something ugly almost always crawls out from beneath these rocks when I turn them over. It's seldom uplifting or pleasant. Get another espresso, and I'll meet you back here."

"Stop," she said. "You're upsetting me. I'm going."

FREDA HAD warned me that Tosha Zeligman was a nervous, fearful woman. "When I left her, she was all in pieces," she'd said. "Maybe this isn't such a good time to visit. Tosha's been rambling, talking about Jacob as if he's still alive."

"Did you discuss the old days?"

I could hear Freda in the kitchen, the water running. A pot clanked in the sink.

"No, no. She was hardly ready for that. Isaac took over a year to die. We were ready. It was sad, but he was suffering and I prepared myself. Jacob was gone in an instant. Tosha left for the store, she returned, and he was dead. She was never exactly a stable woman, Henri. But this? Who can deal with this?"

I had called from Terschelling. Liesel was on the beach, in her sun hat, the breeze lifting the edges of her skirt and blouse, the surf pounding behind her. I stood at the rail of the balcony, in her apartment. She turned and waved.

"Henri, what is it you want? What do you expect Tosha to tell you?"

"What Jacob knew."

"Boychick, I would slap your handsome head if you were in this kitchen. It's the same story for anyone who survived. We suffered, we lived. What exactly do you need?"

I had no answer other than the medallion.

"Isaac wanted me to know," I said.

And she: "Leave it. If he wanted you to know, he would have told you."

"I can't leave it, Freda. I'm sorry."

"Then be careful. And it's not you I'm thinking of. Tosha breaks easily."

ZELIGMAN'S WIDOW left the door to her apartment unlocked, with a note that I should ring the bell and enter. We found her sitting by the window where Jacob had fallen to his death. I presented a box of chocolates. Liesel offered flowers, and we waited until Tosha was willing to speak.

"He was reading here," she said, swaying, dabbing her eyes. "In this seat, his chair. I left him sitting, reading his newspapers like always. On Thursdays and Mondays, I pushed my cart to the market. We waved to each other. I was there—" she pointed to a spot in the courtyard. "He was here. And when I got back, I saw police in the courtyard and upstairs, leaning out our window. They carried him off in an ambulance."

I held her hand. Liesel stood at my shoulder.

Freda had told me that for nearly three decades the Zeligmans ran a dry goods store down the street from their apartment. Not more than a year ago they'd sold it to a young family and retired. "She's a crier and a worrier," Freda warned. "She'll drive herself mad before long."

The widow looked well on her way.

They were originally from Poland; but having lived in Belgium for decades, the Zeligmans also spoke a reasonable amount of French and German. The note on the apartment door had been in French, so that was what we spoke. She had remembered me when I called the week before, and said she would make a friendship cake for the occasion, like in the old days.

In person, she didn't look capable of baking or much else. She stared into the courtyard, where her husband's blood had stained the flagstones, moaning, "*Vey iz mir.*" Woe is me.

And then she was up, insisting on serving tea. She worried over our cups, which were dainty, undersized things decorated with Flemish landscapes. I could imagine Jacob attempting to negotiate a proper tea with his wife and throwing his cup against the wall in frustration. Tosha added sugar to her tea, then milk, then more sugar before making a face and pouring it all into a potted plant.

After thirty minutes of her hand-wringing, I steered our conversation to the war. I had asked specifically, on the phone, if she would talk about those days. She agreed, so I didn't feel ungracious about asking.

"Where was Jacob a prisoner?"

She dabbed at her eyes. "In the camps, to the east. Yaakov was at Auschwitz and Janowska, where he worked with metal. From there they sent him to Drütte, in Germany. He was one of those rare Jews they used according to his talents. There weren't many of us. Usually, they just made us dig ditches until we died. He met Isaac at Drütte. Who's she?"

"A friend," I said. "My good friend. I already introduced you." I felt Liesel's hand at my shoulder when the widow mentioned Drütte.

"He fell right there." She pointed. "Do you see the stones?"

"I see, Tosha. What did the police tell you? What happened?"

"Everybody said *accident*, a terrible accident for an old man. The policeman said he lost his balance and fell when he was getting up to answer the door. Someone was delivering a package. Did you know my Yaakov?" She dabbed her eyes. "A good man. Everybody said so." Her black dress had short sleeves; on her left forearm was tattooed a five-digit number, preceded by the letter A.

Liesel stared.

Zeligman was an old but still powerful man when we met. Isaac had wasted away and needed help bathing and walking at the end. But Jacob, only weeks before, had drunk vodka like a Cossack and walked a straight line when the time came to leave. I would have bet he had years left in him. I patted the widow's hand. "Even oak trees fall, Tosha."

"Freda said you were a good boy. How is she?"

I told her the truth. "Lonely. Sad."

"Yaakov said Isaac worked on a farm before the war and also knew how to work with metal, so they sent him to the steelworks. They both came to Drütte from other camps in the east. We met at Bergen-Belsen in 1945. Jacob had typhus, but I was sick with it already at Auschwitz, so I was safe. I got to be a nurse."

Again, I felt Liesel's hand at my shoulder. If Zeligman and Isaac were at Drütte, then this was without question the Jacob Zeligman who had signed the affidavit. Liesel had gotten, was getting, what she'd come for. She had met the woman who married one of the ten who'd stood as witnesses for her father.

"Did he ever talk about life in the camp?"

"The SS worked them like animals, is all I know. Look," she said. "In those days, people didn't live or die the normal way. Do you understand me? Jacob survived. We met, and we just wanted to live and die in the normal way. He would have talked to you, for Isaac's sake. Now he won't."

She rocked back and forth.

Liesel said, "Tosha, did your husband ever mention a man named Otto Kraus?"

The widow looked at her. "Who's she?"

"A friend, Tosha. I introduced you."

Liesel would tell me later that she put her question in precise German to make sure she was being clear.

"*Deutsch*?" said the widow.

"Yes, Tosha."

"This is a German's *Deutsch*. I know this accent."

"Yes," said Liesel. "I'm German."

"Ach! Nazi. *Killer*!"

The widow began wailing. I tried to talk sense. "Tosha, she was born after the war. She did none of that."

"And her father and uncles? Where were *they*? Burning babies?"

"My father did not burn babies."

"But he knew men who did. Did he stop them? *No*, because if he tried they would have killed him. So he said nothing and lived.

And that's why you're alive, because he lived and permitted children to be killed." The widow struggled for breath.

Liesel fought back tears, but she pressed on. "At Drütte, did your husband know the director of the steel mill? His name was Otto Kraus. Did he speak of him?"

I watched the widow go somewhere in her head, to a special hell that had taken our species thousands of years to perfect. No one who hadn't survived the camps could follow. Her face, by degrees, betrayed horror, grief and finally blank annihilation. I'd made a mistake in coming.

"Tosha, you took time to see us. Thank you."

She grabbed my arm. "The police. The police and my neighbors said he called '*Boża miłość*' as he fell. Three times. What did it mean, they asked. I cried when I told them and cry when I tell you. Because he called 'God's Love' as he fell. They all heard it. Jacob, he wasn't a religious man. But he called to God, and it makes me happy to think so. *L'amour de Dieu*. God's Love. *Boża miłość!*"

She smiled in her pain. "He must have seen Heaven as he fell." And then, pointing a stubby finger at Liesel: "Who is she?"

Liesel didn't move.

"A friend, Tosha. Did your husband ever speak of signing a piece of paper after the war? To help someone—a German?"

"Ach! Who would help a German?"

"Someone who had helped him," said Liesel. "Your husband signed a piece of paper to help my father. His name was Otto Kraus. He was one of the Germans who saved Jews, one of the righteous. He saved as many as he could. Did your husband ever speak of him?"

"*Saved* us?" said the widow, beginning to shake. "Was that before or after the soldiers killed his family?" She rubbed the armrests of her chair. "I cry too much. I couldn't help him. I went to the market."

She looked at Liesel. "*Deutsch*?"

Liesel nodded, and the widow grabbed her arm, digging in her fingernails. "They killed my daughter. They clubbed my brother to death at the rail yard for stopping to help a child. From that day I cried. Who cries for you, *Deutsch*? Who cries for the murderer? Out! How dare you bring a filthy woman into a house of mourning. Out, *Deutsch*. Get out!"

twenty-five

"*I* can't breathe," she said. "We've got to leave Bruges."

We were standing in the courtyard. Above us, Tosha Zeligman sat at her window, rocking back and forth. If I returned in a month, should she live that long, she would be rocking still. Through an archway, we could see the spire of the Church of Our Lady.

"The Nazis were here," said Liesel.

"You told me you'd never been to Bruges."

"You think I don't know German history? I can *smell* Nazis. They overran the city, rounded up Jews, then walked to that church to admire Michelangelo's *Madonna and Child*. How do you *do* this? Kill in the morning and admire a sculpture in the afternoon?"

She held my good hand and led me from the courtyard. "Do you understand, they were here. *Here.*" She stamped her foot. "Sometimes I can't breathe because of it. I love my country, but how did it happen? We were not all monsters! But I can't help myself. I go walking in Munich or Berlin and see a man with white hair, and I wonder how many people he killed during the war. Why do I struggle like this? My father was a *good* man. He was gentle with me. If you knew him you'd know he never wanted to be one of them. He never *was* one of them. Not in his heart."

She buried her face in her hands.

"I need to get out of here. I need air."

WE ROARED out of the city. Liesel drove hard, squealing the tires and opening the throttle wide on the ring road, tears streaking her cheeks. She headed north and, after thirty minutes, found a coastal road.

"Where are we going?"

"Somewhere off this fucking continent. Back to Löwenherz." She began to sob again, this time so violently I couldn't trust her driving. We raced through lowland farm country, past fields of wheat and rye. She braked hard, then pulled the car onto a dirt road.

"Watch out!" I called.

I felt a hard bump beneath the car. She skidded to a stop and we got out.

Behind us, on a road, lay a small dog, a terrier mix. The car had crushed its abdomen and spine. The animal was dying, unable to move its hind legs. When she saw what she'd done, Liesel dropped to her knees and wailed. "Oh, my God. Gott! Gott! For the love of God. *Liebe Gottes.*" She touched the animal. She stroked its muzzle as it closed its eyes, blood pooling on the dusty roadbed.

The dog had a kerchief tied where its collar would have been. Someone's pet, then. Liesel murmured, she spoke softly as the life drained out. "I killed it," she said, looking at me. "I *killed* it. I've never killed anything, Henri." I knelt beside her. "Oh Henri, I've killed this poor dog."

"Liesel, you didn't see. You couldn't stop. It was an accident."

We heard a rumbling behind us, and when I turned a farmer was stepping from the cab of his tractor. "What's the problem?"

I walked back to explain, and the man came to inspect.

"I didn't mean to do this. *Liebe Gottes.*" She broke down again.

Without a word, the farmer returned to his rig for a shovel. Again, without speaking, he scooped up the animal and heaved it into a drainage ditch. "A dog," he said. "There are other dogs." He climbed back into his tractor, pulled around the BMW, and drove off.

I placed my jacket around Liesel, then opened the trunk of the car. The closest I could come to a shovel was a tire iron. I grabbed it, then rummaged through my suitcase for a shirt. I lifted the dog from the ditch. Liesel watched as I wrapped it and scratched out a shallow grave along the edge of a field. My hand and ankle ached.

We didn't make Terschelling that day. I drove to Cologne and we found a hotel. In bed, Liesel cried and I held her until she stopped shaking, finally, and her breathing grew even.

How could I help, I wondered. I could no more remove the stain of war from her German soul than I could swim an ocean. I couldn't speak to her father's complicity, however much he may have helped innocents. I felt her drifting off, but then she startled and looked at me, beautiful even in her pain. She made an effort to smile, then let it go.

"If I died tonight," she said, "if I died, would you cry for me?"

We had been gone a week. In the morning, Liesel called Munich to pick up her messages and discovered that Anselm had tried multiple times to reach her. "*What*?" she said, when they finally connected. "Not again! You go this time. *You* fix it!"

She slammed the phone down.

"What?"

"Our ship-breaking yard in Bangladesh. One of the workers cut the wrong truss with his torch, and a three-ton section fell away from a tanker and crushed several men. One disaster after the next, Henri. *What* is happening? I've got to get back to Munich. Let's go."

"I can't," I said.

She stared at me.

I could hardly explain it to myself. "I need to see Tosha Zeligman again. Something doesn't make sense. Jacob was a strong man. He was old and could have had a stroke and fallen. Even so, something's missing. I need a day or two."

She looked doubtful.

"It's me, isn't it? You can't stand to be with me anymore. It's my family. It's everything. There's too much *shit* in my life." She put a hand to her head as if to stanch a wound and leaned against a bureau. A tray fell, and she kicked it across the room.

"That's not true, Liesel."

"Then why stay behind?"

I couldn't say more because I didn't know.

I held her and forced her to look at me. "I'll return to Munich soon. I'll be with you. I *want* to be with you. Do you understand?"

She choked off a sob. Her pain at the death of these workers was real. I knew then that she needed me.

"Are you OK to drive?"

She nodded.

"Something," I said. "Give me something, a photo. I'm going to keep it in my wallet and I'm going to look at it and think of you."

She wiped her nose with her sleeve and tried to laugh. "You want my picture?"

"That's right."

"And you're coming home soon?"

"I just said so. I am."

She crossed the room for her purse. "Before we left, I picked these up from the photographer, photos from Anselm's party at Löwenherz. There's one of me and you that I'm keeping." We sat on the edge of the bed as she flipped through them. "There's this other one. You don't mind, I hope?"

"Impossible. I'll cut them out."

"No, you can't. They're my uncles."

The photographer had posed Liesel with Hofmann to one side, and Nagel and Schmidt to the other. I asked if I could at least fold the photo. She said *no*.

"They look like trolls, and you look like their prisoner."

"At least I'm smiling, Henri. It's this or nothing. I'll get you a better one when you're back in Munich."

So I took the photo, pressed it between the pages of *Steel and Service: The Life of Otto von Kraus*, and waved as she drove off. The ache I felt as she turned onto the highway and disappeared didn't surprise me, exactly. I thought of other partings. My parents sending each other, and me, off with a kiss. My leaving Isaac for University. Isaac's leaving us. *Get over it*, I thought. *You won't see her for a day or two. Get a grip.* But I couldn't help myself then and can't help myself now. From my earliest days, I have felt that delight in this world carries within it the seeds of its own agony. Nothing lasts.

As Liesel drove off, I recognized the void.

Still, there was work to do. I rented a car and headed back toward Bruges for something important left behind, though I couldn't remember what. In Ghent, I found it. I had stopped for lunch—why hurry if you don't know what's coming next?—when, in the way of things, the world snapped into focus over a random choice. For no particular reason I turned right, not left, out of the café where I had enjoyed a salad and baguette. Fifteen minutes later, I found myself before Saint Nicholas's Church. Strung above the main entrance was a large banner that read "God Loves You" in Belgium's three official languages: Dutch, *God houdt van u.* French, *Dieu vous aime.* And German, *Gott liebt Sie.*

Agnostic bordering on atheist that I was, I chuckled and wondered if just to be safe I should be crossing myself in all three languages. I kept walking but then stopped on realizing, with a jolt, why I'd let Liesel return to Munich alone. Tosha Zeligman said Jacob fell to the courtyard hailing God's love in his native Polish: *Boża miłość.* I turned back to the sign. In German, *God loves* is *Gott liebt.* I repeated the words until they blended and became something else: *Gott liebt, Gott lieb, Gottlieb.* Zeligman hadn't called to God when he died. In his final moments, in the language of his childhood, he had bellowed the name of his killer.

PART III

twenty-six

I went to Argentina.

The Hong Kong project wouldn't begin paying for several months, not until Alec and I began consulting with the architects in Stuttgart. The Bruges public works department could be counted on to pay slowly, weeks after I completed work that wouldn't begin until February. The Argentines, however, promised payment on receipt of my already completed specs for their dive platform. Alec was the one who worried over balance sheets and cash flows, and in the end he prevailed upon me to go.

"Look at it this way," he said. "They fly you first class. You arrive one day, solidify our relationship with the generals, and leave the next day with a fat check. We pay off our bills, we pay ourselves for once, and all you sacrifice is a few days and some sleep."

He had a point, notwithstanding the reputation of the Argentine government. Our work out there, Alec assured me, was attached to a cultural program reappraising South America's colonial past.

I could live with that.

The forced concentration of a transatlantic flight helped me to think matters through. Zeligman had a long life, and who knew what enemies he'd made along the way. What if he *had* been murdered? The possibility alarmed me, of course. But I couldn't explain why I should become involved, especially if the Bruges police had investigated and found nothing suspicious. They couldn't have known about *Boża miłość* because they knew nothing of Gottlieb. That much I could do, tell them on my return. Beyond that, I wasn't so sure. I had no training as an investigator. I had no facts. I had wisps, not even strands, to hold onto. Gottlieb was a phantom who'd disappeared after the war. He was connected to Drütte, and Drütte was connected to Liesel's father. It was all tantalizing, but none of it advanced my one certain goal of learning more about Isaac. Yet if pushed, I would have placed Zeligman, Isaac, Gottlieb, and Otto von Kraus in the same pot.

What a strange soup it was.

My training as an engineer had taught me to distinguish primary problems from secondary ones. Solve for the primary, said my professors, and the secondary have a way of sorting themselves out. Finding Isaac was my first responsibility. The other business I would leave alone or risk, through diluting my efforts, failure in everything. On the long flight to Buenos Aires, I therefore resolved to locate and interview the remaining eight witnesses. If they had died or were scattered beyond my powers to reach them, I would reconstruct Isaac's wartime life in other ways. I knew the Nazis had imprisoned him at Drütte. I would start there.

CALL IT a bad habit, but when I travel to a new country, I tend to avoid well-worn tourist paths and search out spots favored by locals. For example, by that point in my life I'd visited London half a dozen times yet hadn't seen Westminster Abbey or the Tower because I was too busy drinking ale in neighborhood pubs and wandering the ancient market squares. Wise or not, it's the way I prefer to travel, and I had made it into an art. I would arrive and walk for hours, watching everything, eating the food from street vendors, not saying much. Then with questions gathered through the day, I'd chat up the locals and before long would stitch together a promising itinerary. My goal was to travel *in* a place, not dance through the brochures describing it.

It wasn't unusual, then, that on landing in Buenos Aires my radar would be tuned to the streets. I was well aware of Argentina's troubles because of coverage in the European press. Two years before my visit, a military coup had ousted Isabel Perón, who according to the generals lacked the strength to defeat a leftist insurgency. Only a sustained campaign against the guerrillas and subversives of all stripes, many of them students, could save the nation.

What followed was a reprise of Germany in 1933 in which thugs called for patriots to stand tall, then inflicted a murderous, traumatizing order upon their countrymen. On the particular Thursday I landed in Buenos Aires, a media storm had descended to cover the World Cup soccer tournament. The generals enjoyed the attention, yet they showed no interest in putting a gentler face on the junta. Just days before, the Argentine ambassador in Paris had insisted that the French citizens gone missing in Buenos Aires, including a pair of nuns, were terrorists who deserved their fates. Even with the international press in town, police continued to raid homes at night, throwing hoods over suspected troublemakers and hauling them off.

When I cleared customs, I found a limousine driver holding a card with my name. We set off for my hotel, and I eased into my passable but rudimentary Spanish. It was all going well until I saw a large number of people walking down Avenida de Mayo. Police and army trucks had set up toward the end of the avenue, and I thought it strange that in a police state people would be walking *toward* a commotion.

Something was up. I rolled down the window and could hear a woman chanting through a bullhorn, though I couldn't make out the words.

"What's that?" I asked.

The answer, Plaza de Mayo, came in a dead monotone.

I had time before my first meeting with Colonel Batista, my main contact with the Argentine government. "Let's go," I said.

The driver didn't slow and didn't turn. He glanced in the rearview mirror. "My instructions are to take you to the hotel, Señor, then return for your meeting with General Perez. Colonel Batista will take you for a helicopter tour of the river, and the two of you and the general will dine this evening."

I told him I appreciated the plan, then repeated my request.

At the next stoplight, he pulled on the emergency brake and turned to me. "Why there? At this hour, the plaza is filled with the *madres*. It's no place for tourists. We should go to the hotel."

That settled it. "Let me get my bags from the trunk. I'll walk to the plaza and take a taxi to the hotel—or directly to see Colonel Batista. I have the address. It's no problem."

The man implored me. "I'll have trouble if I don't drop you at the hotel. Take a taxi from there. It would be better for me."

He was my age, dressed in the crisp uniform of his trade: black suit, white shirt, black cap, black shoes, black tie. Something dangerous, I knew, was brewing down the avenue. With my French passport, I could find out what it was and return to Paris unharmed. As an Argentine aiding my unscheduled stop, this driver might well be buried in his black suit. His fear was real. I was not ten minutes into my visit when I got my first bitter taste of Argentina.

We drove to the hotel.

It was a fabulous, ornate affair that rivaled the Peninsula Hotel of Hong Kong for opulence. I dropped my bags with a porter, leaving a card and advising him I'd register later. I climbed into the first taxi in the queue and gave my instructions. The driver was an unshaved man in a plaid, rumpled shirt. His cab smelled of stale sweat, and his only reaction to Plaza de Mayo was a raised eyebrow. Fifteen minutes later, he pulled to a curb and pointed east. "It's the closest I'll go. Three blocks that way. You can't miss it."

I walked in the direction of the flashing lights, toward the sound of more chanting. It was late June, winter in Argentina, the air cool. The crowds grew dense near the plaza—which, I'd learned from an in-flight magazine, was the natural and fitting spot for any sort of protest, for it packed into one place Argentina's symbols of power: the great cathedral, the Bank of Argentina, the security secretariat, City Hall, and the Presidential Palace.

Walking slowed to a shuffle as the crowd backed up at a checkpoint that funneled people through metal detectors. Military police were snapping photographs, less nervous-making for me than for the locals, who had every reason to fear that government personnel would be attaching names to faces and opening files. Still, thousands came in support of the *madres*.

The police presence was robust, both along the perimeter of the plaza and milling about the crowd itself. *What are they looking for?* I wondered. *Subversives?* I had no idea what a subversive looked like. I was surrounded by grandmothers holding the hands of schoolchildren, teenagers carrying books, old men walking their bicycles. To the generals, the entire country must have been suspect.

I shuffled along with a few hundred others until I saw a procession of women, many of them carrying placards with images of younger men and women, circling the Pirámide de Mayo. This, perhaps, was the most potent symbol of Argentine independence, the obelisk celebrating the May revolution of 1810 that broke the nation free of European control. The protesters covered their hair with white kerchiefs and walked behind a hand-painted sign strung between poles. It read, "Madres de la Plaza de Mayo."

A woman was shouting into a bullhorn. "Tell us what has happened to our children. No matter what they've done, they deserve to be charged and tried. Let them face their accusers. Let their mothers visit with them in jail." She passed the bullhorn. The next woman, older by thirty years, made the same plea: *Give us news.* And the next woman, and the next. Their children were disappearing. Years later, I learned that the generals had ordered the kidnapping, torture, and murder of two of the founding *madres*, along with a French nun.

This was my client, then, the Argentine government.

The mothers and grandmothers who circled the Pirámide began to sing a lullaby. I couldn't imagine the fear these people endured as they nodded off each night, wondering if they'd wake to the rumble of boots on the stairway. I'd read reports of beatings, rapes, and plucked fingernails at the government's infamous detention center, the old navy yard. Still, the mothers and grandmothers came.

I wanted a photo, just one, to remember it all. I pulled my Minolta from a satchel and drew the lens in on a woman who could have been anyone's grandmother anywhere. Freda, perhaps. Deep creases ran from the corners of her mouth to her chin. She was thick and bent at the waist, aided by a woman half her age, both of them wearing kerchiefs. They circled the monument that celebrated the nation's birth. As I framed the shot, people standing near me stepped away. I'd thought I had little to fear as a foreign national. But the moment I snapped the photo, two men grabbed my arms and hustled me to a perimeter post, by an idling van.

I wanted no part of that van, not if Liesel or my parents wanted to see me again. Four more policemen approached. One cut the strap to my camera and opened it, exposing the film, which he then ripped from its sprockets.

"Identification!"

I presented my passport.

"A Frenchman? What does a Frenchman want at Plaza de Mayo? Are you a photojournalist? Are you preparing some trashy exposé of our country? What are you doing here? What!"

I could barely follow his rapid-fire Spanish. My interrogator, a man in his mid-thirties, had a clean-shaven, intelligent face and wore at his belt all the instruments of authority: gun, club, cuffs, pepper spray, bullets. The leather was shiny; the lead tips of the bullets, dull. I glanced at my camera, which a second policeman had stashed into a bag with a half-eaten sandwich and a glossy magazine festooned with images of large-breasted women.

Exactly how much trouble am I in? I thought. I tried finding out in a language other than Spanish.

"*Español!*" the man roared.

I reached for a letter from the Ministry of Antiquities, printed on stationery with an embossed federal stamp. It had arrived in Munich, *par avion*, the day before I left: instructions, in Spanish, for customs agents to give me every courtesy and expedited treatment so that I could pursue business important to the state. Though Colonel Batista was my main contact, the letter was signed by his superior, General Perez.

The policeman read the letter, looked at me, and read it again. The mothers, meanwhile, had begun another lullaby, something about the seasons—how they know just when to come because the one true God, *el Dios*, loves his children and brings sweetness, in time, to those who wait.

"You have business in Argentina?"

I nodded.

"You have business *here*? In Plaza de Mayo?"

"My business is later this afternoon. Now I'm a tourist," I said. "My guidebooks say, come to Plaza de Mayo if you want to know the soul of the country. It's supposed to be the most beautiful plaza in all Buenos Aires. However—" I pointed to my exposed film on the ground. "I'll have to start over with photographs. Perhaps it's not the right day for photos? My Spanish is not so good. Can you tell me, what are all these women celebrating?"

The man listened closely for cracks in my story. He reviewed the letter of introduction a final time: "It is our mistake, Señor. And no, this is not the right day to be taking photos. You'll find a tourism shop on Avenida de Mayo, one hundred meters that way. Just there." He pointed. "They'll have all the photos you need. My sincere apologies."

I smiled at the news. "I assume there's no need to mention this to General Perez? He and I are having dinner this evening."

The policeman blanched. "No, not necessary. But give him my regards."

I reached into my jacket for a pen and slip of paper. "That would be my pleasure. Please, give me your name."

He thought the better of it and waved me off. "We're too busy for this. One of my men will escort you to the tourism shop. Enjoy your stay in Buenos Aires."

I pointed to the bag with my Minolta. "If you would."

The policeman said: "Manuel, give the man his fucking camera."

twenty-seven

"*El Preciado* . . . It will be our grandest success, Señor Poincaré! One billion in gold and silver coins, if we've read the ship's manifest correctly. And a statue, a life-sized golden statue, of the Virgin Mother!"

What surprised me more than General Perez's office with its intricate cornice moldings and Persian rugs was that the general wore a suit, not a uniform, though his staff, all in army green, addressed him as General. The Ministry of Antiquities occupied the upper floors of an ornate government building three blocks west of Plaza de Mayo. I had seen buildings like it in many European cities. Indeed, Buenos Aires itself had the hybrid feel of this office, part old world and part new. I was seduced by its cafés and handsome parks, its many invitations to sit and talk. Yet what I had seen of the *madres* demonstrated nothing if not the bitter truth that talk in this city was dangerous.

I didn't for a moment doubt that, as in Nazi Germany, informers insinuated themselves into every crevice of society. Where could anyone feel safe? Not at the University, where police hunted down leftists. How about the confessional? Years later, I would read the testimony of priests who apologized for their church's support of the dirty war. If church fathers ministered to the families of the disappeared, they also assigned chaplains to comfort soldiers who showed signs of stress after torturing enemies of the state. So while Buenos Aires invited its people to talk in one lovely venue after the next, I saw no one talking.

"Yes," I answered the general. "I've read all about the wreck of *El Preciado*. I know you're not the first to search for it. But you're the first with a definite fix on her location. Congratulations."

The general had lined his office with artifacts from Argentina's rich history: indigenous handicraft and weapons in one display case; colonial-era books in another; presentations of armor; and, closest to his desk, gold coins mined and minted in Argentina over the centuries. Behind the desk hung a photograph of President Videla and, below that, portraits of the other generals who led the junta.

Perez smiled. "Evidence, almost certainly," he said. "A ship's bell with two letters still legible, and space enough for six more. We're all but certain, Señor Poincaré, that she is *El Preciado*, and we'll need every bit of your skill to reclaim her riches. Colonel Batista tells me the platform you built for the *Lutine* will work splendidly for our application. He says that you and Mr. Chin are the right men for the job. Isn't this right, Colonel?"

The colonel bowed to his general.

I don't believe I've formed an impression of anyone as quickly as I did of Alphonse Batista. A handshake in the outer office and thirty seconds of preliminaries were all I needed to peg him as a honey-tongued weasel who lived to advance his own career. Batista chilled me the way President Videla, staring from his portrait like a latter-day Himmler, chilled me.

"Yes, General. My visit to the dive site in Holland was most impressive. These are the men we need. They've done fine work."

"So there we are," said Perez.

"But nothing's certain until I see the site, General."

In fact, I had seen the site in my descent to the airport. I had read extensively on the tidal flows in the estuary. I knew the volume of water moving through the Rio de la Plata in every season, and I'd calculated the likely stresses on the anchor beams. I'd even read analyses of the geological features of the river basin and knew, for a fact, that the platform Alec and I had designed for Terschelling would work well for the *Preciado*.

Still, I hedged. I didn't like these people. I didn't like what I'd seen in the plaza. "Each site has its challenges," I continued. "I can't guarantee our platform will be the right approach. But let's establish that when we get to the site. It's important that you know all the possibilities ahead of time."

"Of course," said Perez. "But you'll forgive me. I won't be able to travel with you today. My schedule has erupted beyond my control, and I'm afraid I won't be able to meet for dinner either. I understand you're leaving tomorrow. A pity! Please give all your confidence to Colonel Batista. Speak with him as you would to me. I know you'll find a solution that allows us to begin salvaging the wreck next spring."

The general showed us to the office door.

"It's a vast treasure," I said. "I know you have excellent museums in Buenos Aires. Where will you be displaying the coins and artifacts? Many ships have sunk in Rio de la Plata. If this truly is *El Preciado*, you must have plans."

The general flicked a speck from his sleeve. "Señor Poincaré. You may have read that these are trying times for my country. We face labor strikes. Our economy is struggling, and the political situation . . . perhaps you read the papers. Order and stability are threatened. Should this wreck be *El Preciado*, I assure you the Argentine government will find uses for the gold and silver. The statue of the Virgin will go to a museum, of course. As for the rest, a billion is a large number. A treasure this size could help stabilize the economy and provide our nation with the tools we need to restore order. I am Minister of Antiquities, but my responsibilities extend well beyond giving attention to the past. All of us must work for a stable Argentina, present and future. Good day, Señor."

BATISTA DIRECTED the pilot to bank over the soccer stadium. "Look there," he said. "The game begins this evening, and already a long line of cars. In the stadium itself, people are seated. I have a feeling Argentina will do well in this World Cup. It's not so common for the host country to win, you know. But we're confident."

I listened through headphones as the pilot maneuvered the helicopter. A muddy river basin opened before us from a narrow neck in the west to a wide, gaping mouth at the Atlantic: treacherous waters, I knew, with a full catalogue of ships lost over the centuries. The shifting gravel banks of the estuary were notoriously difficult to read. Ships that ran aground would take a beating from violent gusts off the Atlantic, blowing from the east, while the river's current ran from the north and west, creating a devastating shear. Experienced pilots shadowed the far shore, the Uruguayan border, though that came with the risk of submerged rocks. The river had earned its reputation as a cemetery.

The general said they'd found the ship's bell. It was the grail of any dive, definitive in establishing a wreck's identity. I asked Batista about it to keep him talking, for I needed time to think.

My decision whether or not to help them was not a technical one. My problem was the *madres* and the police van and the barely controlled terror on the face of my driver from the airport. The money from this dive was going to fund more boots on stairwells and more vans that took people away and never brought them back. I didn't know what I would say when the helicopter landed. I only half-listened as Batista recounted the improbable story of how a fisherman had found the wreck.

"Over there," he said to the pilot, pointing to an orange circle on the shoreline. I saw several concrete, tin-roofed buildings, a water tower, and a recently constructed pier alongside which bobbed a large skiff with a machine-gun mount. A flag at the end of the pier flew the federal colors.

The colonel pointed to a spot some seventy meters off the pier. "It's hard to believe," he said, "but *El Preciado* is that close. When the general saw this, he said, 'The water looks like mud but will taste like gold.' We have high hopes for the dive, Señor. It is my special project, and I will make my name with it. We are *very* pleased to have you advising us."

I adjusted the microphone on my headset. "I see a problem, Colonel." The pilot turned the helicopter into the wind so that dust kicked up by the rotors wouldn't blind him.

"A problem? What problem?"

"For the barge."

The only problem would be breaking the news to Alec that I'd rejected a rich contract. "The barge we designed is too heavy for this application," I said, inventing one bogus detail after the next. "It draws seven meters. I've studied the average depth of the river, thinking the dive was farther offshore. This close, during the summer, the hull will sit too near the wreck and put your divers in danger."

Batista shrugged. "Let us worry about the divers."

No surprise there.

"The wreck itself could be damaged," I continued. "We could build a smaller barge, but that would require drawing up new plans for a different configuration of sheds, cranes, and the like. We don't have room in our schedule, I'm afraid. I'm sorry, but I didn't understand until now. I'm afraid I've wasted your time. Please tell your pilot to take us back." All this, and beside me, in my briefcase, I had a complete set of workable plans. With a signature, I'd walk away with a check for 50,000 Argentine pesos.

Batista looked at me, amazed. "You don't want to inspect the site? We're here. Step out of the helicopter, Señor. Please."

"I'd just be humoring you," I answered. "I don't want to waste your time."

Batista removed his headphones. "You may have already wasted my time. Come, step out of the helicopter. Humor me."

I followed him onto the dusty riverbank.

"The problem jumps out," I said. "Let me suggest a simple solution that will save you money. Run a cable system with pulleys from the shore to a fixed anchor beyond the wreck. Attach an engine on shore—and run barges smaller than the one I designed back and forth, like a ferry service. The divers and whatever they find will come and go from those. You don't need my barge. In fact, I'd be stealing your money. I won't do it, Colonel. It wouldn't be honorable."

"Honorable?"

"Honorable. Why would I take your money?"

"I saw your operation in the Netherlands. It seemed ideal for our use. Your partner, Señor Chin, thought so."

Alec would, I thought. "He didn't have the advantage of being here. The waters need to be deeper for a fixed barge. I'm sorry."

"Then you will design the pulley system for us, and also the buildings we'll need on the shore to handle all the gold we expect to find. We'll transfer capabilities from the barge to buildings on land. This will work. The general was quite specific that he wanted the same team that Lloyd's of London used. Please understand, this has nothing to do with the expense. We want *you*."

I chose my next words with care. "Our company is backlogged with business," I said. "We couldn't possibly take on this work until sometime next year. This is unacceptable, given your schedule. Please apologize to General Perez for me."

I was thinking of the police van as I reached for my checkbook. "You went to considerable expense to bring me here, and the fault was ours. I have the paperwork for the airfare." From another pocket, I produced a receipt. I was thinking of the *madres* and the driver. I wanted nothing, not a peso, from these people. Batista watched me and made a cutting motion for his pilot to kill the engine.

"Come to the pier, Señor."

He motioned for me to follow.

Rio de la Plata cut through a coastal plain as flat as a dinner table. In the distance rose the towers of Buenos Aires. I was alone and vulnerable. I wanted to get no closer to the water, but Batista was waving me on. To refuse him would bring down a world of inconvenience, or worse, and no letter of introduction would save me this time.

"What is it?" called Batista.

I had paused after the first step. "I'm just a bit hesitant around piers and bridges." I tried laughing. "It's funny. You'd think an engineer who designs these things wouldn't have problems."

Batista made his own attempt at laughter. The river behind him was vast and muddy. Anything that fell in had a very good chance of being lost for a long time. "Yes, Señor Poincaré. We all have fears to conquer."

By the time I joined him at the end of the pier, I was sweating.

"*My* fear," he said, "is looking like a fool in front of General Perez. This is my project. This is *my* promotion. What are we going to do?"

"You're going to look very smart."

"And how's that?"

I dabbed a handkerchief at my forehead. On the back of the paper sleeve that held my airline reservation, I sketched the pulley system I had suggested. I noted the gauge of the cable and the length and shape of the anchor beam. "Colonel, take this to the general and explain why you refused my services. Copy this design in your own hand and tell him an idea occurred to you that could save paying my fee. You will spend a few thousand to build this—" I handed him the sketch—"when you would have spent twenty times that to buy my plans. You'll look smart *and* loyal," I said.

Batista thought it over, and I wondered if I'd be taking a swim in the near future. Like the other man in uniform I'd seen that afternoon, he wore a holstered gun, and this for a desk job at the Antiquities Ministry. His effort at smiling seemed to hurt him. He smiled and nothing cracked: "You were about to write a check," he said.

Alec would be spitting mad.

"So I was. It's only fair."

"In that case, write two. One to the government of Argentina for the wasted airfare. And one in the same amount to me, for services rendered. Round up to the nearest thousand, if you would." He turned to admire the river. "My first name is Alphonse—with a silent *e*."

twenty-eight

*N*ow that I was paying for my hotel room, I canceled the reservation at El Presidente and found a modest guesthouse. I didn't put it past the grim-faced colonel to send a collector to Europe looking to recoup expenses for his *Lutine* visit. But I couldn't worry about that. My main concern was to avoid all interactions with the Argentine police until my return flight Friday evening. I found the Braniff offices and exchanged my first-class ticket for coach and a cash refund. My day would be spent looking over my shoulder for Batista and his cousins.

The walking cure did not work. I was some hours at it, trying hard to look like a tourist by losing myself in crowds at popular destinations. But after seeing one too many monuments of generals on horseback raising a saber to Argentine liberty, I found myself in the Belgrano district with a bitter taste in my mouth and a strong desire to get off the streets. The policeman at the plaza and Batista had worked their magic. I was unhappy and paranoid, and I dug into my wallet for an address I thought I'd never use.

Viktor Schmidt had left his card when he visited the lab with his well-muscled assistant. That visit unnerved me. His delay in calling off his dogs had baffled and frightened me. But unless I was badly mistaken, he had no interest in seeing his goddaughter's boyfriend "disappeared" from the streets of his adopted city. My choice came down to selecting Schmidt and the merely vicious over the Argentine police and the potentially murderous. I convinced myself that I had to keep clear of the police. I stared at

Schmidt's card and realized that I had wandered on my own into the correct barrio.

THE BRICK and stucco Tudor sat well back from a street lined with eucalyptus trees, still green in the mild Argentine winter and smelling of menthol. Absent these fragrant trees, which didn't grow in Germany, I could have been walking in suburban Munich admiring the trimmed lawns of a well-tended neighborhood. I pressed a buzzer. A maid in uniform answered.

"Greta Schmidt, *por favor*." I presented her husband's card.

She appeared within minutes wearing an apron and a broad smile. "Herr Poincaré? I've heard all about you. Please, come in." She waved me into a tiled foyer. "Viktor says you're quite the bright star. Welcome!"

It must be true that spouses, over decades, come to resemble each other; or perhaps all older people tend to look alike, with their slack faces and ears and noses that used to fit, but now seem oversized and attached with putty. Yet for all her wrinkles and mismatched parts and hair so thin I could see her scalp, Greta Schmidt was an elegant, self-possessed woman. Her hair was tinted and coiffed, likely that morning at a salon, her makeup applied with a light and confident hand. She was sturdy like her husband, more fireplug than willow, but graceful just the same, with an expression on the softer side of stern. She clasped my hand in hers.

"Viktor said you might stop in for one of our gatherings, and here you are! I'm so pleased, Henri. Your timing is excellent. Our little gathering is just now enjoying a late lunch. Please join us."

At last, I thought. Even in Viktor Schmidt's home, I couldn't deny my relief at being off the streets. I followed her into a roomful of gray-haired men and women, where Greta introduced me as a special friend of Anselm and Liesel Kraus, and also Viktor, here on business. "Henri," she said, "I present the Edelweiss Society. We gather each week to speak the mother tongue and eat bratwurst, which my husband brings with him from Munich."

Someone raised a beer stein: "To Viktor and bratwurst!"

"Friends, be kind," said Greta. "Herr Poincaré's German is passable. He makes a good effort. And there's something else. I have it on good authority there may be a match in the making with Viktor's goddaughter, Liesel Kraus."

The little group perked up.

"Do you know something I don't?" I asked.

"Don't play sly with us. We all know the Kraus family here. Give us news."

Eckehart Nagel stood in the corner of the room with his arms folded. I saw him at once and we'd acknowledged each other as Greta showed me about the room. "Look," I said. "Liesel's magnificent. I don't know anyone half as smart or beautiful. But it's only been a few weeks. I don't know what Viktor's been telling you."

Greta winked. "Remember, I have a daughter in Munich." *Yes,* I thought. That would be Theresa. "Our Liesel's the right age, Henri, and so are you. Theresa and Viktor say you're both smitten. Dear, you get to be a grandmother and you stop being coy about these things. If you see the potential for a match, if there's an attraction and . . . how do I say it, an agreement about—"

"Values," said Nagel, interrupting.

He looked just the same as when I'd seen him last, or so I thought, on the train platform in Vienna, in a neat suit with a pocket watch showing a loop of gold braid. Here was the same lean, erect bearing and perfectly bald, shiny head. "Shared values," he continued. "If there's an agreement about how to see the world, and if there's real affection, then why not marry?"

"Exactly, Eckehart. You put it so clearly. Henri?" She placed a hand on my arm. "Do you and Liesel see the world the same way?"

"I don't know," I stammered. "Yes, I suppose."

Nagel inspected me. "So, we meet again. Give us news, Herr Poincaré."

Twice I had yelled his name across the train platform. If I'd had any doubts it was Dr. Nagel, I had none now. Why hadn't he acknowledged me? Others standing near him had, which all but proved he was deaf or had willfully avoided me. One could not mistake a man whose skin was pulled tight over his skull. I told him the story and tried making a joke of it.

"Two weeks ago? I certainly wasn't in Vienna. But if I were, I'd have gone straight to the Sacher Hotel for a slice of torte with an espresso. And invited you to join me! Maybe you and I shall do that sometime—meet in Vienna."

"There couldn't be two of you, I suppose?"

"Herr Poincaré, the world can hardly stomach one of me."

He called on the others to introduce themselves. Gustavo and Anna Brandt announced that they lived near the airport and would be pleased to drive me when the time came.

Another couple asked about Munich. "We haven't seen it in so long. The heart aches, Herr Poincaré. But in Buenos Aires, we've done our best. We've found a place to put the nastiness of the war behind us. All of us feel the same way."

"You could visit," I said. "It's as easy as booking a flight."

"Oh," she said, smoothing a crease in her dress. "It never seems convenient."

The members of the Edelweiss Society could not have been more welcoming. Still I felt, as I had at Terschelling, the odd sensation of standing in a room with Germans of a certain age, wondering what they did or saw and tolerated thirty years earlier. It was an ungenerous, though not preposterous, thought. Juan Perón had made Argentina a sanctuary for Nazis, Eichmann included. Doubtless, there were others, though I couldn't think ill of this sweet lady who longed for the old country.

When the women retreated to another room, one of the men turned on the television to catch a World Cup soccer match. "Ach," said Nagel. "It's the Netherlands, those effeminate bastards. Switch it off, Gregor, before I throw something at the set." Nagel turned to me.

I knew something about soccer. "Why effeminate, Dr. Nagel? The Dutch have a good team."

Nagel had a talent for turning strong opinions into direct assaults. "Let me tell you," he said. "The Cup comes to Argentina, and the Dutch soccer authority declares it objects to our politics.

Their team debated. They wrung their hands. They took votes. You should have read the editorials in their papers! All this limp, wishy-washy soul searching and then they came anyway. It sickens me when someone won't step forward to take charge. This world has no use for hand-wringers. Not in dangerous times. None. It's soccer, for God's sake. What has soccer to do with politics? Do you agree, Herr Poincaré? Tell me your view of the matter."

And I had thought sports was the universally safe subject. I was saved when the man at the television changed the channel to a news broadcast.

Nagel erupted again, this time over footage of the protest at Plaza de Mayo the day before. "I can't abide it! I *will* destroy that television! Switch it off, Gregor. Truly, if this weren't Viktor's house, I would throw the damned thing out the window."

"You'd also pay for it, you piece of old shoe leather. I could use a new television. Come, let's walk down the street to my house and wind you up."

"Gregor, you miss my point."

"You're boring Herr Poincaré with politics. Enough."

"No," said Nagel. "He's here to do business, and he should know what he's walking into. Let him get a good dose of it and decide for himself."

"Eckehart, stop," said another. "You're raising the temperature in here."

"Well, let it get hot. Those screeching grandmothers are exactly what's wrong with this country. Here's how it is," said Nagel, grabbing my arm. "I'm a physician. The way I see it, a country is like . . . no, it *is* a body. If a cancer attacks the body, you cut it out to save the patient. You dose that patient with strong medicines and radiation. You set a course to *annihilate* the cancer. It is permissible, in fact, to all but kill the patient to save him, using extreme measures when you must. If you succeed, the patient lives. As it goes with the human body, so it goes with the body politic. Argentina is in danger, Herr Poincaré. Our leaders are strong and our nation is capable of great things. But these women and the leftist guerillas who inspire their marches in the plaza are cancers that must be cut away."

"Eckehart . . . they carry banners, not guns. Open your eyes."

"*You*, Bern, are an apologist. Have you forgotten your history? If they're bold enough to protest, if we *allow* them to think it's their right to protest, in time there will be guns. Mark my words."

"The *madres*? Old biddies with guns?"

"Their sons and husbands will carry the guns, you fool."

Nagel was red in the face by this point. "All right, then. If my wife were alive, she'd have sent me to the kitchen for drinks and then apologized for my behavior. Forgive me, Herr Poincaré, but it's an abundance of love for my adopted country that leads me to say these things. I won't retract a word, but I *will* change the subject. I've mellowed in my old age."

Brandt drew off the foam from his beer. "You should have heard him ten years ago when he was still in the army. He's just a harmless old dog now. Isn't that right, Herr General? People had to listen to you then."

"It was the medical corps, not the army. And, yes, they listened."

"Oh, how you loved a uniform!"

Nagel shook his head. "Ignore these imbeciles. You've come for business, I understand. With whom did you meet today? Perhaps one of us can help. Business in Argentina works the way it does elsewhere, you know. If Viktor recommends you, then you're one of us. If you're one of us, you gain full advantage of our contacts. Which are extensive, I might add. The main thing is to know a place before doing business. You've not been here long, but surely you've formed an impression of Buenos Aires. What do you think?"

The nine men of the Edelweiss Society had been chatting among themselves. One read a newspaper, another was inspecting an aquarium. Each stopped what he was doing and turned as a unit when Nagel asked that question.

With their wives in the next room, the Edelweiss men had relaxed in a way I hadn't noticed before, and I realized that as a group they looked familiar. It was their clubby, easy attitude as much as any distinct memory of having seen them before. I could imagine these men as school chums, legs thrown over chairs, a card game under way. I imagined them smoking cigarettes and drinking their fathers' liquor as someone kept watch at the window. They had aged alone and they had aged together, a fraternity that took root long ago. Thirty years as expat Germans in a new country could make brothers of anyone, I supposed.

As for my impressions of Buenos Aires, I decided against sharing my thoughts about the *madres* or the policeman and his van. Nor would I mention the limousine driver ready to wet himself over my visiting the Plaza de Mayo on his watch or the ever-charming Colonel Batista. Instead, I spoke of the *Preciado*.

"Your government is going to salvage a treasure ship," I said. "They brought me here to consult."

Which was true.

They were amazed at the prospect of riches just seventy meters off the shore of their muddy river, and most of them were happy to discuss the intricacies of marine salvage. But Nagel had attached himself to his interrogation of me like some burr I'd picked up in the forest.

"All this is fascinating," he said. "But what is your impression of Argentina? First impressions matter, son. Surely you have an opinion."

I told the truth. "Buenos Aires is a magnificent city."

"We know that. What else? What do you *see*?"

"Ambition, Dr. Nagel. I see . . . tremendous ambition."

Thank God he didn't ask for what.

twenty-nine

On returning to Munich, I learned that four more of our proposals had been accepted and eight others had made their respective shortlists, with notification expected within the month. My life was about to become a crazed quilt of travel, consulting, and hiring. This was the good news. The bad: not a single new client was based in Germany, let alone Munich.

Liesel had returned from Bangladesh three days earlier, her spirits in shambles. "Before I arrived," she said, "the plant manager and the government had worked out the death benefit for each worker." It was the second time that summer she nursed a Scotch on her balcony, contemplating how Kraus Steel had violated its own. "The families agreed that each life is worth $244 in US dollars. Two-forty-four times fourteen workers. This was our total liability in Chittagong. Our manager didn't understand why I bothered to come."

I asked about an account in the *Times* reporting that three children had died.

Liesel wouldn't look at me. "The teenagers lied about their age. To work they must be eighteen, but no one checks. One of the dead was sixteen. Two were fifteen. Apparently, we hire them to carry off asbestos. Each ship has 15,000 tons of it, and the children break it apart with hammer claws and carry it off with their bare hands, out to the beach. It floats on the tide, then sinks. We pay the cutters, the ones with torches, forty cents an hour US. The men who carry the steel plates to the trucks get twenty-five cents an hour. The children get eleven cents. This is what they die for?"

She turned, her eyes ragged and ripped. "It's *our* yard!"

For two days she hadn't talked of Chittagong. Wanting to be near but to say nothing, she watched me work in my moon suit as I closed out my research on the circuit boards. On the third day, her version of the calamity poured out. *It's our yard.* She said it a good dozen times that evening.

"I see it now. Your work at capturing gold will become another Chittagong and Uganda. Maybe Anselm won't set up his computer salvaging in Bangladesh. But he will somewhere, and the workers won't be wearing a protective suit or gas mask. Will they?"

"He's your brother," I said. "You tell me."

It was not inevitable. Anselm could choose to earn an obscene profit or settle for an enormous profit, depending on whether or not he bought safety gear for his workers and shipped the acids to industrial facilities for recycling.

"My couch," she said, pointing. "Look at it."

We were standing on the balcony.

"It's a beautiful couch."

"Dora was here this morning. Have you looked in the kitchen?"

I had. It was spotless.

She leaned against the banister and sipped her Scotch. Couples strolled in the garden, and we watched just as we had on other evenings. But this time, Liesel could find no pleasure in it. "Chittagong and Uganda pay for all my comfort," she said, more to the treetops than to me.

After a while, I asked about the *Times* reporter.

"The same parasite from Uganda. He's coming after us, Henri. He arrived in Bangladesh before I did. He called me for a comment, then left his card at my hotel with a note on the back—'In case you have an attack of conscience and want to talk.'" We left the balcony.

"I can't stand this, Henri. Come to bed."

"Liesel—"

"No more talk." She threw back her drink. "I want to think about something else." She set the glass down and corrected herself. "No, I don't want to think at all. Don't leave tonight." She studied the Rothko that hung above her fireplace, with its pulsing volcanic reds and oranges. I followed her eyes across the open space of her apartment with its blond wood and polished steel.

Night was falling in Munich. But the sun never set on Kraus Steel. Somewhere in Asia, Africa, South America, or Eastern Europe, at that very hour, men and boys were putting their lives at risk for pennies so that Liesel could enjoy her white leather couch and her Rothko. She knew it. She knew that I knew it. She said nothing as she surveyed her apartment.

What I did that night was more an act of mercy than love-making. She pulled me on top of her and placed my hand at her throat. "Squeeze," she said.

I removed my hand and kissed her.

"No. Choke me. I need it."

"I won't," I said. "Shh."

She found no peace until she slept. Even then, she tangled the sheets and shuddered. I never knew that one could cry while sleeping. But that night Liesel cried. She called for her parents in her dreams, and all I could do was hold her.

—⁂—

VIKTOR SCHMIDT finally got his wish and visited the dive plat-form. Anselm remained behind in Munich to deal with the fall-out from the latest *Times* article, an above-the-fold photo of the sixteen-year-old who had died at the breaking yard. It ran beneath a thirty-point headline: MORE DEATH AT KRAUS STEEL. Apparently, the Kraus manager in Chittagong knew the child had lied about his age and put him on the night shift to avoid queries from gov-ernment inspectors.

Before heading north with Liesel and Schmidt, I called on Anselm to deliver my final report on the salvage of circuit boards. He apologized for not making the weekend trip with the family, but he had fires to put out. "It's a public relations nightmare, Henri. I'll be there for the end-of-season hike onto the flats. I've never missed that since we started, back when my father was still alive. No matter what, I'll be there."

He felt the heft of the report and approved. "Do I have a reasonable prospect for success in salvaging gold?"

"You do," I said. "But read the section on safety."

He skimmed the report, and I reread the *Times* article, one of the three copies he'd placed on his desk. The reporter had focused almost entirely on the events at Chittagong, but he referenced the mine collapse, and in the final paragraph hinted at a broader investigation underway into Kraus's Third World facilities. It was a horror show and, for once, Anselm seemed dwarfed by events. A portrait of Otto Kraus loomed above the fireplace in his office, his right hand grasping a bar of steel and his left resting on a globe of the world. I couldn't have worked with those eyes pinned on me.

He looked up from my report. "A gold salvage could be Chittagong all over again. More accidents, more headlines?"

"It doesn't have to be. But, yes, it could."

He thought for a bit. "I'm not breaking a single law, you know. Not in Uganda, not in Bangladesh, not in any of my facilities worldwide. I've directed my lawyers and managers to observe all local labor and environmental regulations. We're compliant. We've broken no laws."

"I understand."

He walked to the window, where he could see Friedrich piloting the Stuka. "These countries beg me to open my facilities, Henri. My yards bring cash to their economies. I give their people something to do other than scratch the dirt trying to feed their families on a few miserable rows of corn and milk from swaybacked cows. I'm helping, you know."

He wanted to believe it. He turned back to the lawn and watched his son. Franz Hofmann shuffled and tapped across the patio with his cane. He saw Anselm and waved, then called: "That sprinkler head's fixed. Good as new!"

Anselm thanked him.

"The old ways are gone, Henri, and I don't think it's always for the best. Children don't learn at their father's knee these days." He waved to Friedrich. "When I was his age, I was walking the factory floor with Otto. The men would take off their caps and bow."

"Why?"

Anselm turned abruptly.

"Those were difficult days, and the workers knew damned well he was doing the best he could for them. He was more than their employer. He was their leader and protector. That made a huge impression on me—the respect they showed my father. There were soldiers everywhere. These men were scared, of course, but they loved their work. Even I could see it. Now I spend my life in an office, and I'd need to get in a car and drive for hours to the nearest steel mill. In those days, I could open the window and smell smoke from the stacks. You should go to Salzgitter one day. It was a child's paradise."

What world was he recalling? I could barely hold back from shaking Anselm into an honest account of the war. Otto's adoring laborers were slaves. One was named Isaac Kahane. They removed their caps because those who didn't would get rifle-butted in the gut.

I stood in his office achingly close to Isaac. Earlier that week, I had tried to contact the remaining witnesses who'd signed the affidavit. I reached no one. Too many years had passed, and they were gone. Yet here I stood with someone who had lived at the Reichswerke and breathed the same polluted air that Isaac breathed. Surely, Anselm the man knew what Anselm the child could not: that those hollow-eyed souls in their funny, striped uniforms had no love for his father, or for any part of a system that had destroyed their world.

"I learned at Papa's knee," he said.

In fact, I didn't think so. Whoever that man in the portrait was, whether or not he ultimately saved lives, as director of a mill built on slave labor he had to walk the factory floor and look his Jews and Slavs and gypsies in the eye before flushing them down the toilet. Nazis did that, and I doubted Anselm's soul was black enough.

"Will you teach Friedrich the business?" I asked.

He turned away from the window and thought for a moment. "What would I do, bring him to watch me in my office, sitting behind a desk? These days, Kraus Steel is located everywhere *but* Munich. Nothing real happens here any longer."

"Then take Friedrich to Chittagong," I said. "Let him see what you do. Let him learn at his papa's knee."

He studied my expression. "You're being ironic. Say what you mean."

I *had* said it. With all my heart I wanted Anselm to take him. I wanted the child to see that hellhole and ask: Papa, why are these men in rags? I wanted the misery of his own workers to shake Anselm back into himself, the other self I had seen and admired. But I knew he wouldn't be taking Friedrich to Bangladesh or his other yards anytime soon.

He folded the newspaper on his desk, obscuring the face of the boy who'd been crushed. "The *Times* article missed the obvious," he said. "Dangerous work is dangerous. People get hurt. You join the army and go to war, you expect casualties. If you work in a mine, you expect cave-ins. Breaking yards are inherently dangerous places, Henri. No one's holding a gun to these people's heads. They *choose* to leave the farm and break down ships. We pay them. We're legal. But even so, on occasion, accidents happen."

"They do," I said. "You're right."

He handed me a check for the completed report and I left quickly, mourning the loss of this man. I didn't want to believe he'd accepted death as a price of doing business. This was Anselm the CEO speaking. Where was the man who raced across the open sea on *Blast Furnace*, laughing like a child, the one who danced his daughter around the ballroom at Löwenherz?

From the cast of his eyes and his weariness of spirit, I knew he was suffering. His justifications had a rehearsed feel, as if he were presenting them to a group of investors. He wasn't lost completely, I decided. He couldn't be. Otherwise, what was left for Friedrich to learn at his papa's knee? That with work dispersed across a wide world in the most desperate of places, a factory owner no longer had to look anyone in the eye before flushing the toilet? Anselm didn't believe it, and surely he didn't want Friedrich believing it.

thirty

"Treasure!" they cried. "A treasure ship!"

The look on the faces of Friedrich and Magda as they climbed onto the barge was nearly reason enough to have built it. What compares to the wonder of a child? Through their excitement, just as through their father's weeks earlier, I saw the barge anew.

"Show us! Are those really cannons? Can we touch them?"

Liesel's reaction was barely less winning. She laughed for their joy and for her own; and after taking a brief inventory of the sheds, the crane, and a sluice that was pouring tons of sand through a screen as we climbed aboard, she glanced my way with profound approval. I felt a surging affection for her.

Theresa had been timid on *Blast Furnace* during the crossing from Löwenherz. On the barge, she continued to wear her life jacket and insisted the children wear theirs. For his part, Schmidt looked unimpressed. For all the enthusiasm he'd expressed earlier, he was oddly solemn.

Alec emerged from the crew's quarters with a clipboard, binoculars, and a floppy hat that shielded him from the August sun. He was talking with the conservator, Hillary Gospodarek. They headed our way, and I thought I saw him place a familiar hand at the small of her back. I managed the introductions as Friedrich and Magda, losing patience, demanded to climb on the cannons and then see the treasure.

Gospodarek extended a hand to both children and set off with Theresa, Liesel, and Schmidt. When they were out of hearing range, Alec pressed me for news about the trip to Argentina. I had put him off, earlier, when I called to update him on our new contracts.

"How good was Buenos Aires?" he asked. "Excellent or superb?"

I told him about the *madres* and the taxi driver.

"Let me guess, Henri. You walked away from it. If we hadn't just gotten these other contracts, I'd throw you off this barge."

As would have been his right. But I had a vote, too, and I wanted him to understand: "Alec, they drug some of the people they kidnap and drop them out of helicopters at sea. While they're alive. That's what they'll fund with the gold from the salvage. I couldn't let us be a part of that."

"What planet were you born on?" he said. "The generals will get their gold with or without our help. Better that it's with. If you're so bent on foiling them, get the money and fight some other way."

"With my personal navy and air force?"

"Write an article or a book. Scream all you want, but take the money *first*."

I produced Anselm's payment for the completed lab work. "It evens out in the end," I said. But I wasn't so sure, because I couldn't tell which pocket Anselm had taken that money from: earnings he intended to make from the gold salvage, which he might or might not choose to run as a toilet? Or present earnings from Chittagong and Uganda, which *were* toilets? I had no way of knowing. I could have been purer-hearted and refused the check, but it turned out I wasn't *that* pure. I accepted Anselm's money because we needed it. And I accepted it because I didn't want him or Liesel thinking I held myself above them.

But I *was* holding myself above them. And what friendship, or marriage, could endure that?

Alec stared at the check.

"He paid you this for two months' work?"

"Plus the initial check. Generous, right?"

"No. It's stupidly generous. What's with this guy?"

We heard squealing across the barge, where Gospodarek let the children climb on the cannons. Liesel and Theresa helped them to balance while Schmidt watched the crane operator, who swung a long, oxidized rail over a growing pile of metal.

"We found a submarine," said Alec, pointing to the crane. "A U-boat, if you can believe that, blown open from the inside. Two explosions, forward and aft. Our divers came up so excited I went down to see for myself."

"*You?*"

"It's shallow enough so that if the scuba gear failed, I could get to the surface. No decompression issues on this dive."

"But you're terrified of water."

"I had a personal guide."

"Dr. Gospodarek?"

He said nothing.

"What did you find?"

"I didn't go into the sub. For a rookie, it's too dangerous, too many cables and lines drifting around. But the divers tell me there are bones inside. It's terrible, when you think about it."

Alec had made some calls and discovered that Germany maintained a submarine base in Hamburg during the war, not even a day's sail from Terschelling. Those subs left their pens for the North Sea en route to the Battle of the Atlantic with a mission to sink troop and supply ships. The sea lanes north of Terschelling must have swarmed with submarines.

"What no one understands," said Alec, "is why a U-boat would get caught in such shallow water. A storm pushed the *Lutine* onto the shoal. There's a category for that. But the sub would have to have motored in, unless she was disabled at sea and the tides pushed her.

"Geoffrey, our Brit, is on it. He's contacted a German naval office with U-boat records. We don't have a definitive ID yet, and the guys are still looking on their off hours. One team comes up from the *Lutine*, but instead of resting they get fresh tanks and go right back down to the U-boat. Meanwhile, there's nothing but buttons and porcelain coming off the *Lutine*, and Hillary is the only one who isn't pissed. Lloyd's came and went with their film crew. They're about ready to pull the plug if we don't start hauling up gold within a few weeks. Which is fine with me. We've got plenty of other work now."

Liesel, Theresa, and the children entered the conservator's shed with Gospodarek. Schmidt remained on deck, watching crew members remove the sling from the railing they'd hauled up. He walked over to the pile of metal to inspect it, arms clasped behind him. He headed for Gospodarek's shed just as the children emerged, running to him.

"Opa, we held a *gold* bar!"

Their grandfather made a show of excitement, but when we met at the crew's quarters, the air had gone out of him. "We're looking for something on the U-boat with an identifying number," said Gospodarek. "The submarine lies about twenty-five meters east of the *Lutine*. We've got precise coordinates and are supposing the German navy will want to conduct its own dive. But we hope to give them a definitive ID so they can notify the next of kin."

"The ID could come when?" said Schmidt.

She shrugged. "This afternoon. Or never. There's no telling. But from a conservator's standpoint, I hope we can nail this down."

Schmidt was clearly moved by the pile of twisted metal. Perhaps he was recalling his own painful episodes thirty-five years earlier. I decided against asking him how he spent the war. On any side of a conflict, death had to be respected for the absolute, irreclaimable loss it was. Whether he fought with the Wehrmacht or my father fought with the Partisans, I imagined that cradling a dying comrade was much the same for any soldier. Blood is blood; and the mystery of where life goes when the body rattles is beyond our ken no matter which flag drapes the coffin. I figured he was a soldier and left it at that.

Friedrich was hopping in place with joy at having held real gold. "Pirates' treasure!" he cried. "I held pirates' treasure!"

In fact the gold wasn't stolen and didn't belong to pirates, but he didn't need to know that. Dr. Gospodarek grinned and said nothing to change his mind. I liked her for it.

Before we left, Alec pulled me aside. "This Liesel Kraus. She's all right."

"Writing any bad poetry of your own?"

Dr. Gospodarek was laughing with the children.

"Very funny."

"I mean it."

"Then yes, as a matter of fact. I began something just yesterday." He cleared his throat. "'The man stood on the burning deck, his feet were raw with blisters.' I can't seem to find an ending, though 'deck' rhymes with 'Gospodarek.' What do you think?"

"I think spending two months in close quarters has agreed with you."

He showed me a weather map.

"Henri, the sea's calm today, no wind. Freaky calm. The barge feels like we parked it on the Champs-Élysées. But in three days, we'll get a middling storm." He pointed to a wavy line, a low-pressure system. "Next week, we're looking at its big brother. To the west of that, in Greenland, there's a system too large to fit on this map. Plus, I'm following three storms moving across the continent. If any of these meet up, I'll evacuate."

"You should."

"It's been a shitty summer for weather," he said, grasping my hand. "But hey, the *Lutine*'s just about played out. Lloyd's has its raw footage for a documentary and a few gold bars for a display case. Hillary's got her buttons and brass fittings to study. I've got Hillary, you've got Liesel, and the divers have their U-boat. I'd say it's time to get the hell off this barge."

In bed that evening, Liesel propped herself on an elbow. "*Now* I know why my brother is so impressed with you."

"It's my personality. People say so all the time."

"It's your brain," she said, poking me. "My brother and Viktor are both tickled you used our steel as anchors. You say the barge rides up and down on them?"

"At the four corners, that's right. Looped with chains."

"So the barge could just float off the anchor beams?"

"In a Biblical event, it could. Short of that—"

I threw a sheet over me and propped myself up. Ever since finishing the biography of her father, I'd been puzzling over something.

"It must have taken a lot of money to start the steel mill," I said. "I know the Reichswerke survived the war, but it was idle for two years. Where did your father get the money to fire up the furnaces? The fuel and the ore alone must have cost hundreds of thousands. Maybe more."

"Why are you so interested?"

I shrugged. "I was just thinking about it, driving up here."

"Viktor."

"Viktor?"

"Papa knew steel and Viktor had money. They formed a business—a two-thirds, one-third split in ownership. Otto tinkered with new processes and won contracts. Viktor managed production and labor. He's still in charge of that, the labor end of things. He hasn't done such a good job, has he? Anselm's speaking with him about that."

We kissed.

"The children love you," she said. She laid her head on my chest.

I combed her hair with my fingers. "It was a good day, wasn't it?"

The curtains lifted into the room, the sea sheet-glass calm.

"Walk with me onto the flats in the morning, Henri. Low tide's at five. We'll get out and back before anyone wakes up. I need to go. I want you to come."

"How could you *need* to go?"

"I'll explain when we're out there."

So we rose before sunrise and made straight for Terschelling harbor. When we reached the docks, a glimmer of light had lit the east and we could see that the Wadden had retreated to wherever it went at low tide, leaving an absolute wilderness of raw, muddy seabed.

"Just a short trip out and back," she promised. "A kilometer each way."

I could only laugh again at my first steps. My feet sank, and the mud sucked at me as if I'd offended it.

Liesel tuned her radio to a frequency monitored by the coast guard and placed a call. On a second radio, she raised the lighthouse keeper.

"Ditmar, is that you? Liesel here. Going out from the harbor onto the flats, due south off the ferry landing for a kilometer, then home again. One hour out, one hour back. Will check in every thirty. Out."

"Enjoy the morning," came a crackling voice. "And tell your brother he owes me a beer. The Dutch kicked Germany's ass at the World Cup. Over and out."

I followed her, struggling to keep pace.

"Papa insisted that Anselm and I be able to come out here alone," she said. "We all went on hikes together, and when Papa died Anselm took over my training. I was thirteen when he brought me down to the harbor at low tide and told me to walk until we couldn't see each other. My instructions were to stand out here alone for ten minutes, then return. A year later, I crossed to the mainland by myself. I study the maps every summer and recertify as a guide, even if I don't lead any hikes. The tidal creeks change, you know."

She adjusted the straps on her pack.

We hiked for forty minutes on a muddy version of the Sahara. But this desert emerged only at low tide: no trees, no grass, nothing but mud and sky and a thin line at the horizon in all directions. One could almost call the Wadden flats unworldly, but this was the point: it is very much of this world and all the stranger for it.

Liesel stopped and said, "This will do."

She planted her pole, threw her arms wide, and turned a circle. "Try it. But keep your eyes open, unless you want to fall."

I turned a circle.

"Now, tell me what you see."

What I saw was nothing. I said so.

"Exactly! I come when my brain's full up."

I counted the ways. Uganda. Bangladesh. Otto. Viktor and his toxic fairy tales. The Reich. "It's magnificent," I said.

"What it is, is *nothing*. Sometimes, I need as much nothing as I can get." She turned a circle again. "All right, tell me which direction you'd walk to get back. The mainland's too far to reach before the flood tide runs. Which way? And don't look at our footprints. That's cheating. In a fog, you'd lose them in minutes."

My watch read six-fifteen. If we were still on earth, the sun rose in the east. I wanted north. I pointed.

"Not bad. But you'd still miss the island by two degrees and drown. If you ever come out here, bring a compass." She reached into a side pouch and gave me her spare. "Here, put it around your neck. When you leave the jump off—it was the ferry landing for us this morning—take a bearing. Memorize the compass point of where you start, or write that down. That's your line home."

"Got it," I said.

"You'd better. You won't outrun the tide otherwise."

"I'd hardly come alone."

She shrugged. "You never know. And now for the best part." She raised her arms again. "You can scream here, really scream, and no one thinks you're crazy because no one can hear. I want you to love the flats, Henri. I've never told anyone why I come alone or what I do. You're the first. I'm going to scream, and you're going to hear me. Is that okay?"

I grinned.

"I'm full up," she said. "I need to scream like the world's going to end. Scream with me, my love. Scream!"

thirty-one

$\mathcal{T}$he first thing I learned in my undergraduate statistics class is that correlation does not imply causation. No better proof of this law exists than a dog-mangled calf that aches at, is correlated with, the approach of bad weather. Sometimes, as much as a day in advance of a rain-lashing storm, my calf muscles seize up, causing me to limp until I work out the knots. Much as I may have wanted to claim super powers as a child, even I knew that my knotting muscles didn't *cause* storms. Still, I enjoyed turning logic on its head every once in a while and pretending otherwise.

Thoughts of Eckehart Nagel continued to trouble me. The trip to Buenos Aires confirmed that unless my memory had altogether failed, I'd seen him in Vienna when I'd gone to meet Aaron Montefiore to ask about the affidavit and about Isaac. Nagel was lying, and the question was *why*. Though it was a violation of logic to think so, I connected his presence in Vienna to Montefiore's death from a heart attack. It made no sense, and I wanted to be wrong. In the interest of proving I was, I returned to Bruges to test a grim hypothesis.

I stayed on in Harlingen when Liesel and the others left for Munich, explaining that Alec and I needed time to talk through our new contracts. This was only a partial lie. Alec took the morning ferry to town and we met over coffee to plot our strategy for hiring new engineers. When he returned to the platform, I rented a car and headed south.

I met Zeligman's widow in the courtyard of her apartment building, very near where Jacob fell. Caretakers had finally scrubbed the stones clean, but we both found ourselves staring at the spot.

She looked older than when we last met only weeks before. Without a shopping cart to hold her up, she could barely cross the courtyard to the stairwell.

Tosha wasn't going to last long in that apartment. I asked if she needed help moving. She said she couldn't possibly leave Jacob. We climbed the stairs, and she ordered me to sit while she prepared tea.

Zeligman's chair remained by the open window. When alive, Jacob enjoyed a view across tiled rooftops and canals to the bell tower at Market Square. His wife had sewn a black ribbon from one frayed, upholstered arm of the chair to the other. On the seat cushion she'd propped a photo of him clutching a cap and standing on the sidewalk before their dry goods store. Tosha kept to a low-backed wooden chair positioned beside Jacob's.

We drank tea on a sweltering day and didn't say much.

When the time came, I showed her the photo Liesel had left with me from the Terschelling ball: a Liesel sandwich, with Hofmann to one side and Nagel and Schmidt to the other.

"No," she said. "I've never seen these men. But the *Deutsch*, she was with you?"

"Think, Tosha."

"How is Freda?"

"The same as before. Lonely."

"Let me get you another cup of tea."

"Please," I said. "Think back to the day Jacob died. Might you have seen one of these men? A neighbor said she saw a deliveryman that morning, after you left for the market. Maybe you passed someone in the courtyard?"

I knocked on every door in the small apartment building with my questions and got the same vacant stare in response. I was hours at it, walking ever-wider circles from Zeligman's apartment, presenting the photo, asking strangers if six weeks earlier they'd seen anyone who looked like the bald man dressed in a suit or, possibly, a deliveryman's uniform.

I had come to Bruges to prove my theory wrong, and I had. Eckehart Nagel was not Menard Gottlieb. He hadn't pushed Zeligman to his death. And Zeligman had called out God's name, not his murderer's, as he fell. *Good for Jacob*, I thought. Perhaps he'd seen Glory after all.

So my powers of memory *had* failed me, and Nagel told the truth. I had seen someone at the Vienna station, but it was not Dr. Nagel. The news relieved me, frankly. I could end my search and return to Munich, where I'd collect my things, take the train to Paris, and begin the process of building P&C Consulting Engineers from a company of two into a going concern of thirty.

I had worked up an appetite and, for sentimental reasons, found the café where Liesel and I had come to discuss our visit with Zeligman's widow. I was two kilometers from the apartment, well beyond my range for surveying shop owners and hoteliers for a hit on Nagel's photograph. Still, almost reflexively, I presented the photo.

The woman behind the counter called into the kitchen for the owner, who took one look and made a face, remarking on how stern-looking a man Nagel was. "I wouldn't soon forget him," she said. "No, he never came here."

I ordered, admiring the canals and heavy willows and steeply pitched roofs with their fish-scale tiles. A woman turned the corner, negotiating the cobblestones in preposterously high heels. Thunderheads rumbled and Bruges, old as it was, seemed a steady, timeless place. There's a comfort in returning to things that never change, an illusion, I suppose, that a life can be reset, mistakes erased. I was pleased to think I'd be returning for work.

But I could hardly leave before visiting the chocolatier, Anton Dumont. The pot-bellied, apron-stained master himself stood behind the counter when I entered the shop. "My young friend who used to be on crutches," he said. "Where's the pretty lady?"

"You remembered."

"And apparently you don't remember my telling you about my memory? Eat more chocolate, son. It's the oils, the bioflavonoids, that will keep your brain sharp. A lifetime of eating my father's and my own product has bestowed two gifts. This." He patted his stomach. "And this." He tapped his head. "Mark my words, chemists will one day discover that dark chocolate, it must be seventy-percent cacao or better, is restorative. I eat chocolate every day and drink red wine. I'll live to be a hundred."

Isaac put his faith in butterscotch and cognac, little good that it did him. But he enjoyed both. The candy I ate alongside him on our park bench from the earliest days. It wasn't until I returned during my first year at University that he let me drink with him. I had climbed the stairwell at rue Jeanne d'Arc to find my parents out. I left a note, dropped off my bags, and found Isaac and Freda at their kitchen table, reading.

"Tell me," he said, "my big man of the world. What have you learned?" They were so clearly happy to see me. At the door, Freda all but sang my name. Isaac threw his arms wide. He kissed me, then sat me down at the table.

"Wait," he said. "You've had a birthday. You're nineteen! Wait!" He rummaged for three glasses and a bottle of Rémy Martin. "I don't even want to know what you're drinking at school. With me, you'll have a proper champagne cognac."

Freda reached for the bottle. "It's eleven o'clock in the morning!"

"So what?" he said. "Because of a clock I should deny the boy and myself our first drink together?" He poured, then looked at me. "First lesson," he said. "Drink nothing out of a bottle unless you find yourself in Russia in a blizzard."

Freda grinned. "You know, it happened once."

When my parents arrived, Isaac found two more glasses. The four of them toasted my future, all of us halfway to drunk by noon. My father suggested the bistro around the corner, and we made a day of it—the very first day, I recall, that my parents and the Kahanes took me into their lives as something other than a child. In my presence, Isaac and Freda held hands. My mother rested her head on my father's shoulder. The music played. And ever since, I've had a fondness for Rémy Martin.

I looked over at Anton Dumont and considered the boast he'd made about oil of cacao. "How old is Monsieur Dumont, the elder?"

"He died last year at fifty-nine—but he had bad genes."

He said it as if throwing down a challenge, and I bought a box of pre-packaged nougats, Dumont's so-called Bruges Memories, instead of arguing. I also ordered four loose truffles and mentioned that I'd be seeing him regularly, once I returned in the autumn for work.

I was nearly out the door when I set down my bags and laid my photo on the counter above a tray of pralines, which I regretted not ordering. "Pardon, Monsieur Dumont, would you please?"

He reviewed the photo. "Your pretty lady and three men of a certain age. This one I've seen."

He was pointing to Nagel.

"Five, six weeks ago. He complained he didn't get to Europe much anymore, and that he missed the chocolate. He bought our Belgian Memories collection, forty-eight pieces, a superior mix. And also a bag of loose truffles, like you. My male customers frequently do, you know. They buy a gift *de cacao* for the wife or lady friend but can't really present it with three pieces missing."

"Did he say anything else? Did he say where he was from?"

"Not Europe is all I remember. Hey, are you police?"

"No, nothing like that."

"Then is it proper, these questions?"

I felt lightheaded. "It's proper," I said. At a wall calendar by the door, I worked a timeline backwards to the day Zeligman died. I fixed the date in my mind, lifted the calendar off its nail, and presented it to Dumont. "I know your memory is good," I said. "But how good? Can you tell me when this man visited your shop?"

Dumont grew more suspicious. "Perhaps I should call the police. I'm not comfortable, you know. What if this should come back at me? What if the man in the photograph should hear of it?"

I reminded him that Nagel no longer lived in Europe. "In any event," I said, "perhaps it would help if I bought, say, four or five of your Belgian Memories?"

He thought it over. "Which is it, four or five?"

"Five."

"I have just enough inventory for seven."

"Seven it is."

"It is our premier collection, you know, a nicely mixed collection of nougats, truffles, pralines, and our signature dark chocolate *petite maisons*, with and without nuts. I've been experimenting with Madagascan vanilla bean. It makes for a *very* interesting truffle. Look for the one wrapped in gold foil."

He ducked into the kitchen and returned with a file box. "I'm good with faces, Monsieur, but not so good with dates. I record all sales of our Belgian Memories. The Bruges Memories, the one you just bought, is half the size. I may sell thirty of those a week, in season. But the Belgian Memories . . ." He flipped though his index cards and looked up at me. "July eighth."

"You're certain?"

He showed me the card. "We sold two Belgians that day, to different customers, one in the morning, one in the afternoon. I ask for names and addresses, because we've started a mail order business. It's quite profitable, you know. The customer in the afternoon gave me his particulars. But not this one." He tapped a pudgy finger on Nagel's face.

I SPENT a sleepless night in Bruges, wrestling with my newfound information, and placed a call the next morning to Serge Laurent. He answered, and without announcing myself, I said: "How do I know if you're an Interpol agent? We've met three times, and you go by three names."

"Monsieur Poincaré?"

I waited.

"Where are you?"

"That doesn't matter."

"All right. If you're in a city, go to police headquarters. Ask to speak with a detective. Tell that detective you need to contact Interpol. It may take all day. They'll want to know why, and they'll question you. Eventually they'll place the call. When they do, tell them to ask for Inspector Serge Laurent. An assistant will answer. I will call her now and leave this message: Inspector Laurent is in Iceland."

I thought it over. "Add 'hunting seals.'"

"Fine. Now, what can I do for you? Do you need a friend, after all?"

"I need information."

"Don't we all. This could be the start of a beautiful friendship."

Laurent told me that his dossier on Anselm Kraus's use of slave, or near-slave, labor was complete. But he wanted to know about the computers he saw in Hong Kong and their relation to the sordid empire Kraus had built. "Can you tell me about the computers?" he asked.

I could, though at a terrible cost. I could betray Anselm and, in the process, Liesel. But faced with betrayal on the one hand and the possibility of Nagel's getting away with murder, I had no choice. I hadn't forgotten my lessons in statistics: Nagel's presence in Vienna and Bruges on the days two men died proved nothing. Then again, my gut told me otherwise, and I was ready to turn logic on its head.

I agreed to send what I knew of Anselm's plans for salvaging precious metals if Laurent would locate the eight remaining witnesses *and*, I insisted, track the international travel of Eckehart Nagel. If for reasons I couldn't guess Nagel had begun killing the men who signed the affidavit, the others needed to be warned. And I wanted them safe for my own selfish ends. Every one of them who died placed Isaac Kahane that much further from my reach.

We had a deal.

Sure enough, I found the police station in Bruges and learned that Inspector Laurent of Interpol would have to get back to me because he was off hunting seals in Iceland. On my return to Munich, wrestling a final time with the knife I was thrusting into Anselm's back, I faxed my report on the gold salvage to Laurent.

Then I called my father.

I could remember only two or three times interrupting him at work, but I had entered dangerous territory. I needed him.

"Henri? Is anything wrong?"

Alarm in his voice, alarm in mine. I tried to stay calm. "No, Papa. Well, maybe."

The night before, I had dreamed of watching myself asleep in an apartment in Buenos Aires, waking to shouts and boots on the stairs. I heard a boom, then a crash as my apartment door exploded inward. More shouts, and in full riot gear Alphonse Batista, his breath stinking, leaned into my face: *I need more money. You stole my money!* He spoke in machine-gun Spanish. They hooded me, then dragged me to a prison where other soldiers, wearing swastikas at their lapels, questioned me in German.

"Papa," I said. "Do you remember when the dog came after me in the park, and afterwards, when I was better you gave me your present?" I reached for the T in my pocket. It jangled against Isaac's medallion.

"Yes, of course."

His voice itself was a tonic, and I knew that one day I would call and he wouldn't answer. Isaac's death confirmed it. I mourned Isaac all over again, and I mourned my father though he was still very much alive. Was this the price of love, I wondered: to ache with loss even in the presence of the living?

"Papa, when you gave me the T, you said always to face the beast. Never to run. You told me that if I had to I should let it bite me once, then aim for the eyes and throat. You weren't talking just about dogs, were you?"

Dead air.

"What's wrong, son?"

"Please, answer."

I knew what he would say. He had watched Nazis invade the city he loved. He had seen friends killed in battle and former friends collaborate before the Partisans killed them or deported them after the war. He had watched neighbors with names like Epstein and Cohen herded to the transit camp at Drancy before being shipped in cattle cars to Poland.

"Henri," he said. "Beasts come in all shapes and sizes. The worst ones walk on two legs."

thirty-two

*I*t would be our final weekend before I returned to Paris, and Liesel and I decided to see Munich as tourists do. "You live in a place so long that you forget why people come from around the world to visit. I haven't seen half these sites," she said, showing me a "Munich's Top Ten List" ripped from a guidebook.

That morning we saw the Glockenspiel at the Marienplatz and watched a nearly life-sized mechanical knight knock another off his horse. We visited the Viktualienmarkt for a sausage and wheat beer. We strolled and held hands as lovers do, planning her visits to Paris and mine to Munich. We vowed to shrink the distance and visit often, every weekend if possible. In truth, the flight between cities was not even an hour. But despite our best intentions, we both knew what became of most long-distance affairs. Already we were missing each other, and as we walked, we clasped hands all the tighter as if happiness were a tangible thing that could be gathered up and stored against lean times, like wheat. I promised again to join the family at Terschelling for its end-of-summer trek.

"It's only two weeks off," she said. "September arrives, and I always wonder where the summer went."

By midafternoon, we were hot. My ankle had begun to ache where the dogs had feasted, and I was feeling cranky. At that point we had visited eight of Liesel's top attractions, and the ninth was a welcome sight: the Frauenkirche, the Cathedral of Our Dear Lady. Our plan was to step out of the heat and rest a bit in one of the pews before climbing the south tower, where we would enjoy a fine view of Munich and, if the smog was down, the Alps.

At the doorway of the cathedral, a woman in a muddy skirt sat on a paver with a ragged-looking child beside her. As each visitor passed, the woman pushed her daughter forward to beg. The little one made her approach with an open palm and the most miserable, forlorn of expressions. They were gypsies: Roma, stateless, and likely living in a makeshift camp along the river well out of the city.

It's a common-enough scene throughout Europe, repeated hundreds of times each day. When Liesel and I reached the massive cathedral door, the child made her way to us, whimpering like a sick animal. Liesel didn't hesitate. She dipped into a pocket, dropped a coin into the child's outstretched hand, and stepped into the half light of the nave.

What surprised me wasn't the begging but how suddenly annoyed I'd become. No doubt I was irritable from the heat and my gimpy ankle. Perhaps watching tourists offering coins to a child raised to beg struck me as useless because nothing about her life would improve from that exchange. Frankly, I didn't care. After a lifetime of depositing coins in the hands of Roma women who, from what I could tell, did nothing to advance themselves beyond begging, I for once, a solitary, irritable once, wanted to be left alone.

The woman stood and blocked my way into the cathedral. She pointed to a crucifix, then to her child, muttering, "Jesus, Jesus." On cue, the child dropped to her knees in a prayerful pose, lifting her eyes not to God but to me. Her eyes were the eyes of wretched, impoverished children who stare from billboards and magazines. *Give*, they said. *Give!* Tourists behind me waited. How, at the entry to a house of God, could a decent man refuse?

There was no way, not this time. The gypsy beggar cared nothing for houses of God. She had chosen that day's venue as deliberately as the man with a pushcart in the cathedral square, hoping to do a brisk business. Her goal was very clear: to slip the blade of a knife through my conscience, into my wallet. She dared me not to feel guilty in the shadow of a cathedral. I was furious. I felt used. She had ambushed me.

And when she touched my arm, I jumped as if she were leprous.

Liesel had seen none of it. She called after me, but I pointed to the sign for the lavatory and disappeared into a two-stalled water closet that reeked of bleach. I scrubbed furiously to clean myself, and I began to mutter curses. *Get it off. Get it out! Cow*, I said under my breath. *A whole fucking race of beggar cows.* When I looked into the mirror over the basin, the man who looked back was weeping.

Whole fucking race?

The words unmoored me.

I staggered from the lavatory and told Liesel I had to leave, alone, that I was suddenly ill. She pressed me for details, asked if I needed a doctor, asked if she had said or done anything to offend me, cried when she saw my tears.

"It's *me*," I managed, begging her to leave me alone.

I found a taxi and took it straight to my apartment, where I threw myself into packing up the lab, preparing for Anselm's movers. And then, hoping to drain the swamp of my self-disgust, I walked. But I could not walk long enough or far enough to escape what I discovered: an evil seed I'd assumed was a *German* seed. I was a liberal, postwar Frenchman. I was better than the Nazis and the children of Nazis, above the rank hatreds that made the Reich possible. I had *nothing* to do with all that. But there it was: in my revulsion for the Roma, a revulsion for Jews, blacks, this tribe and that tribe. I had felt physical, stomach-churning disgust at the touch of a hated other.

It was a fine summer evening. Streetlamps blinked on. Couples sat in cafés and children chased each other on sidewalks. Dachau was an orderly, handsome suburb no different from a thousand others. First the children disappeared, called in for a bath and bed. Then the couples, arm in arm, ducked into their apartments for wine and lovemaking. The traffic eased, and in time I was left to myself—the very last person whose company I wanted to keep.

I walked, but the cool night air did nothing to ease my fever. I walked blindly, amazed. This wasn't the way I imagined myself in Germany, the one country in the world that prompted me to gird myself, thinking each time I entered: *Forty years ago this place was hell on earth—and these people, and their parents and grandparents, let it happen. You can live among them, Henri, but you're not one of them.*

Apparently, I was.

I walked, exhausted, without a clue where I might be headed and pushed on, hoping to numb myself. Night yielded to a foggy dawn and a procession of people going about their business. Traffic picked up, the streetlamps died. I walked, and in the hollows, the mists gathered about my legs. Through a stand of trees, I saw a bank of lights and headed that way. The closer I drew, the surer I was that all that long night my feet knew exactly where they were taking me.

I saw the guard towers first. I saw barbed wire rising to a height impossible to scale, tacked to concrete pillars buried deep in the earth. I counted barracks. I saw a chimney. I walked the perimeter and found the administration building, with its front gate of heavy iron and its infamous *Arbeit Macht Frei*. In the mists, it might have been a dream. God knows I was tired enough to be dreaming. But this was real. They had done it. Typhus and stench, cattle cars filled with rotting bodies. Death. Gas. Excrement. Hangings. Starvation. Ovens. Blood. History was real. I had come upon the Reich's first Konzentrationslager, Dachau: prototype of the grand experiment, tucked into a pleasant suburb of Munich.

I reached through the gates.

"Isaac. Isaac, I'm sorry."

I couldn't find him. He didn't answer.

"It's in me, Isaac. The seed's in *me*. I'm so scared."

The sun rose. I heard traffic beyond the trees. In a few hours, visitors would arrive and the tours of the camp would begin. The interpreters would explain the Nazi mind, the contempt for others.

I could not do it. I couldn't walk through those gates and face myself. I returned to the apartment and the lab to collect my things. A freight train passed beneath my open window, a long line of cattle cars destined for the dinner table. I smelled manure and heard a low, plaintive mooing. Someone down the line pulled a lever. Tracks switched into place and the train turned east. A whistle blew and the building beneath me rumbled.

thirty-three

*L*iesel had left several messages on my phone. Unable to reach me, she came to my apartment half expecting to find my remains sprawled across the kitchen floor. It was a Kraus facility, so the superintendent let her in. She left a note, and when I appeared at her apartment later that day to apologize, she fell into my arms, then stepped back and slapped me. "I was calling *hospitals*, Henri! What happened?"

A fair question.

I could have told her I now knew why she didn't want children. Or that I saw something in myself that convinced me I shouldn't have them. She asked if we were okay and, again, if she had done anything wrong. I said that the running was my problem, not hers, though I didn't explain.

In the end I told her I saw a ghost.

"You scared me," she said.

I'd scared myself far worse.

Low-budget horror films often feature a long, dimly lit corridor at the end of which is a door that mustn't be opened. Again and again, the director returns to the corridor. We hear cries and whispers. A bare light bulb swings. We approach and retreat until, inevitably, the door swings wide and all manner of grief pours out. People have such doors, I think. I opened mine and found the stuff Nazis were made of.

And Liesel wanted me to talk about it.

I PLANNED one last stop before leaving Germany, the history department at the University of Hanover. Since reading the biography of Otto von Kraus, I had wanted to contact the author, A. Bieler, whose signature was logged immediately before mine on every file I'd pulled at Ludwigsburg.

I was ready to bet that Nagel was Gottlieb, and that he'd come to Europe to exact some sort of punishment. But the logic of the camps would have dictated the reverse, that the tortured would hunt the torturer. Then there was Reinhard Vogt, also listed in multiple captions as Death's Head SS, the one Zeligman had cursed. Their photos had gone missing, and I was hoping Bieler could point me in a fruitful direction.

But I could find no trace of Herr Bieler. He had listed his academic affiliation as the University of Hanover, Department of History. Yet when I called, the secretary told me that no one by that name appeared on the roster of full- or part-time faculty, or as a student. The young man was willing to check records going back five years. I called the following week and received an even more definitive answer. No A. Bieler had ever taught at or enrolled in the university, let alone declared history as a major field of study.

I smelled a fraud in the air, and I was determined to track its source. If the biography was suspect, so too was the temple Liesel had constructed to the memory of her father. And if Otto were something less than the hero his biographer made him out to be, then Isaac's life at Drütte was probably darker than I dared imagine.

I made an appointment with the department head and found her in the former Welfen Castle, set amid the royal gardens of Herrenhausen. The maintenance crews were busy preparing the campus for the return of students. Flower beds were mulched and bursting with color, the grass trimmed and the paint fresh. I paused beside a bronze sculpture, a horse kicking its forelegs, and was seduced, all over again, by university life. Part of me loved nothing better than working in libraries and labs on obscure problems. But another part, a more visceral part, was impatient to see something in the world change for my efforts.

Engineering offered a compromise. I could begin with a problem mundane or glorious: traffic flow at an intersection in London, or the exoskeleton of a seventy-story tower in Madrid. I would study. And using fundamental laws, say, of thermodynamics or the science of stress loads, I could create from thin air a solution, more or less elegant. Then the architect would build in stone or steel or glass, and some problem in the world would go away. It would be settled, and people would stop arguing for a minute or two. They would step inside, through, and around the creation, while I moved onto the next challenge.

Nothing about my world that summer was so tidy.

"Someone wrote this book," said the department head, pointing to the biography of Otto Kraus. "Because here it is. But Professor Bieler had nothing to do with our university. Given that and the fact that Hanover is listed as Bieler's academic home, I'd say someone was trying for a show of academic respectability. So I wouldn't give any weight to any claim made in these pages."

I left her office convinced that Anselm had written the biography himself, or paid some itinerant scholar to craft a fiction, then slap a name and an affiliation on it. It was a puff job worthy of a corporation that profited from business with the Reich. Siemens, Bayer, Ford, and General Motors had all whitewashed their profit-making and use of slave labor during the war. Why shouldn't Kraus Steel? Once I made that leap, Anselm's fraud was easy to see for what it was: an exercise in public relations. Undoubtedly, he or his ghostwriter used the University of Hanover because it was the jewel of Lower Saxony, where Otto was born and Hermann Göring built his steel mill. No library in the world held better information on the Reichswerke or von Kraus's rise, and that same information would be available to me. I settled into a study carrel with three sets of books: general histories of Germany between the wars, histories of Lower Saxony, and studies of the Nazi industrial machine.

The first thing I learned was that von Kraus's story began well before 1939, when Göring chose him to run the Reichswerke. Fifteen years earlier, inflation had grown so desperate in Germany that a loaf of bread cost 670 million marks. People carried suitcases of near-worthless paper money into shops to transact daily business. In November of that year, 1923, with the nation reeling from political incompetence, street violence, and a crushing war debt, Adolf Hitler and a small army of disaffected veterans—including Göring—attempted to seize power in Munich. They called themselves National Socialists. The putsch collapsed, and Hitler was sentenced to incarceration in a luxurious prison where he wrote *Mein Kampf*. In his trial, he offered so forceful a defense of his desire to restore the Fatherland's economy and honor that his remarks, reported faithfully by the German press, propelled him to fame.

Ten years later, as Chancellor of Germany, he built the first concentration camp at Dachau. A year after that, he combined the titles of chancellor and president to become Führer and banned Jewish newspapers from public sale. By 1936, in response to an agricultural crisis, he charged his friend and confidant Hermann Göring to rebuild Germany and re-arm in preparation for war.

This was the moment where German history and the history of Otto von Kraus intersected. Hitler demanded a four-year plan for self-sufficiency, and among Göring's first priorities was to free the nation of its dangerous dependence on foreign ores. The goal: for the Reich, without interference, to produce German steel that could be made into German tanks, German aircraft, and German trucks.

Which was how Göring came to the iron-rich district of Salzgitter. Here, he could control the means of production by mining iron, building mills to smelt the ore, and erecting factories to shape steel into bombs. The Reichswerke Hermann Göring was born. By decree, the formerly loose collection of villages spread across a vast acreage of forests and fields became the city of Salzgitter, a single administrative unit dedicated to making steel for the Nazi war machine.

Göring needed managers. He surveyed the available talent and determined that von Kraus, a man with solid Aryan credentials who owned a small but efficient mill, would do. As if touched by a magic wand, von Kraus rose overnight from obscurity to a position of such importance that the fortunes of the Reich itself could be said to rest as much on his shoulders as on those of its soldiers.

For nations cannot prosecute wars without guns and bombs, and these can't be made without steel.

Von Kraus became a hero. Much was expected of him, and he exceeded quotas with such regularity that Göring called him to Berlin to receive a commendation. There, von Kraus shook hands with the Führer and learned that for as long as the Reich thrived, so would he thrive. None of this did A. Bieler report in his biography.

What I needed was to find someone who *knew* von Kraus, someone from the old days, from Salzgitter. Hanover was only sixty-five kilometers northwest of the town. An hour's drive the next day would put me there.

"So you'll be wanting a man with white hair," said the librarian I consulted. "Someone who didn't move away." He pulled phone books and census data. He consulted municipal registries. On my behalf, he spent forty minutes on the phone with locals who told him that one longtime mayor was dead, though his cousin might be alive. The cousin passed the librarian to an acquaintance, who passed him to the local historical society, whose president pointed to a member raised on a farm in Salzgitter-Bad, one of the original twenty-nine villages. The librarian phoned and spoke with that person's granddaughter, who spoke with her grandfather, who agreed to an interview the next day.

The librarian returned the phone to its cradle. "Done," he said, smiling. The man had a genius for fact-finding. He wrote an address on a slip of paper. "Ten-thirty. They're expecting you."

thirty-four

I parked my car by a barn and approached the porch, where I found two rocking chairs, one empty, and two bottles of beer on a table. Ulrich Bloch didn't acknowledge me. He stared across a pasture to the hills of Salzgitter, rich with ore and history, steel for the making beneath a carpet of wild daisies and ryegrass. His cows grazed, their bells clinking.

"Sit," said the man.

He was eighty or better, his clothing too large and worn smooth from use, his hair a white filament that lifted in the breeze. Bloch was shrinking, on his way to the graveyard I'd passed on the drive to his farm. He didn't look especially concerned about that.

"My granddaughter told me about you."

He couldn't know the particulars because I hadn't shared them with the librarian. I was careful. Bloch was old enough to remember, if his mind was intact.

I tried the beer. "It's early in the day. But it's good, Herr Bloch."

"My son-in-law makes it now. Family recipe."

"You were born here?"

"In 1898, in this house. Do you need to see the bed?"

I tipped the beer in Bloch's direction. "Thanks, no. I won't take any more of your time than I need to. The librarian told me you worked in the mines before the war. I have some questions about those years and about the steel works. Will you talk with me about that?"

He hadn't stopped his rocking, and he watched the pasture more than he watched me. He nodded, or so I thought. It might have been the motion of the chair. His cane leaned against the house.

"Talk? What else am I good for at this age? All I've got left is my mind and those cows. At least they'll be meat one day." He tugged at the turkey flaps beneath his jaw. "Not much of me left. . . . What do you want? Courtesy's a waste for a man who doesn't have much time. Why are you here?"

"Otto von Kraus. What do you know about him?"

"What did you say?"

"Otto von—"

"*Von*? What's this *von*?"

"This is . . . was, his name."

"My ass. He was born Otto Kraus, farmer, just like the rest of us. The *von* he must have taken on after the war. The self-important fool. Bismarck was a *von*. Hindenburg was a *von*. Kraus was a piece of local shit who wanted to puff himself up. What would the British do to a man who anointed himself 'Lord'? They'd eat him alive. Here, somehow, no one cares. Why do you want to know about him?"

Bloch was plenty sharp. My search could end with him, and I wasn't about to play games. My answer surprised me. "I want to know about him because I love his daughter."

"He had a daughter?"

"And a son."

"I knew about the son. Anselm, a major pain in the ass as a kid."

"Opa, it's time for your medicine." A young woman let the screen door slam behind her. "Here's water. The doctor told you not to take pills with beer." She swapped his bottle for a glass, and he cursed her.

"Anselm," I said. "Before the war he would have been—"

"I know exactly how old. Otto's son and my youngest son were born the same year. Mine died while I was off fighting Russians. His didn't. That's what I know. He would have been forty-three in September."

"I'm sorry—"

"Don't say you're sorry when you don't know me and didn't know my son! Don't. What do you need from me?"

His granddaughter called from inside the house: "Opa, the doctor told you not to yell. It's bad for your nerves. Please!"

Bloch placed his water on the table and grabbed my beer, drank half of it, and belched. "She wants to keep me alive for some reason. I'll tell you. First thing, Otto Kraus was a son of a bitch. Hell, in those years everyone was a son of a bitch. We ate turnips for the better part of a decade, and in 1935, we ate grass if we were lucky. But Otto and his cousin and uncle, they ate meat."

"Why, Herr Bloch? Were they wealthy?"

"No, they were cruel. His father died, and the boy lived with his mother and her brother." Bloch turned from the meadow and considered me with slow-moving eyes, much as he'd considered his cows. He had cataracts and a blue, bulging vein at his temple. "Do you know how to shut up?" he asked. "Can you listen and not interrupt? Because I'll talk if you'll listen. Otherwise, leave."

"I'll listen."

"Good," he said. "I never liked Kraus, not even when we were boys. He was a lazy sheep-fucking prick who waited for you to go into the woods and collect berries, then kick your ass if you didn't hand them all over to him at the road. His younger cousin Nils was worse. I didn't like Kraus then, and I don't like thinking about him now. What, I've got a year left, maybe months, and you want me to talk about *that* man?"

I waited.

"Ach. Listen. Hell, close your eyes and we'll pretend it's a bed-time story. That'll wake you up screaming. Ha!" He turned to me again. "Can you listen and say *nothing*?"

I nodded.

"Well, then." He turned to the pasture.

I did close my eyes, and the old man's words played like a movie.

"In those days we all worked in the mines," he began. "We farmed, but the country wasn't so good for it. Raised sheep and pigs, mostly. A bit of feed crop. In the larger families, the girls stayed on the farms. Once we boys reached twelve or thirteen, we went to the iron mines. The ore out here is low-grade shit. But there were a few blast furnaces in the district, one run by a fellow named Frick. His parents died young, and he was an only child, like Kraus. He couldn't manage the farm, and he sold it and bought a small steel mill, and he paid us for the ore. A good man, Frick. Hard worker. He had a wife. They were just starting. This would have been, what, 1928? He was twenty-five or so. Younger than me. He worked like a plough horse, and he had a little business going, for sure, making short beams.

"Otto, me, and the others—we were stupider, so we worked the mines. But Otto's uncle was the mayor of Gross Mahner, and one day at the end of a long shift Otto goes to Frick and says, 'There's plenty of steel business. Let's be partners.' And Frick, he told me this himself, says, 'Go on, get out—who needs you?' Otto tried again and this time brought his cousin Nils. Frick got angry at being threatened. Nils had a reputation as a barrel-chested pair of teenaged fists who'd pound your face raw for looking at him sideways. He ended up in Hitler's navy, a captain of some sort. Died at sea, thank God.

"Anyway, Frick's wife, Kerstin, was sweet and devoted. Pretty. She talks him down, and Otto and Nils leave without any blood spilt. But Otto tells his uncle the mayor what happened, that Frick won't play, and the mayor sends the police out to the mill. Everybody knows everybody in these villages. Hell, the man his uncle sent went to school with Otto and me. I won't tell you *his* name, because he was following orders. I can't find fault with that, even if it was a bad business. The policeman says, 'Frick, you're wanted for questioning.' And Kerstin, she tells me this afterwards, says: 'What for?' And the policeman says, 'Someone reported a health code violation in this district. Did you hurt your hand?' Frick holds up his hands and says, 'My hands are fine. I cut them and bang them every day in the shop. What do you mean?'

"'Come with me,' says the policeman. So there's nothing to be done. Frick tells his wife everything will be fine, that he'd done nothing wrong, and that he'll be back by supper. But he didn't come back for supper that evening or any evening. The mayor, and I know this for a fact, was a National Socialist. Fought in the first war. Was a goddamned zealot for wounded German pride. He says to Frick, 'You've hurt yourself on the job and haven't reported the injuries, as the law requires. This is an offense against the health of the district. What have you done with the bloody bandages?' Frick tells him there were no bloody bandages, that he has no idea what the man's talking about. The mayor says, 'So, now you're telling me that public safety is a trivial thing? You make light of public safety, the spread of disease?'

"And Frick, who can't believe what's happening, says, 'What's this about? You're out of your mind! Go catch criminals, why don't you.' At which point the mayor turns furious. He's spitting mad, he's red in the face, he's snorting. 'Do you dare to challenge my authority or doubt the seriousness of this offense? Herr Frick, this is no longer a matter of exposing the district to disease. You're disrespecting the rule of law. You're dangerous. I will do my duty!'

"And the mayor throws Frick in jail for the night on a charge of endangering public safety. Kerstin goes to visit, Frick tells her it's some monstrous mistake, but he must stay in jail for a few days. A few days become a month. Frick gets congested lungs and dies. He dies! Kerstin is lost in grief. They'd held off having children while he got the business started. She's childless, she has nothing. Frick already sold the farm, and she doesn't know how to run a steel mill. A month later, when she's desperate from the loss and out of money, who should knock at her door but Otto Kraus, with an offer to buy the business for an eighth of what it's worth."

"Kraus set him up? He got his uncle, the mayor to—"

"Shut *up*! Did we not have an agreement?"

I fell silent.

We rocked in our chairs. The cow bells clinked. Far down the road, a truck kicked up a plume of dust. I grabbed the armrests of my rocker as if the chair might fly off the porch with what I'd heard. None of this, none of it appeared in the airbrushed history of Otto Kraus—aside from the purchase of a small steel works in Salzgitter in 1928.

"Kerstin went mad with it," said Bloch. "She just lost her mind at how one day the sky was blue and the next day, black. What kind of hell had she slipped into? A catastrophe that came from nothing! But her shakes didn't begin until she sold the foundry. In town one day she met Frick's cousin, who had a bandage on his hand. She said, 'What's this?' and he said, 'You know, I nearly sawed it off in an accident a few months back. But I'm on the mend, at last. The doctor saved my hand.'

"That's when Kerstin realized that the mayor had heard about the cousin, not Frick, but wanted Frick gone anyway. He made it up, made all of it up so his nephew Otto could own a blast furnace.

"Now I have to say Otto was clever with that furnace. He tinkered with the smelting process and got the shitty ore in these parts to render usable steel. What was it, ten or twelve years later, Hermann Göring himself comes to Salzgitter to build a mill for the Reich, and he makes Otto Kraus his man. Gives him the run of the place. Just like that!"

Bloch tried to snap his boney fingers, but no sound came.

"And the worst of it, that beautiful woman, Frick's Kerstin, goes mad. It was the mayor's town, the mayor's law, the mayor's justice. No wonder Kraus made such a good Nazi."

When I opened my eyes, the meadow was just as lush and fragrant as when I arrived. I waited until I could wait no longer. "Herr Bloch?"

"I'm done. Goddamn it, I shouldn't have remembered that. It upsets me. Otto Kraus and his cousin Nils and his uncle were born Nazis. They were Nazis before there was a Nazi party. They were thugs looking for a club to join. In the Wehrmacht we fought a war, at least we were soldiers. We met other soldiers in combat. We killed like soldiers kill. I'm not proud of it, but I'm not ashamed either. What I won't own is how, when we pushed east and north into Poland and Russia, the SS came in behind us to stabilize the country. Stabilize? They lined up women and children and old men in front of pits and gunned them down. That's not what I fought for."

He brought something up from his chest and spit into a rag.

"The wife," I said. "What became of her?"

"Kerstin? Went to live with a cousin. Her hands started shaking, and they stopped only when she slept. She put it to good use, though. Give her a baby, colicky, whatever. Drop any kind of wailing child into her arms and she'd shake it right to sleep. Touched by God, some people said. A gift."

He looked at me.

"I'm done. Get the hell out."

thirty-five

I stood before the sprawling steelworks that Otto Kraus resurrected in 1947, when the furnaces lay cold and dormant. Thirty years later, rail cars fed the beast with mountains of ore; flatbed cars rolled away, stacked with high-grade beams. The furnaces were roaring again—this time in support of a modern economy, not a war machine. The people of Salzgitter paid their taxes, and they revered Otto Kraus and his son as industrialists who'd brought prosperity to their region.

Inside the steelworks, meanwhile, undisturbed and long forgotten, lay the remains of a darker past, the Drütte concentration camp. The SS had built Drütte within the yard's perimeter so that prisoners wouldn't waste time and precious strength marching to and from the mill in winter.

Isaac had survived this.

In those days, factory managers in sectors critical to the war economy paid the SS for the right to use camp inmates on the production line. Wernher von Braun, the rocket scientist whose V-2 terrorized London and who later helped the United States reach the moon, used slaves. So did Alfried Krupp, who made Hitler's guns and bombs. So did Hugo Boss, the clothier who designed and manufactured the Reich's snappy uniforms. Kraus was no different. He paid in deutschmarks and received slaves fed on thin soup and stale bread. When the prisoners died after the expected four or five months, a never-ending stream of dazed, starving new ones replaced them. Which meant that very near the spot I was standing on, some forty years earlier, Liesel's father had negotiated with SS administrators to compel Isaac and others to work, while on a diet that couldn't sustain a dog.

Yet Kraus *saved* lives, the story went. Could it be? Had he played a double game *that* convincingly—a thug in childhood who, in war, saw the light and turned prince? Ten witnesses had said so. The Allied courts said so when they freed him, even as they were bringing the managers of other plants to account and sentencing them to prison.

For Liesel's sake, I wanted to believe it.

I stood on the side of a road some distance from the mill, recalling from Isaac's funeral how some mourners left stones on the grave markers. The custom was new to me, so at the time I asked the rabbi, a kind, skinny man with a soft beard and a bow tie, what it signified.

"The stone's a marker," he explained, "more for us than the deceased. In ancient times, farmers would bury their kin in the fields and build stone cairns so that others would steer their ploughs elsewhere. Who would sow grain or plant a fruit tree where men are buried?"

Otto Kraus, perhaps.

In the absence of any memorials to consecrate this place, I set a cairn, three stones point-to-point. I laid a fourth on top. It was a small thing. I knelt beside it and thought of Isaac, who once presented me with a stone as we sat on our park bench.

Henri, here's what you do with a stone. Any stone will do. You take it in hand and you think on it for a time. You might give it a thought for someone you love, perhaps for the one you haven't met but may one day love. You could think of a place you'd rather be or a place you've been. I've thought of my parent's farm and scrubbing dirt from my fingernails before the Sabbath meal. And after the scrubbing and washing, I've thought of how at the table my father would bless my sisters and brothers and me. I've thought of sitting down to my mother's bread, the way it steams and the way the butter melts. There are times I would have traded a fortune for a slice of her Sabbath bread! The thing is to give the stone one true piece of yourself, just one, then throw it as far as you can knowing you could never find it even if you went looking. *That's important. If you've been true, the stone, out of sight, will roll and keep rolling until it stops and takes root.*

Uncle, how could it keep rolling?

If it's out of sight, how do you know it doesn't?

But stones don't take root and grow. That's silly!

And you know this for a fact?

I've never seen one grow.

You have, Henri.

Never. What do they grow into?

He pinched my cheek. *My boy, how do you think the Alps got there?*

—⁂—

"You wrote a fine report," said Laurent.

I had stopped at a petrol station on the A2 at nine that same evening, on my way to Ludwigsburg, and phoned Laurent for an update. "Who knew gold could be mined from computers? Kraus, he's a clever one."

"Is it what you wanted?" I asked.

I was standing at an outdoor phone booth, the traffic roaring past. Across the highway rose a forest, its canopy silent and dark.

"It certainly rounds out the profile. I've established his labor methods at eight of his Third World facilities. I'd say I have him nailed. His steel mills in Europe are state-of-the art, a safety inspector's dream. Overseas, it's a bucket of shit. He plays by very different sets of rules."

"But he hasn't built a salvage yard for computers. Not yet."

"You're defending the bastard? When he *does* build his salvage yards for electronic junk, and he will when there's money to be made, he'll choose some desperately poor place like Delhi, some other Chittagong. Do you think he'll make it safe for the men mixing hydrochloric and nitric acid? You think he'll buy his workers the gas masks and eye protection you called for in your report?"

We both knew better.

"In the morning I'm forwarding my dossier to a prosecutor in The Hague. I'm quite sure your girlfriend's brother is running debt slaves. It's against international law, and if you give me a minute I'll recite chapter and verse."

"Don't bother," I said.

At the far end of the lot, I saw a man on the driver's side of a late model Mercedes, stretching. A taller man, also dressed in a suit, rose from the passenger side. They had parked just beyond the sharply defined wash of a lamppost, and I couldn't quite make them out. Others crossed the lot.

"Fair is fair," said Laurent. "You gave me your report, and now I've got news for you. Seven of the remaining eight on your list are dead. Two died from cancer in the sixties. Nothing remarkable about that. But the other five died of heart attacks in the last two months. That's the past eight weeks, if you're hearing me. Ventricular arrhythmias. Add to those five the two you crossed off your list in the last month, Zeligman and Montefiore—who was a confirmed heart attack, I checked—and we've got seven men who died this summer. Suddenly. What's going on?"

I leaned against the phone booth, staring into the forest.

"What about the tenth witness?"

"Witness?"

"Forget it. Did you find the last one on the list?"

"David Grossman? No. He's dropped off the face of the earth. He lived in Innsbruck for twenty-five years, then this past June, during the same time the others are dying, he sells his house and moves with no forwarding address. I've run down tax records, phone records, certificates of death. I've checked passport control in every Interpol member nation. He's likely changed his name. You've got my attention," said Laurent. "What's this about?"

A truck sped past and lifted grit into my eyes. The two men were walking my way.

"Eckehart Nagel," I said. "What about his travel records?"

"Those are a gem. The five whose hearts decided to stop beating lived in Lisbon, New York, Los Angeles, Chicago, and London.

Nagel landed at JFK two days before the first heart attack victim in the U.S., and left LAX the evening after the third. His visits to England and Portugal overlapped the heart attacks in London and Lisbon. I checked. He's a cardiologist."

"How did you get his travel information?"

"The police in Buenos Aires. They asked him to visit headquarters with his passport. Maybe you've heard. When the police ask you to do something in Argentina—"

One of the men approaching me was Schmidt's assistant, from the lab.

"They photocopied, then faxed the passport. Who is Nagel? What are you not telling me, Henri? What is his relation to these dead men?"

I didn't know.

I had already betrayed Anselm and Liesel by releasing the report to Laurent. I wouldn't betray them again by tainting the Kraus name with a murder investigation, not until I knew where it led. I owed Liesel that much, but I was frightened and wanted to spill it all.

"Come on," I said, trying to sound casual. "A thousand businessmen overlapped those cities and countries on the same dates. It's just that we don't know who they are. Nagel's schedule is no big deal. What does it prove?"

Laurent waited long enough for me to appreciate the stupidity of what I'd said. "You asked me to investigate," he said. "Without your list, no one could have linked these deaths. You've got a handful of sixty- and seventy-year-olds dropping dead in different cities around the world. What's the big deal? I don't know. But you've managed to link them somehow, and I'm left with several possibilities."

Schmidt's man and his colleague stopped eight paces from me and waited.

"Let's dismiss the first," said Laurent. "That all this is coincidence. Let's not insult each other. The second possibility: you're way over your head in something you don't understand and can't possibly manage."

The smaller of the two men lit a cigarette and waved. Why had Schmidt sent them? I had seen him not two days ago, on Terschelling and at the dive platform. While he was unusually solemn, he didn't seem particularly angry with me or suspicious. Just out of sorts.

But here were his men, and the sickening thought occurred to me that all this time, after the visit to the lab and his ham-handed effort to have me followed, he *was* following me: expertly now, after a first, obvious warning that he'd meant for me to see. Now his men had tracked me to Bruges and Salzgitter. They knew I visited Ulrich Bloch. They had reported back, and here they were.

"Third possibility," said Laurent. "Grossman, the one who's dropped out of sight, may have killed the others and is now a fugitive. Fourth: Nagel killed them, and Grossman is running for his life. Fifth: You've orchestrated all of this and are using me to trap Nagel or Grossman. You don't strike me as someone who'd hire an assassin, but I've seen stranger things. Where are you now?"

Schmidt's men stepped toward me.

I spoke so that they could hear.

"I'm at a rest stop near the Dortmund exit on the A2, traveling west. I'm driving a yellow Fiat rented yesterday from the GSX Agency in Harlingen. There are two large men in suits standing in my face, not looking very kind. I want you to tell them exactly who you are."

My voice was shaking. I handed the phone to the one from the lab. "It's Interpol," I said. "For you."

The rest stop was busy with late-night haulers and families on holiday. I waited at a table, and after a minute Schmidt's men joined me. We were surrounded by truckers drinking coffee and children slurping ice cream and downing burgers.

"Viktor would like to see you."

"Of course," I said. "I'll call him in the morning."

"Tonight."

I had no doubt they would have delivered me personally but for Laurent. "Is there anything in particular he wants to talk about?"

"Call him."

They left, and ten minutes later I followed. I couldn't find their car in the parking lot, and drove off thinking I was free of them. What I didn't notice was a blue Saab, which followed me all the way to Ludwigsburg.

thirty-six

Gustav Plannik looked like a man freshly returned from vacation. He was tan and the puffy half moons beneath his eyes had receded. He might have lost weight and, if I wasn't mistaken, he'd worked some boot black into his hair. It was a good day to drop in unannounced on the director.

I had no choice, given Laurent's news. If Nagel found Grossman, he would follow the other witnesses to the grave. If I found him first, he had a chance of surviving, and I had a chance of learning something, perhaps, about Isaac.

I needed no reminder that Schmidt had someone at work for him inside the Zentrale Stelle. But I didn't plan to stay long enough for an informer to place a call back to Munich and have it matter. I stopped in Stuttgart to empty the safe deposit box, then headed to the Archive. The risk was that Plannik himself was Schmidt's man, though I doubted it. If I were wrong, so much the worse for me. I had little choice but to tell him everything.

After a bit of negotiating at the main gate, I was buzzed into the compound and was met by the director himself, who'd walked halfway down a corridor to greet me. The bounce had returned to his step, and his seemed genuinely pleased by my visit.

In his office he brushed aside a photo of two soldiers posing beside a pile of bodies. One had a hand on the shoulder of his comrade, who'd set a boot on the rump of a corpse as if it were a lion shot on safari.

Surrounding us on the pale walls, still, were the organizational charts of the SS and Gestapo. Thirty years removed from Hell,

Plannik chose to sit in the middle of it every morning at nine o'clock. Given the photos and sworn statements he confronted daily, Australia seemed about the right distance for a vacation.

Plannik folded his hands. "So," he said. "Still searching?"

I told him I was, and that I had something for him.

Outside the open windows I heard traffic on Schorndorfer Strasse. A utility crew was jackhammering a section of road, and the sound of concrete breaking carried into Plannik's office like a bass-note concussion.

The director leaned forward. "So, how can I help? More time in the Archive?"

I reached into my bag for the list of witnesses, and he reached for his glasses.

"Okay," he said. "I recognize this list from your last visit, when I approved the documents you copied. These are the witnesses in the Kraus affair. One of them, Grossman, is circled. The others . . . they have lines drawn through them."

"May I close your door?"

Five minutes later, having shared my suspicions, I concluded the only way I could. "I don't know why they're dying, Herr Plannik, but they are. I think it has something to do with this place."

"Something to do with Drütte."

I agreed. I produced the file I'd copied on the camp and opened to a group photograph of several SS guards. Ever since my return from Buenos Aires, I was often nagged by the thought that I had already encountered the men of the Edelweiss Society. I'd been busy and preoccupied, and let it slide until early that morning, before I returned to the Archive. Sleep was impossible in any event. I startled at every sound in the hotel corridor, imagining Schmidt's men hunting me down. I thought to call Laurent and ask for police protection. But I held off, concluding for the second time in twelve hours that any talk with the authorities would lead back to Anselm, and I wasn't prepared to betray him a second time.

Nagel was entangled in the murders; but it was a stretch, pure conjecture, to suppose that Anselm was. I had no reason to contact

Laurent, no theory at all on why the signatories to the affidavit were dying.

Much of that night, I reviewed my notes and the photocopied materials before calling on Plannik. Using a large magnifying glass, for the first time I scrupulously studied the photos that hadn't gone missing. It was then I recognized in the Drütte folder eight smoothly shaven faces looking into the middle distance, dressed in the crisp uniform of the SS-Totenkopfverbände, the Death's Head formations. The Edelweiss brotherhood had enjoyed a long history after all. These were not random expat Germans who happened to find each other in Buenos Aires after the war. They'd served together at the Reichswerke Hermann Göring.

I explained all this as I positioned the photos for Plannik.

"You opened files on three of them for suspected war crimes," I said, "but the prosecutors couldn't find them and the inquiries ended. They're in Buenos Aires. I can give you their identities. I know where they meet."

Plannik reached for a magnifying glass, and I followed with my photo of Liesel with her uncles, including Eckehart Nagel. It felt wrong, unholy even, that she should be standing beside that man. When she gave me the photo, I'd promised not to cut the others out of it. So here she was, part of evidence delivered to a man who built dossiers against Nazis. The Zentrale Stelle was not where Liesel should have been, or where I wanted to bring her.

Nagel's bald, grinning skull was bad enough. But the image of a dour Franz Hofmann and a buoyant Viktor Schmidt was almost too much.

"This man, I believe, is Menard Gottlieb, already investigated for war crimes." I produced Gottlieb's secondary file. "You'll notice, no photo—though there had been one because here's a caption on a blank page, and glue marks. It was either lost or someone stole it. The photo I just showed you was taken two months ago. Gottlieb's now a physician in Buenos Aires."

I produced a final file, the thickest yet, on Reinhard Vogt.

Plannik propped his glasses on his forehead. "You've been busy."

I hadn't set out to be, not in just this way. I couldn't begin to re-create for him the tangle that had brought me to his archive a second time. I would have been pleased never to see it again.

"Reinhard Vogt ran the guards at Drütte," I continued. "Your own investigation showed him to be the worst of the worst. I'm almost certain that today he splits his time between Munich and Buenos Aires. I can give you his new name and an address in both cities."

I thought long and hard before giving Liesel's uncle and Friedrich's grandfather to Plannik. I knew only too well the seriousness of making accusations that couldn't be wished away if I were wrong.

I had a compelling case. The Edelweiss Society met at his house. No one who wasn't a guard at Drütte was a member of the society. Only Gottlieb's and Vogt's photos were missing from the Archive, removed almost certainly by the same strong, politically connected hand. I was positive about Gottlieb's identity. That Viktor Schmidt was familiar with these men, that he was Kraus's partner, was undeniable. He was Reinhard Vogt. I was sure.

Plannik rubbed his eyes.

"Who's the woman?" he asked. "I've seen her before. I can't place it."

I told him. "A philanthropist. You may have attended the same events."

"Or seen her in the magazines, I suppose. She *is* pretty."

He sat back in his chair. "I have no reason to doubt any of this," he said, waving a hand at my presentation. "But let me spare you some trouble. Argentina doesn't recognize our extradition requests, and my prosecutors no longer bring cases against Nazis who fled there. Many nations looked the other way in 1948 as they scoured the Nazi ranks, looking for useful talent. The Americans got their rocket scientists. The Argentines settled for smaller fish with the know-how to modernize their economy. It's all on paper, the ratline that ran from the Red Cross and the Vatican right through to Juan Perón's presidential mansion. He made thousands of travel documents available to Germans with uncertain backgrounds. Today, his successor generals won't let us touch them."

"Gottlieb and Vogt travel," I said. "You can arrest them outside Argentina."

"I could be interested," said Plannik. "This is continually painful, you know."

"What is?"

"What? It's continually painful to me how nearly 10,000 Nazis fled to South America, at least half to Argentina, and we can't touch them. Europe was in chaos after the war, with millions of refugees. People had nothing, no food, no papers. Imagine your village is bombed in the night. Are you going to search for your identification papers when the walls are falling in? They ran. In the concentration camps alone, the Allies liberated tens of thousands. Where were they to go? These people had nothing, and the International Committee of the Red Cross set up refugee camps and issued new papers.

"I'm not saying the ICRC didn't do good work for many, many people. But the evidence they required for proof of identity was laughable. All you had to do was arrive at a transit camp with three fellows who'd vouch for you. You made up a name, your friends said, 'Yes, that's him,' and you were issued a piece of paper with a new name and an official Red Cross stamp. That's how Franz Stangl, the commandant of Treblinka, escaped. In some cases, the ICRC knew it was giving passes to Nazis. The system was a disaster.

"And the Catholic Church was a handmaiden to it all. They hated communists more than they hated Nazis. They also wanted to pump up their churches in South America with nice white Europeans, so they issued travel documents. Stangl, in fact, listed his address in Rome, at a bishop's residence. It was more than a ratline. It was a highway leading from the Third Reich through Rome or the Red Cross, to Argentina. So, no, I'm not surprised that you found a cadre of SS guards from Drütte in Buenos Aires. I'm not surprised, and I can't touch them."

He looked like a man who'd returned from a cafeteria line with rancid food, the best he would get all day.

"These two," he said. "Gottlieb and Vogt. You have definite information?"

"I need your help, Herr Plannik. I don't mean to be crass, but—"

"Ah, here's where the bargaining begins."

I felt ashamed.

"There's such a thing as trust in the world, young man. You've heard of it?"

If he was Schmidt's man, I was dead. If he wasn't, I could still be dead, though my chances of living to see my children born improved. "Yes, I'm told there are people in the world who trust each other."

"Why are these men dying, Herr Poincaré?"

"I don't know."

"Contact the police," he said, turning the files back to me. "This office deals in past crimes, not present ones."

If he was turning me out, I had nothing to say. Grossman would be a dead man, and I'd lose Isaac to history. But Plannik made no move to the door. He reached for the photo he brushed aside when I arrived.

"This one was taken at Babi Yar," he said. "The SS swept in behind the Wehrmacht in Kiev in September 1941 and murdered 30,000 Jews—mostly women, children, and the elderly—over two days. They forced the victims to strip, then the SS machine-gunned them into a ravine. They covered the wounded and the dead with dirt and rocks. Later, they killed communists and gypsies at the ravine. A hundred thousand in all. Look at these two, mugging for the camera. We found them, you know. The worst of it is that their consciences are clear. They killed, they said, but it was wartime, and somehow they made it all fit into the constellation of their lives. That was then. No big deal."

He set the photo aside. "This is what happens to vacations. Three days back in the office, and I'm plunged back into the murk. Let me tell you something about numbers that haunt me. I know them by heart. Between May 1945 and this year, the Federal Republic of Germany has mounted 85,802 proceedings against those suspected of Nazi crimes. A full ninety percent, nearly 80,000 cases, led to nothing. The accused couldn't be located, they died in the war, they'd been previously tried and acquitted by one of the military courts after the war, or they fled to South America or to the Arab countries. We *knew* tens of thousands were guilty, and we couldn't touch them. Twelve men out of 85,000, *twelve* were sentenced to death. This itself is a crime."

The number hung in the room before it died, and for a moment Plannik wouldn't meet my eyes. Watching him was like watching the time-lapse decay of a corpse, from life to bloat to festering flesh to bone. His spirits, so bright on greeting me, had gone to a dark place, and I realized that at a Nazi archive a man of conscience like Plannik could only come to grief: grief when he succeeded in bringing war criminals to justice, and grief again when he failed to do so. How could a man come to such work each morning?

And woe to the rest of us if he didn't!

"I'll help if I can," he said, rising from his desk. "You've got me agitated, which is the proper frame of mind for a place like this. Why do you think I can find David Grossman if he doesn't want to be found?"

"I don't know," I said. "I can't think of anyone else."

"Do you appreciate that we have millions of documents in this archive? All that I have would amount to a backwards search. If he just recently changed his name, what help would that be? Moreover, you represent no federal, state, or even local police authority. I'm hanging on the slenderest of threads."

I reached for a pen. "You may not be able to find Grossman's new name and address. I understand that. Here are the current identities for Gottlieb and Vogt. I want you to get these men indicted. Wait for Gottlieb to leave South America and arrest him. Get Vogt now. He's in Munich. You have the files to make these cases. Please, do this."

"It will take time," he said. "The rule of law demands it."

I looked at him. "The same law that forced you to let thousands of Nazi criminals go free?"

He shrugged. "We'd be no better than Nazis ourselves if we just rounded them up and hanged them. Though there are days . . ." He reached into a desk drawer for his business card. "Call me in a week, on my direct line. And leave these here." He pointed to the files. "It may no longer be such a good idea for you to be carrying them. I'll help if I can. If I don't, it won't be for lack of trying."

thirty-seven

I left the Zentrale Stelle with a backwards glance, relieved to be on the far side of the thick prison walls. A guard buzzed me out through the steel doors, but not twenty paces later I wished I could have scrambled back inside. For I saw them: Schmidt's men, one in a car, one on foot, closing in quickly. They had seen me, emerging from the one place on earth that Schmidt had warned me to avoid. I had parked a block away. I glanced over my shoulder and picked up my pace.

The man on foot spoke into a handheld radio, then motioned to the one in the car. Schmidt likely already knew where I was, and I didn't want to contemplate what might happen if they caught me. I considered sprinting across traffic in the direction of the utility crew that had set up along Schorndorfer Strasse. If I kept my wits, I could fall very near them, claim chest pains or a bad ankle, and ask for an ambulance. Or I could sprint straight away and beg them to call the police on their radios.

Instead, I panicked.

I ran down the sidewalk towards my car, a supremely stupid move. The man in the Mercedes zoomed past me; and while my eyes followed him and plotted how I might still escape by bolting into traffic to reach a heavily wooded park, the driver's side door of a blue Saab opened and I crashed into it, crumpling to the sidewalk. Someone pulled me into the backseat, and I passed out.

I woke with a hood over my head.

After an hour's drive, two men dragged me from the car and into a building, where they strapped me at the ankles, thighs, waist, wrists, arms, and chest into a high-backed wooden chair. The first thing I saw when they removed the hood was my empty bag and, on a nearby table, all its contents: maps, keys, wallet, and not a single incriminating file from the Zentrale Stelle: nothing on Drütte, nothing on Vogt or Gottlieb, nothing on Kraus. At the last moment, Plannik had held them back on an impulse that likely saved my life.

It was a large room, another warehouse. I sat alone with a bright light shining in my face and two lights directed to a cart on which I could see a collection of surgical instruments and clamps, in addition to handsaws and several pairs of pliers with different grip configurations. A roll of plastic sheeting leaned against the cart. Beyond this circle of light, the room was dimmed by heavy curtains at the windows, which were closed. The air smelled thick and heavy. I guessed I was in a Kraus facility very near my former lab and apartment.

For thirty minutes I waited, the straps cutting into me.

Then I heard footsteps. Accompanied by three men, the two I'd run from and a third, I supposed, from the Saab, Viktor Schmidt stepped into the room wearing a leather apron over his shirtsleeves. He adjusted his tie, where it remained knotted tightly. He pointed to my bag.

"You and I had an understanding about the Archive," he said. "I told you I didn't want you going. I thought you understood, but there you were. And here you are. Did you think I trusted you, that I'd stopped following after that first time? I made that first surveillance so obvious that even an imbecile could take a hint. You must be a special sort of imbecile."

His apron looked well used, with burn marks and brown stains.

"May I explain a problem to you, Henri?"

I tried to speak, but the impact with the car door had bruised my throat, and my jaw wasn't working right. It was swollen, and I couldn't feel my tongue or left cheek. I knew I was bleeding. I tasted blood.

"My friend in Buenos Aires, whom you met at *my* home— who welcomed you to *his* city—says he was summoned to police headquarters on a request from Interpol. It's a shameful thing for a successful man, a medical doctor no less, to be called in for questioning to inspect a passport. What do you know of this?"

I made a noise meant to sound like *nothing*.

"You're too clever by a half," said Schmidt. "You pressed him about a visit to Vienna. The only reason you're alive is that my goddaughter happens to love you. If it weren't for *that*—" He leaned close enough for me to see where he'd missed shaving that morning. He wore too much cologne. "If it weren't for Liesel, you'd be dead. You went to the Ulrich farm and talked with that old man. Looking for news of Otto Kraus, yes? That came after your visit to the library at Hanover, where you were reading up on the war, I understand, and on the Reichswerke. One of my men stayed behind at your study carrel and noted the books you'd ordered. You went to Bruges and talked with an old woman after *lying* to Liesel and me about what you were doing. Henri, it's not looking so good for you. What were you doing in Bruges?"

If Schmidt knew what Nagel was up to, then he knew very well that Tosha Zeligman's husband had signed the affidavit. He was playing me, probing to know what I knew, and for once in my life I was happy to be injured. For it was my bruised throat and jaw, not Schmidt's sentimental concern for Liesel's happiness, that saved me that day. If I could have talked, he would have twisted a confession out of me with merely the threat of using one of those instruments on his table.

My eyes flashed between the steel and Schmidt's bulldog face. I made a few guttural noises and blinked. He seemed more exasperated than furious, as if I were a son gone wrong. The leather straps cut the circulation to my legs and arms. My entire body was throbbing. But I had news from the larger world: Liesel loved me, he said. It was a thought to keep hope alive.

They had emptied my pockets. Schmidt inspected my father's T. "Fine craftsmanship," he said. He held Isaac's medallion up to the light, and I grew enraged that he touched it. "The old Reichswerke logo. Really, it's strange you should be carrying this."

I made a noise.

"You're a stupid, stupid man. Why couldn't you just have come into Liesel's life, loved her and married her, then gotten rich and enjoyed your life? Now I'm in a predicament." He grabbed an instrument off the table, a pair of clamps—or reverse clamps. I had no idea what they were, but my heart exploded as he approached. "You have no reason to know this," he said. "Before the war I studied to be an ophthalmologist. But history got in the way, you know? Things happened."

He nodded to his assistants. One grabbed my face from behind and snapped me against the wooden back of the chair. A searing pain shot from my jaw down through my legs. Someone cinched a leather belt around my forehead, forcing me to look directly ahead. Schmidt leaned close. "It stands to reason that one cannot do surgery on an unwilling patient. Take the eyes, for instance. The lids must be kept open, but they squeeze shut when the patient senses any foreign object or threat. Do you feel threatened, Henri?"

I was staring at him when my bladder let go. He laughed when he saw that. "So I've got your attention. Excellent."

Without another word, Schmidt leaned in and reverse-clamped both of my eyelids open, so that I was forced to look ahead without a hope of closing my eyes. I screamed, but only a ripped note escaped.

"There's nothing to get excited about just yet. Relax."

He barked an order to his assistant, who rolled in a gurney. On the gurney was a man with his mouth taped shut. He was secured with leather straps, as I was, but held fast to a table elevated at the head. Beneath his feet they laid plastic sheeting in a large square. Directly below the gurney they set a tub, on casters. The man was awake, his eyes bulging. He was also naked, and as he breathed his chest and abdomen expanded and contracted violently. A stink of alcohol and urine followed him into the room. He was pencil thin, bordering on malnourished. I could count his ribs.

Schmidt said: "I found this rodent in the gutter. He's more of an *it* than a man. He's subhuman, a parasite that consumes everything and gives nothing. Why do we even suffer these vermin to exist? Someone must be strong enough to do what I do. It's the way I give back to society."

The man made noises that died in his throat. He was lost and knew it. I, too, tried screaming but nothing emerged. I wanted to say, *I'm here, you won't die alone.* It was all I could give him.

Schmidt snapped on a pair of gloves.

"Who would miss a rodent plucked from the streets? His fellow rodents? They're too drunk and grasping to know the difference. The police? I don't think so. To them, this is one less drunk to haul downtown. I want you to listen and watch closely, Henri. What I do to this half-man I will do to you if *ever* I learn that you've worked to undermine this family or this company. Not one more visit to the Zentrale Stelle. No more visits to Bloch or others from the old days. No more inquiries into my friends in Buenos Aires. No more calls to or from Interpol. Watch and listen. A large and very sharp sword is hanging over you. So help me, it will swing—one small cut at a time—if you disappoint me again or speak a word of what you're about to see."

He circled my chair and tested the leather straps. "A family hangs in the balance," he said. "You could be part of it, or not. It's just the same to me. Now watch and listen, you piece of shit."

MY EARLIEST recollections of swimming are as a child who splashed in the heavily chlorinated water of a community pool. While my family enjoyed regular vacations at the seashore, for many years I was too timid to do much besides jumping in waves that rose, at most, to mid-shin. My father would take me into the surf, and safe in his arms I would squirm, my wet skin slick against his, and scream as he dunked us in the waves.

One day, it was my turn. I was ten, and both my parents swam alongside me out past the breakers as I held onto a floating board and kicked.

"Now!" they said. I let go.

And then came the glory of swimming, really swimming, for the first time in the ocean. I paddled and splashed. I floated and watched sea birds and clouds as a living mountain heaved beneath me. I was a matchstick, a leaf carried on a vastness both incomprehensible and, with my parents near, benevolent.

In the course of an hour, Viktor Schmidt plunged me into a different sort of ocean. He tortured, then ministered to that man, keeping him alive for as long as he could using clamps, cauterizing irons, and even intravenous drips. Strapped into his chair, I grasped instantly and purely the presence of something in this world as real and vast as the ocean of my childhood.

I HAD every confidence that, in time, Gustav Plannik would indict Viktor Schmidt. But I was not sure I could wait the months, or more likely years, it would take to convict him. Nor had I any confidence that I could persuade the police he'd just committed a murder. Schmidt was correct: the victim had been a nonentity, missed by fellow drunks, perhaps, but not by anyone rich or connected enough to demand an investigation. I'd been hooded on my way to and from the warehouse. I had no idea where to point anyone for what little evidence remained of the crime. Without physical proof, I'd be dropping a bomb onto the Kraus family only to see Schmidt vindicated and Anselm and Liesel appalled—at what, I wondered, my lack of loyalty?

What, exactly, did they *know* about this man?

"The engines of justice turn slowly," Plannik had said. Wise in years, he must have also understood that young men are not known for patience. Schmidt enraged me. His very existence offended me. As I lay crumpled amid crushed coffee cups and brittle leaves, dumped into the filthy corner of a hospital parking lot in Ludwigsburg at two in the morning, I vowed to see him dead.

And yet.

I had come searching for Isaac Kahane ignorant of the depravity he faced. Yes, I had read of the war and seen the films and photos; as a schoolchild, I dutifully wept as I was expected to weep.

But I confess to a kind of dumb incomprehension and weariness as I wrote my solemn essays on evil. I nodded, we all nodded, and said, *We must never forget!* And then the bell for recess sounded and we played football.

Viktor Schmidt's laboratory had been my classroom. I would never know, nor did I ever want to know, the horror that Isaac and Freda endured. No one who hadn't survived the camps could know. But I had learned enough. I learned, finally, what men can do to men. For the first time in my life, I trembled.

Everything changed for me.

PART IV

thirty-eight

Of all the places in a wide world. Innsbruck.

Somewhere in his millions of documents at the Zentrale Stelle, Plannik found the one slip of paper that Interpol, with all its resources, could not.

The story Plannik told strained belief. In early April 1945, with the Allies about to overrun Salzgitter, the SS evacuated the Drütte concentration camp. They crammed sixty or more inmates into each of eighty open-air boxcars headed to Bergen-Belsen. The transport stopped at Celle, a town of 65,000 north of Hanover, where it joined other prisoner transports. On a nearby track sat a train hauling fuel and munitions.

The Allies had already bombed Celle and its train depot a month earlier. On April 8th, a Sunday, they attacked again with 132 American B-26's. The devastation was immense. The munitions train exploded and engulfed the prisoner transport, burning hundreds alive. Those who survived the initial blast climbed from the boxcars to face a storm of bullets fired by German soldiers. Everyone in Celle knew the British would soon overtake the town. Still, the soldiers fired. Many prisoners escaped to a nearby forest.

Over two days, a posse of local police, firefighters, soldiers, enthusiastic citizens, and elected officials went hunting. In time, the massacre would be called the Hasenjagd, or hare hunt, of Celle. Its vigilantes, including Hitler youth as young as fourteen, shot prisoners wherever they were found: running in fields, hiding in bushes, cowering in bombed-out cellars. "Just like hunting rabbits," one participant said.

More than a thousand men and women died that night and the next day. But not Grossman, or any of the others who signed the affidavit for Otto Kraus, and not Isaac. They had survived both the Konzentrationslager at Drütte and the massacre at Celle. Little wonder Isaac couldn't find the words for a child who shared a bench with him at a pleasant park. Men wearing swastikas had murdered his first wife and children. Other men wearing swastikas beat and starved him into making steel for Hitler. Still others, dressed as civilians and determined to make a last, grand gesture for the Fatherland, hunted him as they would an animal.

Three days later, the British liberated Celle.

"Finding Grossman was easier than I thought," said Plannik when I called his private number. "We often copy the names in one file to a master index so that we can connect events and people across files. When we took possession of the Kraus affidavit, we indexed all ten witnesses, including David Grossman. Just two years ago, a series of long-neglected letters became known to us, and we opened a case against one of the magistrates at Celle who helped organize the rabbit hunt. We checked our index for anyone who'd been imprisoned at the Salzgitter camps, including Drütte, and survived the bombing and the hunt. Our state prosecutors reached out to all ten witnesses. Two died in the sixties. Of the eight remaining, only Grossman was willing to testify.

"The trial began last year, and as of this past June, Grossman still hadn't been called into court. These things take time, and I believe the case is scheduled to resume next month. In June, Grossman contacted the prosecutor and gave him a new address. Apparently, he had to move from his home rather quickly, but he wanted us to contact him when the time came. He said he wanted 'to help bury the bastard.'"

Plannik gave me the address.

"They shot men running in the fields?"

I couldn't see his face, but the bitterness in his voice was thick. "Herr Poincaré, I could recite for you details of a hundred massacres you've never heard of. When only a thousand die in a Nazi atrocity it doesn't make news, not compared to what happened at

Babi Yar or in the camps. Some of the townspeople fed and sheltered the prisoners, as you might hope. Most didn't. So yes, they shot at men running in the fields.

"Perhaps the new address will help you. Gnadenwald is a village that sits on a plateau just above Innsbruck. If you meet Grossman, remind him we have a case to prosecute. History demands it. Tell him he must stay alive not only for his sake, but for ours."

thirty-nine

"It's a ghost ship, Henri. We've ID'd the sub as U-1158 and sent the information to the U-boat archive in Cuxhaven. Our divers pulled up plates stamped with Nazi eagles and swastikas, cutlery, and medical kits. There are many human bones. There's also a metal schematic diagram of the boat, and that's where we got our ID. Cuxhaven's sending a diver and some paperwork out here before we tow the barge back to Rotterdam. There'll be a crew roster. That will give us some closure, I think.

"Our guys want to hold a service and read the names of the sailors who died. They were Germans," said Alec. "But even I get it after living on this barge for two months, a feeling for anyone who makes his life at sea."

I lifted the curtain edge in my hotel room, scanning the street for signs of Schmidt's goons. One was leaning against his car, smoking. There was no need to play hide and seek any longer. At some point, Schmidt would give up his surveillance, and I would be free to move about. Not yet. With Grossman's address in hand, I needed to leave the hotel—soon and without company.

"The dive season's over," said Chin. "Lloyd's is done. We know we're sitting over the *Lutine*, but I can't for the life of me find any gold on that wreck. Either we're missing it, which I doubt, or someone got here before we did."

I set the curtain in place.

"It's no huge deal to Lloyd's," he said. "Retrieving the gold was a long shot to begin with. They've got a few shiny bars for their display case and a documentary underway. They're calling it a win. What makes them happiest is that they didn't insure the U-boat."

"When?" I said. "When will you leave?"

"There's bad weather on the way, and no one wants any part of it. Soon."

He gave me a week and a half to visit.

I'D SLEPT for the better part of two days after the emergency room doctor released me with advice to stop running into car doors. I promised to watch for them, and he wrote a prescription after explaining that I was concussed and would be groggy even when I wasn't taking the codeine for my aching jaw and ribs. I was badly bruised and dizzy, he concluded, but not broken. Bright lights hurt my eyes, which had dried out from being unable to blink. Over the course of a week, I let fast food cartons pile up on the bureaus. I hung a "Do not disturb" sign on my door.

When I did rouse, I fought the impulse to call Liesel. She would have asked about my health, which was battered, and my voice, which had barely returned at that point. Dullard that he was, Alec didn't think to question that I had a bad cold. Liesel would have sensed my trembling and pushed for information. In time, I knew, the whole long tale would tumble out, but I wasn't ready to speak.

I assumed that whatever information Plannik gave me would find its way to Schmidt, either through his informant at the Zentrale Stelle or one of his other sources concerning all things Kraus. It was possible that he or Nagel had been a guard on the prisoner transport at Celle, in which case he might have been following the trial of the magistrate and known that Grossman was scheduled to be called as a witness in September. Who cared where Grossman had disappeared to if he was going to testify in a Hanover courtroom?

My one advantage was time. I still had Nagel's contact information in Buenos Aires, so I called for a phone consultation under an assumed name and was advised to call back because the good doctor was busy with patients. For the moment, then, there would be no threats from that quarter. I merely needed to evade Schmidt's surveillance team a second and final time. If caught, I'd be taking the place of the man on the warehouse gurney. But I didn't intend to be caught.

I placed a call to Serge Laurent.

forty

Where the valley climbed from the Inn River to the mountains, the roads narrowed and the distance between farms lengthened. The pastures were as green as any on Terschelling. Cows lazed, and the sky was a broad, unperturbed blue. I stopped as tractors maneuvered around me. A few farmers had begun mowing their fields, and I could smell freshly cut grass. Not twenty minutes out of Innsbruck, I reached Gnadenwald and saw a single church spire set amid fields and a few isolated homes. Forests claimed the hillsides, and beyond that granite. The Alps began in earnest here.

My plan was to find a local hotel from which I could hike past Grossman's new home. Grossman had no idea who I was, and if he saw me I would appear to be just another tourist with a backpack and a walking stick enjoying the fine air. I passed the house twice, once on my way out to an overlook that gave me a commanding view of the village, and once back an hour later. At sunrise, on the morning after I arrived, I waited in my car for Grossman to leave his house. He might find it less threatening, I reasoned, if we met for the first time in a public place. I would follow him and find the right moment to introduce myself.

So I was up early that day, and while I waited I replayed my little drama of the preceding twenty-four hours. My escape from Ludwigsburg would have been comical had so much not depended on the outcome. After my call to Laurent, I waited in my hotel for an unmarked police car to fetch me. I checked out of my room and stepped into the car with my bags. As the driver, a detective out of uniform, drove off, three cars followed: one directly across from the hotel; one, which must have come from the alley behind, watching the rear exit; and a third from up the street.

What Schmidt's men didn't know was that the police had first sent an unmarked car to the hotel twenty minutes ahead of my escort. This first policeman spotted the three tails and made a radio call to four marked police cruisers. With lights flashing, uniformed police stopped Schmidt's surveillance team to conduct registration checks. My escort looped back to the hotel to drop me at my car, and I was gone well before anyone connected with Schmidt could guess my intentions.

"A clean exit will cost you," Laurent had warned. I knew it would, and I learned something important about him when he agreed to spring me without demanding an explanation. When he called the Ludwigsburg police for an intercept, he told them he needed to protect an Interpol source. "So I'm expecting you to be a source," he said. "Do what needs doing, then call me."

Given the crimes Viktor Schmidt had committed, I no longer had any problems with that. Within weeks I expected to be telling him everything. But for the moment I needed to find the tenth witness. Laurent didn't push me, and I was grateful.

GROSSMAN LEFT his house just after seven o'clock. Parked some distance away, off the road and behind a stand of trees, I followed him to the parking lot of the church I'd passed on my way into Gnadenwald. I watched him descend a stone stairwell to a basement room. Others drove up and did the same. Meanwhile, no lights shone in the church above; I saw no movement there. After the cars stopped arriving and ten minutes had elapsed, I grasped my father's T and made for the stairwell.

The entry smelled of loamy earth and rot. The light over the stairwell was out, and the metal banister had rusted off its anchors and lay useless on the steps. Through the door, slightly ajar, I heard chanting.

The men stood with their backs to me, in prayer shawls. As I entered, each turned and looked up from his book without breaking rhythm. Their lips moved in a language that would have gotten them shot in this very place decades earlier. They nodded their helloes. One man pointed to the top of his head and then to a basket by the door. I reached for a skullcap and stood when they stood and sat when they sat. For thirty minutes more they mumbled and chanted, and then it was over. Nine men filed past, wishing me a good day. Only Grossman remained.

He turned and said: "Are you the one they sent to kill me?"

forty-one

He asked that I empty my pockets to prove I meant no harm. He examined the T and set it aside. He held the medallion to a light too dim to read by, then walked to a half window hermetically sealed from years of neglected dirt. He passed his fingers over the stamped metal, turning it in his hands.

Still, Grossman couldn't make it out. Cobwebs hung in the corners of the window well. Lower on the wall, a wood shelf sagged with cans of paint, and he used that as a ladder to get at the glass. He spit on his fingertips; he reached, the dirt smeared, and a bit of sunlight leaked into the room. It took him a moment, but when Grossman recognized what he held, the past stained his face like ink from a tipped bottle.

"Where did you get this?"

He was my height, thirty years my senior and thin, thin as though after three decades out of the camps his body still didn't know how to metabolize a decent meal. The years had cut canyons across his face.

"Where did you get it?"

"My uncle. Isaac Kahane."

Grossman lowered himself to a bench.

"Did you know him?"

He looked up. "Isaac lives?"

I smiled sadly.

I had forgotten how beaten and truly frightening I must have appeared with my bruises and rough voice. Grossman had every right to be wary.

"Isaac lost his entire family. He wasn't your uncle."

I explained it all. I explained the park bench, the gifts and the medallion he placed in my hand without a word. Stories poured out of me, stories confirming my love of the man and my sorrow for what he had endured.

When I was done, Grossman looked at me. "It adds up to one thing or it doesn't, young man. After the war, did Isaac live and die the normal way?" I followed his eyes to the basement walls and the crumbling mortar. A mouse skittered across the room. At the sound of footsteps overhead he startled. The priest or caretaker had arrived.

"In the camps," he said, "nothing about life and death was normal. They beat us when we followed orders; they beat us for not following orders. They starved us. If we didn't die of hunger, we died of disease. If we didn't die of disease, they eventually shot us. What I want to know is if Isaac had enough to eat and if the police ever came for him in the night. Did he have a *life* after the war?"

I found it difficult to speak.

"And what of his death? After a year, the designated time, will there be a marker on his grave?"

At the head of the room was a cabinet that held a scroll covered in a deep red velvet. Before leaving, each man put fingers to his lips and touched the covering. Grossman now spoke to the cabinet, letting his focus go soft. "Isaac was one of the oldest at Drütte and I, one of the youngest. It's a wonder either of us survived. I lost my parents, he lost his wife and children. We found each other and held tight."

"Tell me about him."

"Not here," he said. "Come. I walk after morning prayers."

HE WAS born in the east, a small town in Hungary that was destroyed in the war and can no longer be found on a map. At Auschwitz, he survived the initial selection by lying about his age. For a year he made fuses for a Krupp munitions factory in the camp. Then he was transferred to the burial detail. We were walking shoulder to shoulder at that point, in the woods beneath a canopy of beech and oak.

"My job," he said, "was to salvage gold from teeth. The guards would exhaust the gas from the showers, and we'd pile the bodies and cart them out to the crematoria and burial pits. But we made a stop, first. A guard showed me how to do it, how to cut from the corners of the mouth out to the ears. This way, when you pull the jaw down, it hangs open and it's much easier to get at the fillings. I could pull the fillings from your mouth in ninety seconds. You have to do it before the body turns stiff."

I stopped.

"What? You said to tell you."

"About *him*."

"You think it was any prettier for him? None of us knew the particulars of other prisoners' lives. Still, everyone's story was more or less the same. Maybe not yanking gold from people's mouths. But it was *all* detestable, and all anyone wanted to do was live. I saw boys abandon fathers because they were too slow. Brothers abandoned brothers."

Two hikers approached. "*Grüss Gott!*" they called, waving. Grossman returned the greeting. From the shade of the trail we looked across a freshly mowed field. Beyond that I saw a road, a stream, more fields, then a gradual rise to woodlands and mountains.

"Young man, I generally can't abide people asking what the camps were like. I don't need others to use my suffering to have a good cry."

Was he talking about me?

"What, I should lose my family so some pisher studying the Holocaust at the university can make solemn declarations about evil? Evil doesn't *mean* anything. Evil is someone's boot in your teeth, a knife at your eye for the fun of it. I survived the Warsaw ghetto. I watched my sister, eight years old, flushed from a basement by soldiers. She was terrified, searching for a kind face. She saw a soldier and ran to him crying, for help. Surely this man would help. He stuck a bayonet in her throat and lifted her into

~ 245 ~

the air. I watched this from across the street, in hiding. I couldn't make a sound, I couldn't save her.

"I've stopped talking about all this. I didn't suffer so students can get drunk reading *Mein Kampf* and cry how awful the world is." He patted my hand. "But for you, for Isaac's sake, I make an exception."

He spoke the unspeakable for an hour, pausing to ask if I wanted more, if I could stand it. I wanted it all.

And then it ended.

"One day the British came. They said, 'You're free.' They expected us to figure out how to live in the world again after all that. As if we still weren't surrounded by barbed wire and rotting bodies. Tell me, young man, what does living an ordinary life look like after the camps?

' "I walk down the street and have no idea what's inside the head of another man. Is he looking at me and thinking: *Jew*? Does he want to kill me? Does he think of me as vermin, as subhuman? Will he report me to the authorities? One moment I find myself happy, playing with my grandchildren. Then I stop to check that the doors are locked. But then that doesn't help because the police break down doors, you see. They come crashing in at night and yell: *Out! Everyone out!*"

Grossman lit a cigarette.

"I saw you praying," I said.

"Every morning, yes."

"You believe in God?"

"You seem like a bright boy. Why should my prayers suggest I believe in God?"

"Do you?"

"That's between me and God."

We walked for a time, and he began again. "From Auschwitz they moved me to Buchenwald. From there I went Drütte, to the steelworks. Isaac and I shoveled coal into furnaces for two years. When I was sick, he shoveled my load so the guards wouldn't notice. The ones who got sick disappeared, so Isaac and I covered for each other. It was Isaac who saved me in the woods at Celle and hid us from the hunters. He grew up on a farm and could read the woods. He found a hollow, and he pulled leaves and branches over us. All that first night we held each other, listening to the screams of the dying.

"We waited until the shooting stopped. Three days. When all was quiet and we heard planes overhead that weren't dropping bombs, we staggered out of the woods. The British had come.

"They moved us to Bergen-Belsen. If you drank or ate too much, you died. So we ate spoonfuls of soup at first. Isaac held me back when I grabbed for more. In the camps, I'd been a wild animal who'd do anything to survive. When were back among the living, I wouldn't leave his side. When he got ill with typhus, I stole clean water from the British until I was caught, and a soldier said: 'Son, take all the water you want. You don't need to steal anymore.' I looked at him, not quite understanding.

"As Isaac recovered, I told him stories to keep his spirits high, true stories of how the British made former SS guards use their fingernails to dig graves for the dead. There were thousands of dead. They made the *Deutsch* carry rotting bodies on their backs to the burial pits. Some of the guards couldn't take being prisoners, being treated the way they treated us. I saw one jump into a ditch and drown himself. I told it all to Isaac to improve his spirits. And do you know what he said?"

I waited.

"He said, 'Don't.'"

"Don't *what*?" I asked.

"'Don't become one of them.' After the war, we sent each other postcards the first few years, but that stopped. It happens. I would have come to his funeral, if I knew."

Two more hikers passed. "*Grüss Gott!*"

Grossman returned the greeting.

A steep hill rose to our left, pastures to our right. "What does it mean, *Grüss Gott*?"

He didn't break stride. "Roughly, 'I greet the God in you.' It's what Bavarians and Austrians say. In the north of Germany, they laugh at us. They think it's quaint." He smiled.

"Come, I'm hungry. We should eat and discuss my upcoming murder. It's not exactly news, you know. The others were greedy fools who invited all this trouble. I told them they were playing with fire."

"The others?" I said.

"Three of the other witnesses. They got the bright idea to black-mail Kraus Steel."

I stopped. "Why would they do that?"

"Why do any blackmailers blackmail? Money."

"They had damaging information?"

Grossman turned to me. "Young man, the paper we signed was a hoax. They paid us to lie for Kraus. That bastard ran the mill. By rights he should have stayed upstairs in his office. But he walked the factory floors, and I can tell you this. He was worse than the guards."

forty-two

Grossman stood my world on its head that morning. He could read my distress. "You didn't know?"

I didn't know.

"They call it the CIA now," he said. "Back then they called themselves the OSS, Office of Strategic Services. They knew survivors of Drütte were at Bergen-Belsen. About a month after the liberation, the Americans came looking for anyone who'd worked at Göring's steel mill. They found eleven of us, and they said all of Europe was wrecked but we could get a head start on our new lives with some real American money. Isaac was the oldest and the only one who could think to ask, 'Sign what?' And they said, 'A statement that Otto Kraus saved people and was a good man.' Isaac wouldn't stand for it. He begged us not to sign the affidavit. He knew exactly who and what Kraus was.

"Of course, Kraus was notorious. With my own eyes I saw a worker collapse onto the floor of a mill, by the furnaces. Kraus made the rest of us watch as the guard marched the man up through the catwalks, put a bullet in his neck, and dumped him into the furnace. Kraus yelled: '*This* is German steel! We will have no weakness on this floor!' He had quotas to meet. He told us the next person who collapsed would be thrown straight into the furnace without a bullet.

"For three thousand American dollars, a fortune, ten of us signed. We knew it was a lie, but we also knew that American dollars could help us make a new start. I asked the OSS man why they needed the affidavit, and he said: 'In about six months we expect to be at war with the Russians. We need a strong Europe. We need steel, and we need Otto Kraus.'"

I listened to Grossman and knew it was true. Just as Plannik had said, the Americans had scoured the Nazi rosters for scientists who could help them defeat the Soviets. They found von Braun and brought him to Huntsville, Alabama in Operation Paperclip. I had no doubt they protected Kraus. But rather than ship him to the States, they kept him in place to make the steel that would rebuild Europe and saw to it he won plenty of contracts.

As we drove in Grossman's car back to my hotel for breakfast, he was perfectly at peace about his role in the deception. "Later, I learned how the OSS used the paper we signed to free Kraus from prison. Before the Nuremburg trials, each of the Allied powers held war crimes trials in the sectors of Germany they controlled. The Americans arrested Kraus for crimes at Drütte, and he would have been hanged. But the OSS stepped in with our sworn testimony that he was a good man, and he walked free."

We arrived at the Michaelerhof Inn, and Grossman greeted the young woman behind the reception desk with a hearty "*Grüss Gott.*" She was wearing a dirndl, her costume for the tourist trade. She curtsied.

"*Grüss Gott*, Herr Cyngler."

I looked at him.

He shrugged. "Martin Cyngler. The name goes with my new address."

She showed us into a breakfast room, a glass alcove that overlooked a garden. A number of other guests had already worked through a buffet of smoked meats, cheeses, and dense German rye breads.

"So Kraus walked free," he said as we took our seats. "He returned to his mill and built an empire. The ten of us who saved him from the hangman got three thousand dollars apiece while he made hundreds of millions. Look," he said, holding a hand over his plate. "What do you see?"

I looked.

"Tell me."

"What do you mean? I see a hand."

"Do you see these burnt spots? Last week, a doctor cut off two skin cancers. We were getting old, the ones who signed, and three of us grew bitter that we made Kraus wealthy and got next-to-nothing. They called a meeting to renegotiate with the corporation. There were eight living signers by that point. I told them it was a bad idea, that these people are vicious. The three insisted that Kraus Steel provide us with an annuity. Zeligman was the worst. He sent the letter, and a month later the killing began."

Grossman piled cheese on a slice of bread and took a bite.

"Which was when you changed your name and moved."

"Who wouldn't? Well, that's not true. They didn't. I had a wife and family to protect. But so did they, the fools. They thought all the killing was over thirty years ago. Why should they have expected anyone to change? The Nazis didn't go away because Germany lost the war."

I thought of the Edelweiss Society in Buenos Aires. I thought of Schmidt. I watched Grossman. Thirty years gone, and the war smoldered.

"The man who's coming for you calls himself Eckehart Nagel," I said. "He was a guard at Drütte, which would connect him to Otto Kraus and his family." I shuddered to think Anselm was capable of murder. Schmidt, on the other hand, must have been in direct contact with Nagel.

"His real name is Menard Gottlieb. He lives in Buenos Aires. He's a doctor and will come to you, I believe, dressed as a delivery-man. He will try to administer a drug of some sort that will stop your heart. It will look like an arrhythmia killed you."

"Clever," said Grossman.

"Why's that?"

"We were all fairly religious, and observant Jews don't believe in autopsies. The body is not to be desecrated and must be buried quickly. So if it looked like a heart attack, everyone must accept it as a heart attack. They likely read up on Jewish burial practices. Gottlieb, you say?"

"Jacob Zeligman called out the name before he died."

"Do you have a photo?"

I went to my room, where the photo Liesel had given me remained neatly pressed between the pages of the Kraus biography. I could have burned that book. I studied the picture and put a finger to Liesel's face. To be born into this madness, fed lie after lie until she built her father into a hero. Someone would have to tell her. It wouldn't be Anselm or Schmidt.

When I presented the photo to Grossman, he exploded from the table. The chair fell backwards. Plates scattered, the staff scrambled. "Vogt! Reinhard Vogt!" He was pointing at Franz Hofmann. Grossman rushed from the breakfast room, and I found him pacing in the garden.

"That man lives?"

Yes, he did. But if Vogt was Franz Hofmann, the living corpse kept on like a pet by the Kraus family, who was Viktor Schmidt?

"Vogt ran the SS guards. He was a monster."

"Have you ever seen this one?" I pointed to Schmidt.

"No. Never. But this other one, maybe."

I had made a grave mistake in denouncing Schmidt to Gustav Plannik. Schmidt was guilty of one murder that I knew of—in August 1978. He hadn't served as a guard at Drütte, at least not as Reinhard Vogt. But he had founded a steel mill with Otto Kraus and, thirty years later, counted Vogt and Gottlieb as friends. Uncle Viktor ran with a murderous crowd. Still, he was not Plannik's business. Not yet.

forty-three

"*P*erhaps I saw this Nagel or Gottlieb or whatever you call him. The Reichswerke was large. There were thousands of us and many guards. But Vogt? Everyone knew him. You trembled when you saw him. Tell me where he lives."

I hesitated.

"I could beat it out of you."

I didn't doubt it. "Vogt walks with a cane, now. He had a stroke."

Grossman thought it over. "He despised infirmity. Tell me, is he bitter?"

I nodded.

"Good. That will do for the moment."

I explained how I had found him through the Zentrale Stelle. "Now that the court schedule in Hanover is published and you're slated to appear, Nagel will find you, too. He doesn't know yet what you look like. That's your advantage. He'll come to court to identify you on the day you give testimony against the magistrate from Celle. Then he'll come after you."

Grossman shook his head. "Zeligman and the others were greedy bastards. I have to run from my home and change my name because they decided Kraus could afford to pay them? Zeligman said he was doing it for my sake. Now he and the others are dead, and I could be, too. This war won't let me go."

"The police will be there to arrest him." It was a promise I had no right to make.

"He must never learn where I live. I can't allow it. He cannot follow me home, to my family."

"He won't."

"Can you guarantee it?"

This was not possible.

"Then I'll take care of the creature myself. Even if they arrest and convict him, why should he enjoy the luxury of a prison cell with three decent meals a day?"

"There are laws, Herr Grossman."

He smiled. "You're joking."

I wasn't.

"I'll tell you something about laws," he said. "When Hitler wanted to strip the Jews of civil rights, he passed the Nuremburg Laws. When he wanted to set the Jews apart as a despised race, he passed the Law for the Protection of German Blood and Honor. When it came time to kill us, he legalized murder. So don't speak to me of laws. Nagel does not deserve a warm bed and food, even in prison. I'll make other arrangements for him. And for Vogt, in time."

"The police will be looking for Nagel. Don't *you* get mixed up in it."

He laughed at me. "I'd say I already am!"

A car pulled into the lot adjacent to the garden, and a couple stepped out. They opened the rear doors and three children tumbled onto the asphalt. Americans.

"It's beautiful, Mommy," said the youngest, a girl. She was pointing to the flower boxes at each window of the inn. The family was black. They seemed like any other family on a tour of the mountains.

Grossman stared. "How is it possible," he said under his breath, "that they should be allowed to sleep in the same beds as you and I? These *schwarzes.*"

The young receptionist stepped into the garden in her dirndl, a model Austrian hostess. "Mr. and Mrs. Patrick, welcome to Gnadenwald. We've been expecting you. *Grüss Gott!*"

forty-four

Who is truly innocent?

No course in my engineering studies could have prepared me for what I encountered that summer: torture and death, serial murders, a shameful historical fraud, and learning that both the Catholic Church and the Red Cross helped Nazis to escape justice. Worse, I discovered that America, moral beacon to the world, rewarded men who rose to prominence on the backs of slaves. Yet it was Grossman's disgust with that family and my own disgust for the gypsy woman and her child that rang loudest in my ears.

I left Gnadenwald for Harlingen feeling as bruised inside as I was outside.

Alec welcomed me onto the barge with real alarm. "Henri, what the hell?"

I struggled up the ladder.

"You should have seen the other guy."

"Really, what happened?"

Hillary Gospodarek joined us and winced when she saw me.

"All right, enough! I wrecked my rental car. I hurt my ribs and jaw. I have two black eyes, and I actually feel worse than I look. But I'm here, so stop with the third degree. In fact, I don't even know why I'm here."

"Shall I tell him?" Alec slipped an arm around Gospodarek.

Behind them, the deck was empty, the sluice silent. The crane operator was nowhere to be seen. Even the dive shack was quiet. Light and plenty of noise spilled out onto the deck from the crew's quarters. A farewell party, then. Alec was shutting down the barge.

"Hillary and I are getting married," he announced. Before I could congratulate them, he added: "You know what my parents will say? She isn't Chinese. But when she proposed, I couldn't refuse."

She elbowed him in the ribs.

I had seen it coming. I joked that forced seclusion on a barge at sea made Alec a more promising prospect then he'd appeared on dry land. "Try him out back home before you commit," I advised her, "when you can compare him to a reasonable cross-section of adult males."

She leaned in close to her fiancé. "Yes, well, he's looking pretty good at the moment. Your *Lutine* dive isn't, however. We're done, Henri. I've catalogued everything of interest. Three gold bars, two handfuls of coins, and plenty of buttons and broken clay pipes. But no treasure to speak of. Time to pack up."

Voices spilled from the crew's hut. I pointed. "At least I can say goodbye and thank them." Long rolling waves from the northwest lifted the barge. The weather was calm enough for the moment, but I had checked the reports in Harlingen before visiting and a major storm near Greenland had already overwhelmed two tankers. Worse, a low pressure system over the continent was pin-wheeling north, and forecasters were predicting the systems would join over the Dutch coast.

"There's something you'll want to see," Alec said.

We walked to the hut, and at last I felt as though I was getting my sea legs under me. As the barge heaved on the waves, I adjusted my step without a thought. I might have stayed the night had the coming weather looked reasonable.

"The Cruxhaven U-boat archive sent their guy out yesterday," Alec continued. "He inspected the sub and confirmed its identity. He brought a copy of its final orders, issued on April 2, 1945. The commander was to run to the North Atlantic and interrupt sea traffic. After he fired all his torpedoes, he was to ram his sub into an American troop or supply ship and sink it. It was a suicide run, Henri. Germany had lost the war by that point. What a stupid sacrifice."

"So what were they doing here? We're a long way from the North Atlantic."

"That's just it," he said.

We walked into the galley.

"No one knows. The diver from Cuxhaven confirmed what our guys saw. Two blasts from the inside of the sub, forward and aft, sank her. U-1158 wasn't lost to antisubmarine warfare from the sea or air. Something happened on board. She shows all the signs of being scuttled, but that makes no sense because there are bones enough to account for an entire crew."

The divers and the equipment operators on the barge were a friendly, hard-working lot who enjoyed a good-natured joke, often at my expense because of my seasickness. But they watched in silence as I joined them at the galley table. My battered appearance must have alarmed them. Who knew, maybe they respected me for surviving a fight.

But that wasn't it.

On the table before me was a copy of the sub's orders. In a folder beside it was the crew roster. I opened it and scanned a list of names. In a second folder was the officer roster. A thermos and a clean mug sat on the table. I poured myself a cup and sipped, looking from face to face to pay someone a compliment for an excellent brew. They were still staring, though, and it was only on opening the second roster that I understood why.

There, smiling from the page, was the U-boat's handsome young captain, Nils Hauer. *He looks familiar*, a few had told Alec when they first viewed the documents. Some thought he looked like the man who had visited a few weeks earlier. Indeed he did, for Oberleutnant Hauer was a younger, more handsome version of Viktor Schmidt.

Alec was shaking his head. "You go hunting for gold and there's no telling what you'll dredge up."

forty-five

$\mathcal{T}$he one quiet place in a storm is its center, and that's where I went. Liesel shouted in alarm when I entered the sitting room of Löwenherz. She rushed to my side, and when we embraced I said, "Careful, twenty different parts of me hurt." My voice was husky but returning.

"What *happened*?"

"Car accident. The hike is on? I told you I'd make it."

We hadn't seen or spoken with each other for a week, and my injuries hurt less when I stood beside her. I wanted nothing in this world more than to leave with Liesel and forget everything I'd discovered.

The children hung back and stared. Anselm, looking as if he were carrying a heavy load, approached and with real concern said: "What's this? What happened to you?"

Theresa went for a medical kit. It seemed she was always going for a medical kit when I was around.

I tried making light of the injuries. "My rental car looks worse than I do. I don't think it's going to pull through. A truck ran a light."

Schmidt poured himself a drink. He snapped his fingers and released Albert and Hermann to come sniff me. He appeared as sympathetic as anyone. "Thank God you're well," he said, clapping a hand to my shoulder. "You're a resilient young man, Henri. Nine lives, eh?"

All I wanted was one life, with him out of it.

"We're still set for the hike, I hope. I promised. I'm here."

"Really," said Liesel. "In your condition?" She made me sit and brought me a glass of wine.

What a sorry charade it was. A heavy grief was descending on this house. Despite the children's laughter and all the blessings wealth had bestowed, the family must have felt it. Anselm, for one, looked stricken. The news from Bangladesh and Uganda had unleashed a storm of criticism. Fresh accounts of conditions at Kraus facilities began appearing in newspapers worldwide. With his haunted eyes, Anselm could have sat for a portrait by his beloved El Greco.

"You said nothing stops the annual hike. I'm fine, Liesel. I just look awful."

"That's the spirit," said Schmidt. "Low tide's at 6:11 this evening. You've arrived at exactly the right time."

Friedrich approached, pointing at the bruise on my jaw and the yellowish-purple rings at my eyes. "Can I touch?"

A servant announced lunch.

After we ate, Liesel took me to her apartment for what she hoped would be a quick tumble in bed. But the moment I lay down, I fell asleep. When I woke, I found her head on my chest. I ran my fingers through her hair.

She felt me stir and said, "Henri, I love you."

FRIEDRICH WAS the first one onto the mud. He squealed with delight as his feet sank to his ankles, and he promptly picked up a globful and smeared it over his legs. "Look at me!" he cried. For once he couldn't be a Stuka. The mud wouldn't let him move that fast or nimbly.

Liesel insisted I hike beside her. It was Anselm's turn to guide the group this year, but he handed the honor to his sister. "Not this time," he said, looking nothing like the buoyant, assured man I'd met that first night on Terschelling. "I've been making decisions every hour of every day for the past month. For once, I want to follow. You guide us, Liesel."

She noted the time and stated for all to hear that the tide would turn at 7:10. We'd need to be headed off the flats by 6:30. Her goal, once again, was to go far enough out to lose sight of land. She took a bearing on her compass. She asked that I do the same with the one she'd given me.

We were off.

Even the dour, gray-skinned Franz Hofmann, the estimable Reinhard Vogt, made an effort to join us on the flats. But at the verge of the seabed, where the concrete landing gave way to mud, he poked his cane in and decided to wait for our safe return. "I'll count you off when you leave and when you return," he said.

The children wore life preservers, which protected against falling into the tidal creeks, something I'd done on my hike with Liesel. The dogs didn't understand the mess of it all. They whined, but at Schmidt's urging they followed him onto the seabed. The children were soon flinging mud at each other, and no one spoke a word to stop them.

"We let them run wild out here," said Liesel, walking beside me, reaching for my hand. "You know, every other spot on earth has its rules. They must do this, they can't do that. As long as they stay safe out here, we let them do whatever. There should be at least one spot where you're totally free."

Schmidt walked ahead with the dogs.

We all struggled with the mud, the dogs especially. Hermann and Albert sank to their chests at times, but they pushed on and struggled at Schmidt's urging. Ten minutes into the hike, we were all caked with mud.

That was when I told Liesel I loved her.

She stopped. "If you're saying so because I did, that wouldn't be good."

Schmidt was ahead of us; Anselm, Theresa and the children, behind.

"I'm very sure I mean it," I said.

"And you waited until now because—"

"Because I could have died in the accident; and when I realized that, what made me saddest was the thought of losing a chance to spend time with you. I didn't have a chance to say so. We went to your room, I fell asleep, I woke, and you beat me to it. I wished I had told you first. Does it matter?"

We kissed. I took a handful of her hair and brought it to my face. I inhaled and closed my eyes to remember her, this magnificent woman who chose the wrong father. I had come to Löwenherz to do a nasty but necessary job, and I doubted she would want me when it was over. I held her close. We lost our balance and tumbled onto the mud, a soft landing. The children pointed and laughed. Anselm and Theresa walked by, holding hands.

"Shimmering birch," I said, looking into her eyes. "I meant it."

She took a handful of mud and rubbed it on my swollen jaw. "It helps, you know. The fishermen swear by it." She laughed. "Not even clay. You're my man of mud. That's Henri." There we were, nothing but seabed and sky and each other, and I wondered if a man had ever been so happy and so miserable in the same moment.

I told her I needed to speak with Viktor. I walked ahead while she hung back with her brother and his family. In ten minutes I had caught up with him. I whistled, and he turned.

"I'd like a word," I called.

He stopped and invited me to walk beside him. "I was hoping we'd get a chance to debrief, son. You know, have a meeting of the minds. I see how fond Liesel is of you. You and I should bury the hatchet. I did what I did out of a stern affection for you. I'm hoping you can understand. It's for the best."

"I'd like nothing better than to bury a hatchet," I said.

We were a long stone's throw ahead of the others. Liesel called after us to mind the clock. They were turning back early, she yelled, to make sure the children would have time if they tired out. I waved and blew her a kiss.

Schmidt's Boerboels walked between us, their paws sinking in the mud. They lumbered on, just as Schmidt and I did, every step a struggle.

"Nils Hauer," I said. I stared at the desolate ring of horizon before us.

Schmidt stopped: "What's that, you say?"

"I called you by your name. Nils Hauer. That's your name, isn't it?"

Albert and Hermann looked at him, waiting for a command or a treat. The flats extended away from us in all directions, no trees or grass, nothing but mud and sky. I could see Liesel and the others receding in the distance. Aside from them, Schmidt and I were as alone in each other's company as two men can be.

"My late brother, who died in the war," he said. "A submarine commander."

"I'm afraid not, Nils. I had a lawyer check the birth records in Salzgitter. Otto Kraus had one cousin. That was you. Nils was born to Hedda and Tomas Hauer in 1914. No other children. You are Nils Hauer."

"And if I am?" said Schmidt. "Many of us changed our names after the war."

"To escape the authorities, I know. The men of the Edelweiss Society, for instance. Franz Hofmann, too."

"You've been busy, I see."

"That was not my intention, at first."

"No authorities were after me. I was in the navy. I committed no crimes that were not acts of war."

"Would that include scuttling your submarine with your entire crew aboard? You're listed as presumed dead, Nils, along with your crew—in the North Atlantic. The archivists at Cuxhaven were amazed to find U-1158 just off Terschelling. Do you know what most amazed them? That two explosions from the inside of the sub breached the hull and drowned those men, all thirty-one of them. They counted the femurs. Sixty-two. But thirty-two men went out on patrol. The naval authorities want to talk with you about that, about how you survived when they didn't. I spoke with the people at Cuxhaven before I came to Terschelling, you know. I'm not really up on navy protocol, but I thought a captain was supposed to go down with his ship."

Schmidt reached into a pocket for a plastic bag. He leaned over and held out meat for his dogs. He was looking at them, not me, when he said: "I don't know what you're talking about."

"Whatever you say, Nils. I watched you watching the crew on the *Lutine* barge hauling up pieces of your boat. You didn't expect that, did you? Our dive on the *Lutine* was really the worst luck you could have had. The divers were bored silly because they couldn't find any gold. They swam wider and wider circles, looking for anything of interest off the *Lutine*, until they discovered a U-boat. With bones aboard. You murdered your own sailors."

"You lie!"

The dogs perked their ears.

"The navy will determine that. And I should tell you that Lloyd's of London has gotten very interested. I called them, too. You know why? My guess is that you salvaged about seventy million in gold bullion and coins that belonged to them, and you used it to bankroll cousin Otto's steel mill after the war."

Schmidt began walking, putting distance between us.

"You disobeyed your orders, Nils. You never went to the North Atlantic. You and Otto both knew the war was lost, and Otto knew about the wreck—he had since he was a boy. You made a pact, didn't you? If you could find the gold, you'd both be set. Isn't that right?"

I heard him whistling. His dogs begin to whine.

"Lloyd's is sending an attorney to Munich next week to investigate how Kraus Steel was capitalized in 1947. Liesel said you were the money man. But how could you have been? You grew up in Salzgitter with Kraus, both of you poor. You ransacked the *Lutine*, using your crew and your sub. I bet you promised the men they'd share in the spoils. Was that how you got them to cooperate?"

"They were dead anyway," Schmidt snarled. "It was a suicide run. The admirals sent us out to die!"

"Then you should have died with them. Lloyd's is going to want its money back. Kraus Steel is large, but Lloyd's is larger, and they're old as dirt. They won't quit, Nils. They're going to make their case and squeeze seventy million out of the company. Anselm will settle when he sees the evidence. It won't ruin him, but it's going to hurt. What's going to hurt worse is the murder investigation."

He emptied the plastic bag into his hand and let both dogs eat.

"Tell me something," I said. "Look at me."

Schmidt raised his face.

"Did Anselm or Liesel know about the murders—about the attempted blackmail and what you paid Nagel to do? Did they know?"

The question moved him. I had crossed some kind of line, and the muscles in Schmidt's neck quivered. He strained towards me but held himself back, as if he were chained. "Do you think I'm mad?" he growled.

I paused to confirm the earth was still spinning beneath my feet. For that, I realized, was the worst of it. Viktor Schmidt was not mad. Everything he had done, *everything*, was done with a cool, rational head.

"Anselm passed the letter from the blackmailers directly to me. I told him I'd deal with it, and I did."

"Did he ask you how?"

"Not once."

"And Liesel?"

"She never knew about the letter."

I thought of Schmidt as being many things, but not as a protector of the ones he loved. Yet there it was in his eyes and trembling lips. I had wounded his honor. He had kept the hands of his son-in-law and goddaughter clean. She didn't know about the blackmail attempt, and Anselm was willing not to know. Plausible deniability. The man whom Ulrich Bloch remembered as a pair of fists in search of a fight loved his children. It was nearly quaint.

"The press will crucify Kraus Steel," I said. "And it will be deserved, Nils. I've made my calls. Interpol knows about the list and the murders. Gottlieb will be picked up when he lands in Europe to kill the tenth witness. They won't know what to charge him with first, thirty-year-old war crimes or seven current murders. The navy knows about your suspected murder of German seamen. Lloyd's wants their money back. I'll try to convince someone you dismembered that drunk, but I probably won't have any luck. And your overworked, overburdened son-in-law, who looks as if he's about to drown, won't be able to suppress the news about the OSS. They sprung Otto to fight their cold war, and no one was ever supposed to know. Now they will.

"And if all this isn't bad enough, Anselm may be facing a slave labor charge at The Hague. Whatever you've touched has turned to shit. Absolute shit. So go and have a nice day. See you back at the mansion."

I turned away from him. Liesel and the others had hiked out of view, and the gray sky showed no hints of sun, offered no help to anyone trying to find his way home. I pulled Liesel's compass from my pocket and set a course back to Terschelling. Behind me, I heard Schmidt whistle. When I turned, I found the dogs looking eagerly at him as if expecting another bag of meat. He called to me.

"You're too clever by half. You know what I think?"

Flanked by his lion killers against a screen of mud and storm clouds, I saw it. I found what I had come looking for: a glimpse of Isaac's world during the war, in every direction a Viktor Schmidt or an Otto Kraus, a nation of them, a continent of blood and brutal dominance. The man was sane and had always been sane. Even the dismemberment had had its cool method, and I was its object every bit as much as the poor man who suffered and died.

Is this the world, then? I wondered. *Is this it?*

He patted his animals and cooed their names. He scratched them behind the ears. Then he raised his hand in my direction and yelled: "Henri, I believe it's time for both of us to die. Albert, Hermann, Zind!"

His arm swept towards me, and I reached for the T in my pocket.

forty-six

*T*hey would have killed me but for the mud. The Boerboels could get no traction on the flats. At Anselm's home in Munich, they had been tawny, graceful streaks racing across a firm lawn to protect Friedrich. On the Wadden seabed, their paws sank as they tried to gain a foothold.

Schmidt meanwhile had turned away, walking south into the void.

Had there been a tree, I would have climbed it. A door, I would have slammed it shut. I checked my watch: 6:35. To the west, the tide was stirring, more dangerous, even, than the dogs. I could outrun neither, and unless I killed or maimed the animals quickly, I would drown. So I gripped the T and set my stance as first one and then the other leapt.

I let them bite once, then went for the eyes.

Hermann lunged at my throat, and I blocked with my left forearm. At the same moment came a searing pain in the meaty part of my thigh. I screamed, but ignored it as best I could. Both animals kept their eyes open and bit hard. The bone in my arm snapped. I screamed again as I hammered the T into Hermann's skull. He wailed but didn't let go. The next time I aimed, and the jelly of the one eye popped onto my fist, which I brought down again and again until I heard another wail and left the animal blind. Still, it hung on until I hammered its muzzle, then came underneath for its throat. Hermann fell limp.

Albert had ripped my thigh open. The blood ran, and I prayed it wasn't the deep artery pumping what was left of me into the mud.

I killed him.

I took my belt and closed the wound at my thigh. I shook my head to stay conscious. I pulled the compass from my pocket and set a course to the island. But my leg was no good. I began to crawl.

6:58.

Before I felt or heard the flood tide trickling, I smelled the water as a silent, subtle onrush of air. I was an animal myself by that point, on hands and knees with a broken arm and gaping thigh, alone. That's when I realized the earth didn't care if I lived or died, wasn't partial to either me or Schmidt. The mud could suck me down or spit me back, and the tide would run that night and the next and the next. I lifted one paw then the other, panting. I smelled water. I felt the planet spinning and the tide stirring. I made for dry land. I wanted to be human again and to live.

What is this place, I thought, sniffing the air.

In the west, a yellow stain broke through the clouds. I checked my compass and crawled north toward Liesel. By the time I saw Terschelling harbor, the tide was running in earnest and the water had covered my hands. Soon it was at my elbows. By the time I reached the landing, it ran chest deep. Ten minutes more and I would have succumbed. I pulled myself onto the landing.

Tap tap shuffle. Tap tap shuffle.

I heard him before I saw him: the three-legged beast, Reinhard Vogt.

forty-seven

"Where's Viktor? Where are Albert and Hermann?"

He didn't wait for an answer. He raised his cane and brought it down hard across my broken arm. I hadn't let go of the T. Even though I was sure I had killed the dogs, I feared they or something would come for me—Schmidt, perhaps, rising from the deep. But it was the stroke-hobbled half man, Reinhard Vogt, Liesel's beloved Uncle Franz, who inflicted the crushing blow.

I nearly passed out.

I brought the T down hard on his foot and felt bones crack. He went down without a grunt. Vogt clawed at my face but I fought him off, panicked that he was pulling me into a grave. I gave him nothing to hold onto. I lunged with my father's weapon. I hit him again, in the knee.

Liesel saw it all. She ran from the parking lot for me, then Vogt. "What *is* this?" she cried. "What's happening? What are you doing? Where's Viktor?" My eyes began to roll, and she stuffed us somehow into the backseat of her Land Rover and raced across the island to Löwenherz. "Talk to me," she pleaded, as Vogt mumbled curses and lifted one limp fist after the next, punching me in the face.

ALL MY life since, I have regretted this ending.

We took the morning ferry to Harlingen in advance of the storm. I had gone into shock at Löwenherz. I could offer no words of explanation for a night and a long day, not until the clinic in Harlingen stabilized me and sent me off to Amsterdam and a proper hospital. The reckoning didn't come until two days later, as Liesel and Anselm sat at my bedside.

"They found Viktor in the marsh grass yesterday. And the dogs," she said.

I told them everything, and Anselm's and Liesel's reactions confirmed what Schmidt had said: they hadn't known the worst, that Schmidt had dispatched Gottlieb from Buenos Aires to kill the eight living witnesses. Anselm wept at the price his father-in-law had paid to save the good name of Kraus Steel.

What was worse was the news that Schmidt had funded their father's business with bloodstained gold. No one would ever know the details of how he did it, what combination of diving bells and pulleys he had used to haul the treasure off the *Lutine*. But over the next year Lloyd's very clearly established that one Viktor Schmidt, whose existence could not be traced before the war, had appeared in Otto Kraus's life with a fortune sufficient to re-launch the Göring steel mill at Salzgitter.

An inquiry began. Without admitting guilt, Kraus Steel paid Lloyd's not only the millions it had used to capitalize the company in March of 1947, but also the millions more the gold was worth in 1978. The corporation was large enough to absorb the blow. Its bankers issued stock, which an eager public was willing to buy because the business world knew that Anselm, burdened though he was, still had a gift for making money. Kraus Steel issued even more stock to establish a reparations fund for the slaves Otto used during the war.

"It is a stain we are just now discovering," said Anselm in a press release. "This history grieves us, and we will do our very best to make amends." His new public relations office had prepared the release.

Serge Laurent came to my hospital room with the news that the prosecutor's office in The Hague had declined to take on the slavery case against Kraus Steel. It turned out that Schmidt and Anselm were right: the subsidiary facilities in Bangladesh, Uganda, and elsewhere met all local laws to protect workers and the environment. It made no difference that these laws were considered scandalously deficient in developed nations.

"To hell with it," said Laurent. "I gave my entire file to that reporter from the *Times*."

Indeed, a month later, a major exposé hit the newsstands, reporting that for years Kraus Steel had been using a form of debt slavery to staff its facilities around the world. BARELY LEGAL ran the headline. Once again, Anselm pled ignorance. In a second press release, he said:

> I visited these facilities as they opened, when the operations were clean and safe. Little did I know what our vice president for globalization would let them become. But ultimately, as chairman of Kraus Steel, it is my responsibility to ensure safe and clean working conditions, and I failed. We will do better. My sister, Liesel Kraus, who sits on the corporation's Board of Directors, will bring a higher standard to bear for our workers worldwide.

They issued yet more stock to fund cleaner, safer facilities. In the end, buying a good conscience amounted to spending breadcrumbs for Anselm and Liesel. On paper, fixing their troubles cost them many tens of millions. But on paper, they were still worth hundreds of millions.

forty-eight

"Welcome to the world," said Laurent some months after my release from the hospital.

We sat at a café in Paris, where he assaulted a marble table top with his thick fingers, driving home an appeal he wanted me to consider: that I abandon the profession of engineering for a career at Interpol. "You have a talent," he said. "Seven deaths by heart attack, in seven cities, over two months. No one could have connected those dots. You cracked a subtle case, Henri."

"Without knowing I was on a case. That's not talent."

"Call it beginner's luck," he said. "My superiors and I don't think so. They want you to begin your training in January."

His appeal moved me. Still in my twenties, I had trained for a profession that brought technical answers to difficult problems. When rivers needed spanning and foundations needed shoring, I was your man. Give me a dive platform to build and anchor over a treasure ship, and I could do it. Viktor Schmidt was a different sort of problem. For him I had no answers, yet the world needed answers—or at least more men like Gustav Plannik.

I talked it over with Alec. Our consulting company was flush with new business. Of the fourteen proposals I had written earlier that summer, fully ten were accepted, and in months we grew from a pair of engineers to more than fifty. We were launched, Alec and I, with clients on four continents. P&C Consulting Engineers promised to become the company we had trained for and dreamed of.

"You'd give up all this success for international police work? Go," he said, "if it makes you happy."

Happiness I wasn't so sure about. But it's what I wanted.

"The irony of it," said Alec, "is that you'll leave just when we're large enough to send younger guns to go vomiting on barges at sea. We'll never have to do *that* again." He thought it over. "On the other hand, you never know where you'll meet your future wife."

The *Lutine* project had worked out well for Alec and Hillary. They married and brought children into the world, and I was happy for them.

Liesel and I didn't get nearly that far. Indeed, we didn't last another month. I was pleased to recuperate at her apartment in Munich. I gathered my strength as she and a busy Anselm jousted with the press over the suddenly notorious operations of Kraus Steel. She returned home in the evenings exhausted and despondent over the turn her company had taken. She vowed to do better, and I believed she meant it. All the while, neither of us spoke of my role in exposing Kraus Steel; but as I expected, a veil as much of my making as hers was falling between us.

One day, we were seated on her white couch. She was nursing a Scotch. I drank a beer.

"Who is A. Bieler?" I asked.

It was the one discovery I'd held back in the hospital. Broken as I was, my arm splinted, tubes running into me and out of me, I hadn't the strength to push this final, awful legacy into the light: that her brother had lied to her. That he was Bieler and had cemented the sainthood of Otto Kraus with an official-looking but spurious biography.

For weeks Liesel resisted the central fact on which all the bad news of that summer rested. Yes, she asserted, the affidavit was real. Yes, three of the witnesses had attempted to blackmail the company. Yes, Schmidt to her infinite regret had directed Nagel to murder the witnesses. All that was true, she acknowledged. But why should she take the word of a bitter David Grossman that the OSS had arranged for her father's release and revived his career? The company requested documentation from the Americans but received no official response.

Liesel insisted that Anselm had handled the blackmailers correctly: he, too, claimed that the OSS charge was false, but he had to respond to spare the company embarrassing publicity. That the response was disastrous and Schmidt had stained Kraus Steel was not in dispute. But the murders, in themselves, did not prove the OSS had made a deal for her father. Liesel continued to insist that Otto saved lives.

The time had come.

Saying nothing committed me to a lie that would drive me away from her. And speaking committed me to a truth that would drive her away from me. I wrestled with the dilemma and when I finally asked about Bieler, the question came of its own. I hadn't planned the day or hour. I hadn't rehearsed. Some part of me thought we were ready, and I asked.

We were seated on her couch by the window, overlooking the garden. The first trees were changing color, announcing a new, chillier season. I had propped a pillow behind my head, but felt the raised stitching of needlepoint. It was the present Liesel's mother had given her, and I set it aside as Liesel had once asked me to do. Once more, I noted the initials: A B L v K.

"Bieler is my father's biographer. You know that, Henri."

"Liesel," I said. "There is no A. Bieler. I went to the University of Hanover, which Bieler listed as his academic home. They never heard of him, not as a student or as a teacher, full or part time. I have an idea who he is."

She kept a copy of the biography on the bookshelf, and I retrieved it.

"Let's go for a walk," she said. "I'm feeling cooped up. You know, all this business with the press, and my expanded role. I need air. Come, it will do you some good to raise your pulse a bit, to get the blood flowing."

She found a sweater and hat.

My pulse was already up, and my blood warm. I flipped through the first hundred pages, looking for Bieler's description of Otto Kraus in Salzgitter, meeting Anna, his wife. Liesel was tugging at my bad arm. It hurt, and I shook her off.

"Please," she said, "let's go."

"Just a second." I flipped a page, then another, and found it.

I was ready to present well-ordered facts that she could not deny: Anselm had written, or paid someone to write, the flattering portrait, and had convinced university libraries to place it on their shelves. I assumed the news would wound her, but she had to understand that her father was a perpetrator, not a saint. The complete story, the real story of Kraus Steel, had yet to be written.

Why it occurred to me only then to scan the book for information on her mother I don't know. The lettering on the pillow, perhaps. But there it was, on page 132: an account of how young Otto had met and married one Anna Bieler. Anselm had played an inside joke.

"Here," I said, pointing to the page. "A for Anselm, Bieler for Anna Bieler. Your brother gave a hundred twenty pages to Otto's life before the war, twenty pages to the war years, and two hundred thirty pages to life after. Anselm knew exactly what happened at Drütte. Otto *was* rescued by the OSS. Schmidt knew it, and he ordered Nagel to murder the blackmailers because they had actual dirt on the company."

The hat fell from her hands. She took the biography from my hands and closed it. I followed her eyes to the pillow her mother stitched.

"You told me your given name is Antonia?"

When she nodded, I knew.

Plannik had said when I showed him the photo of Nagel: *I recognize this woman from somewhere. I just can't remember.*

I slumped into the couch. I looked past her to the trees of the Englischer Garden and their last bright shout of life. "How did you get the ID made?" I asked. "They let no one into the Zentrale Stelle without an ID. Every document I found listed A. Bieler. You read every file. You knew everything."

She shrugged. "The ID was left over from my school years, when I was underage. I paid to have it made so I could go drinking with my friends. We all did it, Henri."

"Did you steal the photos of Gottlieb and Vogt?"

"No, they were gone by the time I got to the Archive. As I was growing up, Ecke and Franz were friends. They were my uncles, like your Isaac. They were sweet, if you can imagine Franz as sweet. Before the stroke, he could be . . . with me. You're not suggesting I knew what they did during the war? It was monstrous. I could never—"

I hardly knew what to believe.

"And Schmidt. Did you know about him?"

"Viktor was Anselm's father-in-law. Did you investigate your parents' friends or relations? I grew up with these people. I didn't need to know more than that. Don't ask me to turn away from my family." Her voice was rising, shaking. "Everybody has a past, Henri, and I gave them theirs. What's so terrible about that? What is it you need from me?"

I stared at her.

"You think it's wrong that I loved my father? He was my *father!*"

She dug through a drawer and found the ID that gained her entry to the Archive. I studied the photo on the card, and I studied her. At that moment, everything hung in the balance: between Liesel the child who didn't know enough to ask and the woman I loved, standing before me, who had chosen not to ask. In Bruges she said that she wondered about German men of a certain age. Yet she hadn't wondered about *these* men and what they did during the war.

"You were twenty-three or so when you went to Ludwigsburg?"

"I looked enough like the sixteen-year-old on this card, if that's your question. I don't look so terribly different now, do I?" She tried hard to change the mood. She wanted the old me and the old us. She grabbed the ID and mimicked the pout of her younger self.

"Antonia Bieler Liesel von Kraus. A. Bieler."

I saw it. I was sick.

"Do we really need to go through this, Henri? Anselm was too busy, and we decided I should write the biography. Siemens, Bayer, all the big German companies were rewriting their histories of the war years. We had to tell our story. Otto *was* a hero. He helped save Europe from the Soviets. Everything else is negotiable." She reached for my hand, and I shook her off. "We couldn't put our own name on the biography. How would that have looked?" She reached again. "Dearest, do you think we've gotten where we are without knowing who our father was? Those were bad times, and people did bad things. But the world turns and we move on. Otto did good things, too. Great things. Did you think I didn't know? You've got to take the whole man in the balance. I loved him."

I closed my eyes.

"And all your protesting to me that the blackmailers were lying about the OSS?"

"We thought it was what you needed to join the company. That's what Anselm wants, and that's what I want. But we were waiting for you, Henri. I've been waiting." She smiled. "There's so much we can do together. Come."

She held out her hand. "Tell me you love me."

forty-nine

*T*he statute of limitations never runs out on murder. It's the law's way of saying that memory matters and that we must stand for who we are and what we've done. Viktor Schmidt did what cowards do. He killed himself rather than stand and face history. Like Hitler. Like Göring. I suspect Schmidt held the world in contempt until the end, cursing ordinary mortals who would not bow to his superior method. We are well rid of him, though the daily newspapers are evidence enough that his spirit is alive and well.

Sometimes I think of David Grossman, the tenth witness, and how the police had blunted his designs on Gottlieb. He so wanted to kill the man and make him, and Vogt, suffer. I attended the trial that day in Hanover when he testified against the magistrate from Celle.

Gottlieb entered the courtroom, unaware of the trap Laurent had set. I watched the police surround and cuff him. And what should they find before settling him into a holding cell but the tools of his trade: a powerful synthetic opioid delivered as an aerosol to knock victims out with a puff, and three syringes and as many vials of potassium, which administered intravenously crashes the heart into a fatal arrhythmia. Zeligman, ox that he was, had fought him off and staggered to his window, where he fell and called out his murderer's name. The others succumbed according to plan. Court-ordered exhumations of the recently buried witnesses confirmed the presence of excess potassium, and Gottlieb was convicted.

Grossman did have the satisfaction of confronting his would-be killer. Before they hauled him out of the courtroom, he approached Gottlieb and introduced himself.

"Germany lost the war," he said. "Did no one tell you?"

A year later, he testified against Reinhard Vogt, who was convicted of crimes against humanity and died an old man, alone, behind bars.

I LONG mourned my decision to leave Liesel. She and Anselm would have welcomed me into the bosom of Kraus Steel had I accepted Otto's wartime record as a necessary evil. The demand for their steel remained high. And, indeed, as the personal computer market matured, they entered the business of salvaging precious metals from circuit boards. The last I checked, their operation outside Delhi was an open sore that, nonetheless, exceeded local safety and environmental codes. In her new job, Liesel ran her offshore facilities more humanely than her rivals ran theirs. She installed infirmaries and enforced the laws against hiring underage workers. She doubled wages, not that that amounted to much. No doubt she believed she did the best she could in a business that demanded ever-more handsome returns on investment.

The following year, she married Hans Kellerman, the pharmaceutical magnate she avoided that day at Löwenherz by bringing home a summer experiment. Me. She'd been right about his wealth. Mr. Bayer controlled twenty percent of a company that, during the war, manufactured Zyklon B. He had money, he had a home with a name, and he came from good Austrian stock. *Grüss Gott!*

They never had children.

I lived in Paris for a few months before moving to Lyon to begin my career with Interpol. I visited with my parents and with Freda as frequently as my case load allowed. On Sundays, after sharing a meal, I would sometimes visit the park where Isaac and I met. Our bench was still there. I would sit and wait, but nothing came to me, no voices, no visions. I didn't know what to expect, but I waited for a sign nonetheless. Perhaps it was a stranger I needed, someone well-tuned to the ether who could have walked up to me and said: "You did what you could. You told his story.

He's proud." But there was no stranger and there were no signs, save for the sun and the wind and the children playing.

Yet, in these, Isaac was near.

He had given me the medallion to say what he could not. And that summer it spoke, though the story is far from fixed and is hopelessly tangled with the story of Kraus Steel. There's so much I don't understand.

I don't understand what it means to say that six million souls perished in the camps and that since, in the Gulag and Cambodia and Rwanda, millions more perished and that tens of thousands at this moment suffer the whims of tyrants. I can hardly comprehend the mystery of a *single* soul. Here by the fire sits my bride, dozing, the one with whom I have shared my life and for whom I would gladly give it. Claire bore my son. She shares my hopes and sorrows. I love her beyond telling. Yet in her essential, beautiful self, she is a mystery to me. She is perfect yet unknowable. What, then, can it mean that a million, twenty million Claires were murdered?

The mind cannot hold it.

Joseph Stalin, who knew about such things, must have been right: a million dead is a statistic, a single death, a tragedy. Which is why on Christmas Eve I light candles for the children of Isaac and Freda Kahane, who died in the winter of 1940 well before their time. Freda lost her daughters, Fanny and Rose, to the twins' experiments at Auschwitz. Isaac's sons never made it to the camps. The SS shot them into a freshly dug pit. They had names. Samuel, David, Julius, Lipman, Bernd, and Louis. I did not know them, but each year I light candles and claw them back.

ONE SUNDAY I chose to visit the cemetery instead of taking lunch with my parents and Freda. It had been a year before I was ready to approach Isaac's grave with a last, vexing question. How, after everything, could he have chosen kindness? After the Reich and the murders, after Drütte and Celle, he chose to be a gentle man. How did he do it in a world of Viktor Schmidts? And now that I had joined Interpol and was committed to hunting Schmidt down and confronting him again and again, how could I?

During that year, as I made my long approach to the cemetery, I gathered stones from my travels. Some came from the coast of England, some from a scree field at Mt. Blanc, a few from a park in Lyon. I carried a pocketful of stones as I approached the grave. I built my cairn before the bronze marker, then knelt over the remains of Isaac Kahane and opened my heart. The day was beautiful, the air sweet, and I cried and cried. I will not report what I said, for words of love offered to ghosts are written in fire. So were the deaths of millions.

But so, too, I swear it, is love.

Author's Note

The Tenth Witness builds on certain facts worth noting.

In 1799, HMS *Lutine* sank off the Dutch coast (near the Wadden Sea) with a thousand bars of gold. When Lloyd's of London paid on the loss, it assumed title to a vast treasure. Despite many salvage attempts, the bulk of the gold was never recovered. The salvage recounted in this novel is fiction, as is the existence of U-boat 1158. Many German submarines sank during the war, though none as far as I know in the vicinity of the *Lutine*.

From 1939–1945, the Hermann Göring Reichswerke of Salzgitter, Germany produced steel for the Nazi war machine under the direction of Paul Pleiger, not Otto Kraus. The SS built the Drütte concentration camp on the premises of the steel works, using prisoners as slave labor. During the forced retreat of April 1945, many of these prisoners died in the notorious "Rabbit Hunt" of Celle. Postwar, the Reichswerke was renamed Salzgitter AG and, after several reorganizations, remains among the largest steel producers of Europe. Not until the 1980s did the company drop its Nazi-era logo, the so-called Gö-ring, ♀, which resembled the Hermann Göring coat of arms.

The role of the Catholic Church and the International Red Cross in aiding the escape of Nazi perpetrators to South America and elsewhere is well documented. So, too, is the role of U.S. intelligence services in recruiting Nazi scientists—some of whom, like Wernher von Braun, used slave labor during the war. Dispiriting in a different way is the anti-Semitic "Jew Among the Thorns." I quoted from Margaret Hunt's 1884 translation of Grimms' *Fairy*

Tales. For good reason, "Thorns" is seldom found in modern translations of Grimm; but locate Volume 2 of the 1814 edition, and there it is, tale 110.

The salvage of precious metals from crushed circuit boards was more promise than fact in 1978. Thirty-plus years into the personal computing revolution, the use of harsh chemicals and burning to recover value from e-junk has blighted the countries where this work is done. No less toxic or dangerous is the business of ship breaking in places like Chittagong, Bangladesh. International commissions have tried setting safety standards for the salvage of old ships, but working conditions remain abysmal.

I WANT to thank those who generously shared their expertise as I researched *The Tenth Witness*. Dr. Tobias Herrmann, director of the Zentrale Stelle der Landesjustizver-waltungen zur Aufklärung nationalsozialistischer Verbrechen (the Central Office of the State Justice Administration for the Investigation of National Socialist Crimes), welcomed me to the Archive in Ludwigsburg, Germany. Once I arrived, historian Volker Reiss introduced me to the methods used in building cases against Nazi perpetrators. Closer to home, Megan Lewis, librarian at the United States Holocaust Museum, helped me locate accounts of the Celle massacre, both in print and in videotaped survivor statements from the USC Shoah Foundation Institute.

Chris Macort of Orleans, MA, professional diver, advised me on explorations of historically significant wrecks; Elizabeth Hirst, doctoral student in chemistry at Boston University, devised a process for salvaging precious metals from electronic junk; Hillary Gospodarek provided translation services; Mishy Lesser translated the chants of the *madres* of Plaza de Mayo and shared harrowing accounts of the Argentine terrors; Lester Lefton, Laura Tracy, and Sonia Nevis offered insights into the psychology of adult children whose parents committed war crimes; and doctors Gerald

Rosen and David Cohen identified agents that can immobilize and dispatch a victim while presenting as a heart attack. I've tried to remain faithful to the advice received from these and other experts; but where I've misstepped, the errors are mine.

A number of writers I admire read and commented on sections of the manuscript or otherwise advised me. I thank Douglas Starr, Larry Behrens, Chris Knopf, Arthur Golden, S. J. Rozan, Reed Farrel Coleman, Bruce DeSilva, and Joe Finder. I thank Clair Lamb for her expert, critical eye, and also Jeff Chin, Larry and Suzanne Heffernan, James Jones, Stuart Koman, Richard Marks, Bob Morrison, and Frank Sladko. I owe an ongoing debt to literary agents Eve Bridburg and Todd Shuster for their sound advice and encouragement. Once again, I offer heartfelt thanks to publishers Martin and Judith Shepard of The Permanent Press, who have been friends and tireless advocates. To their entire team I extend my thanks: Lon Kirschner, Cathy Suter, Felix Gonzalez, Sarah Flood, Brian Skulnik, Joslyn Pine, and Susan Ahlquist.

And a special thanks to Brigitte and Jorg Purner, who took me on glorious walks through the hills above Innsbruck, and Renate and Bernd Wunderle, who introduced me to Munich. These children of the war suffered as children will. Jorg's and Bernd's fathers were conscripted into the Wehrmacht and died on the Russian front. Jorg was *in utero* when his mother got the news; Bernd may or may not remember a man in uniform who tossed him into the air and smiled. Renate recalls learning the Nazi salute as a child and being shushed while attempting that same salute for the Allied conquerors. What could it all mean to a six-year-old? These good people were moving and articulate in both expressions of love for their countries and their ongoing pain at reconciling that love with the legacy of National Socialism.

During my childhood in the 1950s and 60s, the bogeyman behind the closet door wore jackboots and a swastika. In writing *The Tenth Witness*, I finally opened that door, and I could not have done so without Linda Rosen. Every day for two years I immersed myself in the twisted legacy of National Socialism. And every night she greeted me with its opposite: sanity and affection. Her very presence was a reminder that this world can be, and frequently is, a sweet and decent place.

Leonard Rosen
Brookline, Massachusetts

About the Author

$\mathcal{L}$eonard Rosen lives and works in the Boston area. He has contributed radio commentaries to Boston's NPR station, written best-selling textbooks on writing, and taught writing at Harvard University and Bentley University. *The Tenth Witness* is his second novel. His first, *All Cry Chaos* (also featuring Henri Poincaré), is a much-praised award winner in both the literary and mystery/thriller categories. Len enjoys corresponding with readers and meeting with book groups online. Contact him through his website: lenrosenonline.com.